My Crazy (Sick) Love

Drica Pinotti

My Crazy (Sick) Love

Book and Cover design by DMAM Consult and Design
Illustrations by Megan Tamaccio from iStockphoto.com
Text edited by Jessica Gallagher

To Sammy B,
For believing in my talent and my ability to accomplish
my dreams.
Thanks for being my biggest supporter and for
smothering me with all that love.

1

When the alarm went off at six-thirty I thought my head was going to explode. Not that I had never expected that to happen someday. That the veins in my brain would just erupt, like some sort of sleeping, devious volcano, waiting for the right moment to leap into action and whisk me away, from my bed to a coma, and from the coma to another astral plane, once and for all. But in reality, it was just a pounding headache. What scared me was that this was no simple and pure case of cephalalgia. If it had been a migraine, two aspirins and I would be good as new. But, this was different. My stomach was thrashing about from side to side, like a washing machine with only soap and water, no clothes, going back and forth, up and down, leaving me with a feeling that needed no medical genius or specialist to diagnose as nausea.

I stayed in bed no more than five minutes, carefully analyzing all the symptoms, a total of four, to be absolutely certain my liver was a rotten mess. That's because the night before I had spent just three short hours having a few drinks with friends at a new bar that opened on the corner of 83rd and 3rd. Cool place, with good music and beautiful people. But, a little dark for my eyes, which we all know could destroy my sight. Well, you might as well know right from the get-go that although I panic every morning after thinking I have cirrhosis or cancer of the liver and pancreas – just so you have an idea of how vivid my imagination can get – I go right on drinking. I must confess that I also enjoy a cigarette after a good cup of coffee or a meal fit for a king. It is this combination that gives me a month full of reasons to believe that one day I am bound to have serious throat problems or lung cancer.

Back to my liver. I woke up and decided to make a checklist of the symptoms before my thoughts short-circuited and I fell into despair. The indisposition alone was enough for me to not want to get out of bed. I had every sign of a liver problem. I also felt a pain in my stomach, right there on the right side, under my ribs, lots of nausea, and I even threw up (three times I had counted so far) I could feel my liver pounding in my chest, alongside my heart, and they both gleefully skipped about and danced in perfect harmony in my rib cage. And that made me very, very nauseous. Although I knew precisely what the doctors were going to tell me, since this was not the first nor will it be the last time I thought I have cirrhosis, I went and called one. Actually, I called many of them.

I opened my phone book, which my friends call DD (dial a disease). I have an updated A to Z list in there with the best doctors in town and their specialties. There are also other possible health care professionals and entities to which I may need to resort to. Such as hospitals and customer service centers of more than 50 reliable laboratories I was able to catalog. Drugstores, all of which are open 24 hours a day and within a 20-mile radius of my apartment. Under the letter H, I had all my hepatologists.

I tried talking to Dr. Richard Ember – with whom I have the most contact with and one of the few who still answers my desperate phone calls – over the phone. But he wasn't in, so I left a message on his answering machine.

"Dr. Ember, this is Amanda Loeb. I need to talk to you urgently. I have cirrhosis. I'm sure of it, but I need you to confirm the diagnosis. Please, get back to me as soon as you can. It's really urgent. Thank you."

With those I didn't know as well, I tried to set an appointment for that same day, early, before they even began working at their office. After all, it was Friday, and it doesn't look good at all to miss work, especially on a Friday. I confess I find this sort of "veiled" protocol pretty stupid. After all, it isn't as if we can choose the most appropriate day to get sick. I was only able to get squeezed in at one of them. I had to practically beg the secretary to find me a little opening in the doctor's extremely tight schedule, according to her.

"Brenda, your name is Brenda, right?" I asked trying to win her over.

"That's right. Amanda, unfortunately Dr. White's schedule is booked for the day. I'm certain he would love to see you, but it just won't be possible."

"Brenda, please! Take another look. Check if someone hasn't confirmed an appointment? I'm having a liver crisis. If my diagnosis is correct, I only have a few months to live. In that case, waiting one week for an appointment is out of the question. Please understand, I don't have much time," I begged.

"Look Amanda, what I can do is schedule you as his first patient since I can't squeeze you in anywhere. I'll tell Dr. White to arrive 15 minutes earlier than usual, but if he can't, you may have to wait to be seen if the other scheduled patients arrive on time. Is that all right for you? That's the best I can do."

"That's great for me. I'll get there before Dr. White starts seeing his patients. Thanks a lot, Brenda. You're an angel." I said, clearly trying to flatter her. Many people in Manhattan hate that type of buttering up, but I could tell she liked it.

That's when I paused to reflect. I had never stopped to think about so many people, who like myself, suffer from silent cirrhosis and have their symptoms masked by a Thursday night of drinking with their friends.

After insisting I truly had all the symptoms of cirrhosis in its critical stages, and that perhaps I would be dead by next week, Brenda reluctantly agreed to give me the first appointment of that morning. And so, I went.

First, of course, I needed to study my case so I would be ready with technical terms and arguments when it came time to give my report to the doctor. I have to feel confident about my own diagnosis. So, I went to my personal library, my collection of health care books that range from: *YOU: The Smart Patient* to *Merck Manual of Medical Information* (the updated version!) and including *The Complete Manual of Things that Might Kill*

You: A Guide to Self- Diagnosis for Hypochondriacs, where I saw my disease as crystal clear as mineral water. I had now completed my diagnosis and knew precisely what I had. It was a lesion in my liver cells, the hepatocytes, which results in the formation of fibrosis. There was no cure and it could EVEN lead to cancer. There you go. CANCER. That was just the word to drive me completely insane! I have cancer!

I called my mom. Actually, I do that every time I go into a crisis. After all, being a mother goes beyond giving birth. It is necessary to participate.

"Help, help... You're not going to believe it (*I think she thought: I bet I won't!*), but I'm going to die.

"Good morning to you too, Amanda." She answered calmly, before hearing me out.

And after one of my nosophobic speeches, I made the poor thing go to the doctor with me. I swore this time it was true. She would hear right from the mouth of a specialist that I have the worst of all diseases found in humankind (a malignant tumor had taken over my liver!) and I only have a few months to live.

***

How it all began...

I really can't pinpoint when this all began. Can anyone tell me when depression sets in? Precisely when someone becomes an alcoholic or drug addict? When anorexia takes over a healthy creature's body and soul, transforming it into something pale and corpse-like and full of vanity? Which was the first drink or first drunken

11

stupor that led to an alcoholic existence until the person realized he had to go to AA meetings? Can anyone do that? I can't either.

When it hit me, I was already refusing to greet people with kisses on their cheeks, claiming I had a horrible cold. I would place my hand over my mouth and simulate a cough and hoarseness. And that was just to avoid contact with anyone's dirty skin. Who knows what sort of virus people are carrying! Who knows what their habits are in terms of hygiene, if they have any at all? Carrying around my own viruses is more than enough, and Interferon is an extremely expensive medication! Besides, in my research I have already read that a person's mouth is a source of countless forms of contamination. That a bite from a human being (how ironic) can even kill. I am an intelligent person and as such I have decided to not run any unnecessary risks. When I understood I needed help, it was already too late and I was walking around with my antibacterial hand sanitizing gel in my handbag, disinfecting my hands after opening each and every one of the thousand doorknobs between the ground floor of the building and the room where I work in a nonprofit company.

My mother tells me that when I was about five years old, I would watch her carefully take care of my grandfather who was suffering from a serious case of pneumonia. It was so strong he didn't make it. She often diminished her functions as a housewife and mother to a maid. She dedicated herself exclusively to grandpa. I remember how that bothered me. I loved him too, but I didn't understand his pain. I was just a child, and as such,

I couldn't understand why she, of three children, had to abandon her husband and daughters to dedicate herself full-time to this task. Obviously, today I understand.

Months later, she says, I had already demonstrated my first signs of insanity. I would feel feverish and get the chills just to get her and my father's attention. While my youngest sister, beautiful and so talented, only had to smile, I had to succumb to pharyngitis or, in extreme cases, tuberculosis. And all I had to do was cough twice and the world would begin spinning all around me. Now you can begin to fathom why my little sister "hates" me to this day.

However, as only natural, I disagree with this version of my sickness saga. I can't accept the fact that the truth could be so simplistic: A girl develops a very serious mental disorder just to call her parents' attention. Just to get ice cream and toys or to miss a few days of school.

What I do remember is that at the age of 14 I was already walking about with a clinical medicine book under my arm. I loved reading works like *The Pill Book* or *The Johns Hopkins Complete Home Guide to Symptoms and Remedies*, while my friends read those sugar sweet novels by Nancy Drew or books that were *in* like *Christiane F.* I watched every episode of *Mysteries of Medicine*, and I'm still obsessed with every medical-based TV series. I would discuss the most whimsical syndromes with my doctors to the point of driving them and my mother insane. My friends thought I was going to study medicine. But, people could never understand that reading about medicine was not my hobby nor something that gave me pleasure. It was downright despair. By the way, that is how, ready to begin a brilliant medical career, I went to study Law at Yale Law School in New Haven, Connecticut. And during the time I wasn't going nuts because of every pore in my body that was functioning improperly, I was studying to be the best in my graduating class.

In other words, I have no idea how my paranoia began. What I do know is that I am far from well and my panic attacks are getting more and more frequent. I've been able to make totally insane associations. I can transform a simple toothache into maxillary cancer. An itchy elbow becomes an urticarial eruption, and a simple sneeze, pneumonia. That's why I have already thought about joining a help group, like HA – Hypochondriacs Anonymous - to give vent to my "many probable diseases," neuroses and eccentricities. And who knows, maybe I can find a boyfriend who can put up with me for another three crises. The other probable hypothesis, speaking rationally, is to surrender to my mother's constant pleading and finally seek help from a psychiatrist. Which I absolutely refuse to do!

***

Just as I was walking out the door, the phone rang. It was Dr. Ember. He had heard the brief report about the case, gave me a short list of exams, which I carefully took note of, and promised to take on my case. Now a little calmer, I went for my appointment with Dr. White.

I met my mother in the lobby of the building. As soon as we got to the right floor, we could see Brenda. She was sitting behind a counter organizing medical charts in a file. As soon as she saw me, she blurted, "You must be Amanda?" *She most certainly detected the despair in my eyes.* "Yes, I am." *I answered a little uneasily.* "Dr. White hasn't arrived yet, but he shouldn't be long. Please sit and wait," she said.

Of course, I'll sit and wait. Where does she think I can go with my liver in this state? Does she think I have somewhere better to be? Perhaps a party? Or that I have the physical disposition to run a marathon?

When Dr. White arrived, my mother and I were still the only ones in the spacious waiting room. So, as soon as he settled in, he came right out to call us in.

Both of the doctors I consulted asked me for the same things (I think there is some sort of medical conspiracy against my person and I need to reorganize my phone book, perhaps including doctors from New Jersey to break up this cartel).

Blood tests, an assessment of hepatic enzymes, an ultrasound, and a few others. "And the biopsy?" I shouted before the visit finished as he had yet to ask for that exam, crucial in my opinion.

"Isn't anyone going to examine a piece of my liver?" I would not calm down until someone came in with at least minimal knowledge of our language—as we all know, that is not a strong point for doctors—to explain my problem, or lack thereof, in details.

"Amanda, calm down and let Dr. White do his job." *My mother was visibly embarrassed.*

"Amanda, what you have cannot be cirrhosis, don't worry," said Dr. White.

Don't worry? I thought. How could I not worry if the only thing I do is worry. Day and night studying and thinking about the next perfidious illness that was going to attack me and leave me in a bed for the rest of my days. While I was fighting my thoughts, he continued explaining my case to my mother, who listened attentively.

I ran all the required tests and waited for the results. Two hours later, without further delay, the visit continued more or less from the same point it had stopped earlier.

"The exams we've already analyzed are sufficient to ensure us that what Amanda has is no more than a heavy hangover." *He said that almost smiling.* I could feel my mother's eyes burning into me, wanting to exterminate me. Meanwhile, he went on.

"A patient with real cirrhosis (and he looked at me) will have redness in the hands, red blotches on their stomach, enlarged liver, edema (swelling) in some parts of the body and a series of altered results in lab exams." *He spoke slowly.* Besides my dizziness, nausea, vomiting, and pain, which by that time were already affecting my soul, I had nothing that could be considered a symptom of cirrhosis.

I paid for the appointment up front because Dr. White is one of the best in his area, and as such, he does not accept health insurance plans. I paid in cash, while my mother watched, bewildered by yet another blow to my finances. This time nearly six hundred dollars between the visit and exams. I will uselessly try to get my health care plan to reimburse me, and, as always, I can already see the rejection letter.

"We are sorry to inform you, but these expenses are not reimbursable, blah blah blah blah..." And I'll just have to deal with the health costs on my own.

I walked back to the office, just fifteen blocks from Dr. White's. My mother angrily abandoned me at the subway station on 77th and Lexington. On the way, I stopped at Crumbs Bake Shop to get a large decaf coffee with "plenty of sweetener" and a large slice of cake with "plenty of fat and sugar." I know how absurd that seems, but what can you expect from someone who swears a hangover is actually cirrhosis? To be sensible? After all, I had to take advantage of the fact that my liver was in such good shape. I continued towards the office on 72nd and 3rd. In my hands, I held my snack and a prescription for two medications: an analgesic and an antacid, and the recommendation to drink plenty of water.

I was still unconvinced my illness was not something to be taken seriously. I arrived at the office and went directly to the chapter on liver diseases in my clinical medicine bible (I keep a compendium at home and one of those pocket books in the drawer at my office). If I don't have cirrhosis yet I am at least going to begin preventing it! I need to give my liver a vacation! Tomorrow (if there is one), I will become a teetotaler. I will not drink anything with an alcohol content greater than 1%. I will begin a diet (tomorrow!), with little protein, little salt and little sugar, so my liver can rest. Since there is no shortage of medications for the liver, thank God, I will leave conventional treatment for when the disease stops being so stubborn and shows the doctors, especially Dr. White, that it *is* there, hiding, silently, waiting for the right moment to leap out and attack. And I truly hope that day comes quickly, otherwise, it may be just too late for me.

2

Horrible start to the week. It went against all my expectations, because I had promised myself I would start my week in a healthier fashion. No doctor's appointments, which would have been my first Monday free of doctors' offices in five months. I spent all day Saturday without taking the slightest peek at any article about diseases. I did not read the obituaries in the *New York Times*, and as a result, I finished the weekend taking only three capsules of a powerful antibiotic (because no one can convince me I do not have a urinary tract infection, and I have already heard that I could lose my two kidneys with a crisis like this one). I also took one of those whatchamacallits because my gastritis (I think I'm on the verge of an ulcer) just won't let up. And Saturday night, I only spent two hours on the Internet, a record for me, looking up details on a new super powerful flu virus since I heard on the news that next winter it is going to be stronger than ever. It's probably going to infect the entire city with its new mutating version, transforming my body into a walking incubator.

It all seemed perfect, a dream-like weekend. I was even beginning to think how lucky I was, can you imagine? Forty-eight hours without a single medical incident. That's a dream come true! But perfection doesn't exist, so you don't have to pinch me. All hopes were destroyed on Sunday! And now it's eight twenty-five on Monday morning, and guess where I am? You're right if you said it: sitting on a comfortable white sofa next to a pile of magazines on health, yoga, and getting in shape. Besides, of course, those frightful gossip tabloids about the lives of celebrities! (*Madonna switched boyfriends again! How could I ever go on without that information?*). There is a chubby, smiling receptionist in front of me in the sizable lobby. She can't stop eating her cereal bars packed with chemicals. But, they are DIET bars, so she thinks she's going to lose weight healthfully. In other words, I am at the office of Dr. Linda, my new gynecologist. And for those who have yet to notice, I must say: I am on the verge of a nervous breakdown!

I don't like to blame anyone for my anxiety crises. Far be it from me to say the one to blame for my being here now is Julia, my best friend of more than 5 years. But I cannot deny it. She *is* the one to blame. All because on Saturday, she had to go and invent a party to celebrate her 30th birthday. She claims it is as special as anyone's 15th birthday, and she had to be debuted to society for the second time. How ridiculous! When I hit 30, which will happen in three months (if I'm still alive by then, because the way things are going, I can't guarantee anything), please, forget about me! I've already told all my friends and enemies alike: don't send me flowers, unless I'm dead. And don't look at this as some sort of lack of gratitude (although it may look that way), but how can I thank anyone who sends a biological weapon into my house? That's not a present. It's an attempt on my life! Flowers are like bombs to my immunological system, triggering a very serious allergic reaction in me. No one can imagine how I feel. It's more or less like this: flowers give off pollen, a cloud of almost invisible dust that floats about the air. Well, that pollen gets stuck in my throat, attacks my bronchial tract, causing an inflammation in my airways, and I begin to suffocate. A few minutes later, if I don't get immediate medical attention, I could become just another cadaver among the statistics. Now tell me. Is that a present to send someone? I don't want anyone calling either. I'm too busy and don't have time to waste. Send no emails! Do nothing! Please understand. I will be extremely ashamed and depressed for having crossed the finish line for old age. Being just a few years away from menopause and including geriatricians to my list of doctors are not pleasant thoughts. So, I will have no motive at all to celebrate, but rather one to lament. And the only present I'll love getting, if someone wants to give me it, is a week at the Mayo Clinic in Jacksonville, Florida. That way, I can get a complete check-up, from the tip of my toes to the last cell in my brain. And I will know precisely about all the evil that has been afflicted on my organism by advanced age.

But, back to the facts. Julia included Diego among her guests. A really super cute guy I dated for a long time, like about two weeks, three days and 4 hours. And after taking me to the hospital for the third time in that enormous stretch of time, he decided to break up with me. He decided, all on his own mind you, that the relationship was no longer viable and disappeared without leaving a trace. That's right. I also think people nowadays show no sympathy towards the health of others. I remember my last crisis in front of Diego as if it were yesterday (and from the looks of how he stared at me when he entered the party, I think he did too). I was suffocating. My lungs didn't have 1 ml of air, and I was thrashing about against the wall, in total despair. At the same time, I was forcing my index finger down my throat towards my trachea, trying to perform a tracheotomy, with no success at all, in search of air. He went white as a sheet and almost fainted. Dreadful, I admit, but rather than help me, he went and dialed 911. Can you believe that? I was dying, my lips purple and my face pale as a ghost and the guy didn't have the guts to shove a pen tube into my throat! Talk about insensitive!

I never heard from him again after that. He didn't accompany me in the ambulance and never even gave me a call to see if I was okay. He didn't even have the nerve to do that. And now, there was Diego, standing in front of me, gorgeous, with the whitest smile I had ever seen, which is why I had imagined he'd be the right guy for me. He has a beautiful smile, healthy mouth, and consequently fewer bacteria than all other men on Earth. *I remember thinking, which is, by the way, the biggest mistake made by humankind, the second good reason I had stayed with him for so long: the sex.* The sex was just incredible! He made a point of wearing EXTRA thick condoms. Which was a glad surprise! And he was so clean (so was that!), beautiful, well-groomed feet, good smell of deodorant... yummy... And then that... Those memories would have sufficed, but once I added the three shots of some distilled alcohol that blended right in with my anti- inflammatory medication and went straight to my head like fireworks, there I was groping Diego again.

You know all that you kiss me and I'll kiss you, you rub me here and I'll rub you there, I took a couple of breaks to powder my nose and gargle efficiently with Listerine. After all, I had to reduce any risk of contracting herpes or something like that, so gargling with mouthwash was absolutely necessary. After an hour of shaking about to the sound of that loud and unbearable music which pierced my extremely delicate ears, Diego finally invited me to go somewhere a little quieter. We went from there to Mr. West, a new lounge in Chelsea, where Julia decided to gather her friends and share the onset of her decadence, straight to my place, or better, to my bed. From there to my discovery was just a hop, skip, and a jump! Or a fright! I had dried up! I was frigid!

"Amanda, are you okay?" He asked, frightened. "Of course, I'm fine." I answered, but I was unable to be very convincing.

"You're not going to have another one of those attacks, are you?" He was even more frightened.

"Attacks? What attacks?" I said trying to change the subject.

As he tried to get back to the initial maneuvers of what promised to be an exceptional night of sex, I was thinking of ways to first get him off of me and then out of my apartment. A thousand thoughts rushed through my mind. Why don't I feel anything? Why do I have that horrible feeling that I'm doing something against my will? I want to be here. I invited Diego to my apartment. So why? Why don't I feel anything? *Questions, questions, thousands of questions and no answers. I had to act. I had to understand what was going on with me.*

The first thing to do was to get Diego out of my apartment as he was getting ready to take a shower. I tried not to do anything scary, because this time he would never forgive me and would go about telling everyone I was some sort of half-dead version of Glenn Close in Fatal Attraction. I am a respectable attorney. I have to keep my reputation intact, regardless of how many Prozacs it takes. I quickly began to fake a few sneezes and invent some highly contagious virus. *Didn't you hear the news? Everyone in NY is coming down with it.* I mentioned it, without trying to sound weird, but I don't think it worked.

As soon as he went through the door, grabbing his Urban Outfitters jacket, and visibly upset, I was certain I would never see him again. Nevertheless, I then took my second precaution and called my kid sister. I know that because I'm the oldest I should be the most experienced in these situations, but my sister has always been the more mature between us, you see? Lauren has already been married for almost five years, an eternity according to the words of her own husband, Eric. They have a beautiful and normal daughter, although she does already simulate her first cramps, but nothing too serious yet!

I called Lauren and asked her a question of utmost urgency and importance, ranking an 8, and only exceeded by degrees 9 and 10, Cancer and Death.

"Can you tell me how many women suffer from frigidity? I've already searched the Internet and the results of all my research are inconclusive. *I said with some indignation.*

"I have no idea how many women suffer from frigidity, but I imagine it's a small number. And if it's big, I think many women don't admit the problem, out of shame, I don't know. *She answered as calmly as possible, as if we were talking about a hair loss problem.*

I cannot understand and I find it very worrisome how a person can live like Lauren. She never thinks she can get sick. She never tires of bragging about her perfect health and she says she only accepts dying of old age. She almost never goes to the doctor. Besides routine visits and exams, she refuses any sort of preventive treatment or new natural experiments. I confess that at times I envy her normality and apparent calm in the face of issues like death. Just mentioning the word sends a chill up my spine.

I spent almost two and a half hours arguing with Lauren, who irritatingly tried to convince me that the fact I had not had an orgasm with someone who was practically a stranger was absolutely normal. She kept saying I had no need to worry. But at that point I was already convinced that all of the arguments she was using were just part of her role as a sister to calm me down, or a way for me to stop pestering her anymore with my sexual crisis.

I hung up and went straight to the source that has always satisfied my thirst for knowledge, or as my mother says, the source of all my problems, the Internet.

Since research on the subject was not unreliable, I decided to read reports from women who openly admitted to suffering from the lack of sexual pleasure, like me. Then, I tried a chatroom to discuss the matter, but whenever I brought up the topic, the women began to sign off, one after the other. I still haven't been able to understand this taboo. But for me, someone who has just been diagnosed as frigid a mere few hours ago and who has no intention of "embodying" roles (because no one can convince me that most of these "multiple orgasm" cases are actually true. I think it's a bunch of lies or just pure delirium.), there's only the right to remain silent so my words cannot be used against me.

Among reports and co-reports, I found the explanation I needed there: "Frigidity is a sexual disorder in women, characterized by a lack of desire and any sexual response even when stimulation is adequate" (and here I must be fair with Diego, the stimulation was far beyond adequate). Well then, if it's a disorder, in the language I know quite well, it's a disease. And if it's a disease, I have it!

Researching a little more, I realized there is also a line of reasoning by some doctors who do not think this way, and they do not consider it a disease, which in my opinion is a purely chauvinistic attitude! You can bet that study was conducted by some man with nothing to do. You mean to tell me only *their* thingee deserves treatment??!! Pathology, prosthesis, tons of medication, surgeries, then Viagra, Cialis... And what to do when we are unable to receive pleasure? With what dries up? With what doesn't thrive? Tell me. Show me a little light at the end of the tunnel.

Whatever it is: disease, disorder, emotional problem, "inability" or "inexperience" (the last two refer to the partner, of course), doesn't interest me. I am frigid, and if it is temporary or definitive, I still have no means to know. For now, it is only a verified fact, and that's enough for me to enter into a state of consummation.

What matters in all this nomenclature is my total lack of desire to have sex and my own private desert, my semi-arid being, which is on fire, but not out of pleasure. I want treatment! I need urgent treatment! But who should I look up? A sexologist? A psychologist? Or gynecologist? A priest?

Well, based on my literary findings, this condition may have a physical, psychological, emotional or religious (the reason for the priest) cause, and it is common to have a combination of two or more sources. Among the psychological causes, depression (I have), stress (I have a lot), and relationship conflicts (I don't have, but would sure love to) are the most frequent. The physical causes may be thyroid disorders (I think I have), an increase in the prolactin hormone, which is directly related to the hypothesis (it is involved in the production of milk – I am a woman, so I must have that), lack of feeling related to diabetes (I eat chocolate all day – could it be diabetes? Just to be sure, I need to check that, too), alcoholism (yes, my occult cirrhosis will not allow me to lie) or the use of anxiolytics and antidepressants (I use them all!). I don't think the emotional causes need to be checked right now, after all, I feel completely fulfilled, emotionally speaking. And religious ones? I am honestly much too concerned about my own health problems to think that having sex could be some sin and that my frigidity could be some sort of punishment. I decided to be practical and removed the priest and confession from my list!

Going back to my symptoms, I must point out that anxiolytics are an absurdity to me: if the lack of sex transforms me into a pool of anxiety, and the use of anxiolytics can cause frigidity, anxiolytics – medication that should control anxiety – are the actually root of my anxiety! That's pure logic!!

I also learned that frigidity may also be caused by discomfort produced by a bladder or vaginal infection (just as I suspected, I have a urinary tract infection!), or by an endometriosis (when cells from one of the layers of the uterus are deposited outside it), "surgical removal of the ovaries or estrogen deficiencies in menopause" *I read out loud.* Menopause. I knew turning 30 would not bring me wonderful things like everyone had insisted would happen. Maturity, bull, it's called old age. Who do these people think they're fooling? *I thought.*

With my head full of theories, I decided to visit a gynecologist first. If in general the changes are to occur from the inside out, so be it. Besides, my health plan doesn't cover

psychologists. Medicare probably thinks it's a luxury, and a mind as good and well resolved as mine doesn't need "superfluous treatment."

Once in the room, I explained my case to Dr. Linda Kayes, in detail (I don't think I'm ever going back there). My anguish led to me choosing a doctor's office that was not part of my daily routine and I thought my fame as a hypochondriac had yet to reach those neighborhoods. But I guess I was wrong. Those receptionists who answer at most ten calls per day must sit around gossiping with each other all day long because they have nothing else to do. That's it. They must be spreading the news about me. Now, besides being sick, no one believes me.

"Amanda, the fact that you had unsatisfactory sexual relations once does not mean you are frigid", she said, obviously minimizing my state.

"So, what's going on? This is something I've never had. I know I have many health problems. But when it came to sex, everything always went well. And now this..." I was saying, when she interrupted me.

"I don't think it's anything serious. But Amanda, if it *is* an infection, we can treat it with antibiotics. Let's run a few tests and depending on the results, we'll know what to do", she said patiently.

"How many tests?" I asked anxiously.

She laughed and continued her explanation in a condescending tone, like a first-grade teacher. And I felt like that stupid little student who needed the slow explanation in order to understand any subject.

"If any hormonal alteration shows up, we're going to correct the problem calmly," she added.

Calmly? I thought. She must be nuts! Like I said, I don't think I'm coming back here.

One week of waiting for the results, no infection (I think my warrior bacteria are in such a state of inanition that they are feeding off of any other bacteria that dare to get close), and hormones at ridiculously normal levels. *This is impossible. Either this laboratory doesn't do a good job, or they went and changed my exams with those of some perfectly healthy girl. Do I have to change labs again? I changed labs five times just last month and I'm running out of alternatives.* I promised myself I would start believing in the lab results. BUT, I CAN"T! My symptoms are so obvious that I can't understand how, with all the technology involved in lab work nowadays, they still can't detect my diseases.

I only know I arrived at the doctor's office wanting some sort of miracle pill (some sort of sexual stimulant) and I left with the following instructions: "do pelvic muscle exercises, which can help you feel more pleasure during sex." Yeah, exercises with my pelvic muscles... in other words... "Amanda, you need to start masturbating." That's a good one! The lady charges $200 per visit and dishes out that kind of advice.

I need something a little stronger than that. Doesn't she get it? Something like a shot of Oxytocin, for example. I know it doesn't exist. But, it sure would be great if people with problems creating ties or having good sexual relations could use a medication that would increase their levels of Oxytocin, the hormone related to love. Imagine! An injection of hormones that shoots straight to your brain and charges your emotions, and five minutes later you have become the most loving creature in the universe. It could be used as a violence inhibitor. *Amanda Loeb, you are a genius. I must patent the idea.* I could call it the Cupid Drug, or the Love Pill, who knows? *Yes, I am a genius!*

I was upset the entire week, but tried to follow Dr. Kayes' instructions. I only stopped all movement down below when it was time to eat, so I wouldn't choke. Twenty-four hours of daily contractions!! I actually think I felt cramps!! And every once in a while, a little sign of pleasure, I must confess.

Now, I can only think about one thing, since I've already gone through so many self-tests. I urgently need to try it out for real, with a real partner. I thought of calling Diego and asking him to help me out with this – but I quickly decided against that. I think it highly unlikely he'd agree to help me give my reputation a new start, but I must try. The worst that could happen would be for me to get a big fat NO.

I decided to put that matter aside for a while and occupy my mind with other thoughts. Temporarily forgetting about the matter seemed to be the most intelligent and healthiest thing to do for now. After all, I need the other part literally involved to solve my case. And as you can see, I have no one to help me out right now. When you really think about it, who needs a man when you have a stock of Godiva chocolate in the closet?

3

I wake up almost every morning at the same time, 7:15. Normally *indisposed.* I get up with just enough energy to slowly crawl from the bed to the bathroom. After I expel the first morning toxins from inside of me, I truly wake up.

I have to pay more attention to my morning chores. And, with my eyes still half asleep, I analyze my entire body in search of any signs of abnormality or symptoms of illness. Whenever I wake up feeling *good* (which rarely happens!), I immediately think I may have one of those taciturn, silent diseases, the worst kind, you know? If I wake up with a headache, I quickly take an Extra Strength Tylenol. And, if it's almost miraculous effectiveness does not quell the pain, I begin to despair. I no longer see the symptom as a simple little headache. I start from the principle that a resistant headache may be a migraine or even an aneurism. And if I must choose, I go for the second option, of course! I begin a countdown, expecting the worst to happen. In this case, the worst is a CVA (cerebral vascular accident, or stroke). And if I wake up feeling *really bad,* call the medical team, a priest, and my family members, because there is no doubt this will be my last day.

Then, I recover my mental sanity and what's left of my dignity (I need to rescue both each and every day). This is generally after I talk to my mother on the phone, which is already part of the routine, since I talk to her every day. I decide I don't have an aneurism and I don't need a doctor, and brush my teeth instead. I try to find some way to move on to the practical part of my life. I hang up and drag myself into the shower, in search of a hot bath. But nothing in my life is that simple. I spend a long time examining every square inch of my body and only after the third check do I finally feel ready to turn off the water.

Every day of my life begins this way. It's the first sign of my disorder. It's what I remind myself of every day: "Yes, you have a problem. You have a serious problem. You need professional help. The kind you refuse to get."

I take another ten minutes trying to decide what to wear. I must admit that unlike most women, this is a rather banal task for me. I'm a practical person. And, as such, I have all my clothes previously arranged in my closet. Just like my medicine cabinet, my wardrobe functions with a color code and by order of priority. Clothes fit for work are organized in outfits on the right. Clothes fit for weekends and leisure on the left. And clubbing clothes and eveningwear are in the middle. The pieces are put together on hangers, forming matching outfits, by color and style. Shoes are positioned right under each hanger, which also makes my life much easier each morning. Some people would say this is a symptom of OCD (obsessive-compulsive disorder), but I prefer to believe I am only pragmatic, and I refuse to waste my time in front of a mirror every morning.

I make my own coffee in an Italian coffee maker that Eric, my brother-in-law, got me for Christmas. It is incredibly versatile. It grinds Colombian beans I buy at Dean & DeLuca and boils the water and prepares my coffee the way I like it, strong and full-bodied. I love that good coffee smell that permeates the apartment every morning. At times like this, I even feel like a normal person. Seated at my tiny kitchen table for two, with my "I Love NY" mug in one hand, I calmly skim through *The New Yorker* with the other.

I follow my routine, taking my pills. A pack with 8 capsules of a vitamin complex I've been taking for two months. Ever since I visited a GNC store and was convinced (rather easily) by a clerk that I should take them because they are the *in* thing. "*All the celebrities are taking them, didn't you know? I swear. You know that actress from the film... what's it called? Can't remember now. But she's 60 and has the face and body of a 35-year-old. These vitamins are really amazing. And they combat free radicals and the effects of aging.*" She said as she analyzed my skin. And as always, she didn't have to give me a very elaborate line for me to buy two extra-strength kits, enough for two months. I paid $49 plus tax for each. That could be added to other expenses made in such a manner (irresponsible!) and blow my credit card limit again. But who cares about money when we are talking about health? Eight gigantic pills I shove down my throat, every morning, right after enjoying my cup of coffee and bagel with olive cream cheese.

I'm not someone obsessed with slimness. But everyone knows obesity is also a disease. And as such, it also enters my life, unfortunately transforming food into an enemy of pleasure. So, I try to control my weight with some strict rules. I do it with actual pain in my heart, because I love to eat! During the week, I eat little and only healthy foods. I always have those vitamin compounds at home, the kinds that say they replace a meal. Shakes and soups that alternately enter my menu during my weeknights. They help me maintain my BMI (body mass index) at an acceptable limit for my bone structure. And then on weekends, I let it all go. Everything goes, from brunch with Eggs Benedict and bacon, to a fat, juicy hamburger for lunch and potato soup with cheddar cheese for dinner. And then, if I begin to feel guilty, I jog for two hours in Central Park and feel forgiven. Three kilos lighter, in my head, and I feel ready for another week.

Physical exercise is a challenge for me. At this point, I am able to infringe upon three of the eight capital sins. First, because whenever I think about it, I immediately get lazy, something that happens a lot. Just talking about it makes me tired. The association with vanity is obvious. Don't believe anyone who says they spend 4 hours (minimum) per day at a fitness center just for health reasons. I can't understand those people! How can they spend their days and nights off in a crowded room, full of strange equipment and sweaty people, thinking it's awesome? Some even think it's a cool place to pick someone up. Do you believe that? Here's where I violate the third sin. I die of envy of people who have the disposition to care for their body with that much dedication. But, what can I do? I'm lazy, and my health doesn't help. I know that physical exercise is fundamental for aging with dignity, without arthritis, diabetes and circulation problems. Not to mention flaccidity, cellulite and other things that drive women nuts. But seriously, having stretch marks is not a sin, and cellulite is not a violation. So, I see no need to move my body from the soft sofa I have sitting in the corner of my living room. On a rainy weekend or in the winter, absolutely no way. I'm an assumed sedentary woman. Jogging increases my blood pressure. Swimming? I hate it. Soul-cycle? OMG! My legs hurt. Muscle-building? Boring. The only parts of my body I exercise every day are my fingers, on my computer keyboard. An average of fifty words per minute, which I'm proud of.

First, I check my iPhone to see if I've received any messages during my reinvigorating nap. Then, another look at my agenda. Professional commitments and doctors' appointments are always the first part of my day. My day, which beings on some waiting room sofa, or at a work meeting outside of the office and ends up in my living room, surrounded by thousands of papers at around 8 at night. Every day.

I leave home and walk the streets of Manhattan. I live just eight blocks from the office. That really facilitates my life since I also suffer from claustrophobia and many other imaginable phobias. This makes it impossible to use the subway or public transportation in general. I've already tried. Unfortunately walking the station's corridors wearing my anti-virus mask just doesn't work. The kind the Japanese also wear to avoid contamination. Here, I need to make a small observation: I love Tokyo. It's the cleanest city on the planet. The day I decide to leave Manhattan, I will certainly move there. But, back to the facts. Unfortunately, they – the masks – are not considered stylish in New York, and the sound of contained laughter as I pass by wearing mine is extremely intimidating. I admit it may be slight exaggeration, but don't forget: I'm sick!

So, I prefer walking, something I enjoy a lot. Sometimes, I allow myself to pause in the middle of the rat race just to observe people, cars, in short, the life of the city in movement. My brief respite is suddenly interrupted by a sharp horn blaring, almost puncturing my eardrums. Typical New Yorker, waking me up and making me get out of the way of the taxis to avoid an exposed fracture.

When I moved to the city five years ago, I began a true crusade in search of the perfect apartment. Everyone knows the Manhattan real estate market is insane. Absurd prices for studio apartments the size of a pantry. And the brokers actually say that renting "that" is a great opportunity. What's worse, depending on location, state of conservation and competition to live in the "food closet," it ends up being true.

I immediately contacted several brokers and told them about myself (not a lot), my work, and my demands (if we can call them that) for the right apartment for me.

"Yes, that's right. I need an apartment very near a hospital, a big hospital with all the specialties and a good Emergency Room. *I kept repeating over the phone until convincing them my request was no joke.* No, no. I don't have any contagious disease, nor am I going to live with some elderly person. *I repeated several times until tiring.*

But only one very nice broker, called Tim, actually took me seriously. He was efficient and discrete right from the beginning.

I know it may sound strange. After all, the normal thing is to ask for parks for the children to play in and good schools. Or even a party neighborhood for the younger crowd. Tranquility for the elderly. But, I only need a good hospital close by to feel comfortable. Maybe, next time, I'll ask for a building that expressly prohibits pets. Not that I don't like animals, but one episode in particular made me look at them in a different light, that of the enemy. But, I'll tell that story later. Some brokers I spoke with insisted on questions like: Are you going to live with your sick parents? Or, do you have some horrible disease? (In the latter case, we will not rent an apartment to you! Let that be understood). Or even, could you give me details about the reason for your demand? *Others would ask, with even greater curiosity.* Tim was the only one who simply said: "I know exactly where to start looking and I'll call when I find something just right for you." Two weeks of back and forth, and nothing. I visited about fifteen apartments. Some even had some potential to become a decent home. Others that had noisy neighborhoods, dogs, cats, or children (all probable hosts of creature hostile to my health) were immediately rejected. Very old buildings may actually have some charm, but living among rats and neighbors with dubious hygiene, let's be honest, I could only do if my good sense abandoned me like all my others have already done. I continued my tireless search until the third week, when I received a euphoric and, by then, exhausted phone call from the broker saying he had found what I was looking for.

"Amanda, I need you to come here immediately. I can't hold it for long, but I guarantee you're going to love it."

"But I'm in the middle of a meeting at work now, Tim. I can't just run out of here." *I said trying to argue.*

"This is Manhattan, Amanda, you'll get used to it. If you can't come by 4 p.m., I'll unfortunately have to show it to another client, who is also interested in this apartment, but I'm giving you preference because I believe this is the apartment for you."

"All right Tim. Give me a few minutes and I'll call you right back, ok?" I quickly hung up and was slightly excited about the chance to finally put an end to my days on that dusty pull out bed in the guest room of my mom's house where I had been living for more than two months.

I hung up and called the only person more interested in my search for the apartment of my dreams than myself. My mother. She couldn't take any more of my crises, panic attacks, and cleanliness manias (make up part of my set of measures to prevent infectious-contagious diseases). She flipped when I told her I had made an explanatory handout that had to be followed – with my medications spread about her living room, bathroom, and kitchen. And every time the phone rang, she would go, irritated yet excited, because only the probability of Tim finding the ideal apartment could fill her with the hope of being able to get rid of me one day. And, it seemed that day had arrived at last.

"Mom?" *I asked, even though I was sure it was her on the other end.* "Tim called me and said he has finally found the right apartment for me. The problem is he needs an urgent answer and I can't leave the office now. (Before I could even finish the sentence, or had the chance to ask her to please go take a look at the apartment for me, she offered). *I'll go for you.* She said happily.

"Mom! If I didn't know you love me, I'd be offended, you know that? But thanks anyway. I'm going to call Tim and tell him you're going in my place. And when you are there, please call and tell me all the details about the place, ok? Don't forget anything. Observe every little detail... Mom... look at the details. *I insisted because I knew she might miss something.*

A half hour later, I already had my Zip Code and address in the Big Apple (64th Street – Upper East Side – Manhattan – NY). It was just eight blocks from Cornell Hospital and thirteen blocks from Lenox Hill Hospital. In an emergency, I'd only take sixteen minutes to walk the longest distance, health permitting. Or nine and a half minutes with normal traffic, six minutes at night or on weekends. If I needed an ambulance, according to my calculations, and if the ambulance driver was not some snail, four minutes and twenty-two seconds would be enough for the paramedics to be knocking at my door.

Perfect. More than enough time to save a life, and in this case, mine.

Decoration was comprised of a few pieces of furniture, all in light hues, well-lit and good ventilation. Some stuck up decorator could even call it *clean*. But, the fact is the decoration of my apartment is like that not because I follow some sort of minimalist trend. Perhaps, I follow the decorating style of a hospital! But, that is because it is much easier to identify and destroy a focus of contamination or some undesirable guest (rat or cockroach).

The neighborhood is excellent. It has several doctors' offices with every kind of professional. One Walgreens, two Rite Aids, three CVSs, two GNCs, one Pharmacy and more than a dozen Duane Reades. And even my favorite, East Side Drugstore. Five Starbucks guarantee my shots of caffeine and relaxation on weekends and an "Au Bon Pain" or an H&H Midtown Bagels East, on the corner of 80th and 3rd, to fulfill my carbohydrate ingestion needs. I had to take a good walk to get there, just for the pleasure of eating them, but even with my thoughts on the fact that so many carbohydrates could lead to type 3 diabetes, I still run the risk.

That's how I try to stay alive, day after day. Living with normal problems and existential conflicts just like any other girl my age. But I also (try to) peacefully live with my disorders: hypochondria. That's my drug. It depresses me, and commands me, and dominates me. It is my vice, controlling, and asphyxiating me.

I know that all those stories they tell you about, you know, about disease maniacs, may even seem funny.

I must admit they are truly funny and I have to confess I feel pathetic for being the reason behind the laughter. But, what can I do? I'm nosophobic, so excuse me, okay? And for those who don't know that hypochondria or nosophobia is a disease, here's a little information. It's right there, triumphant, in the manual of mental disorders. It's not just in my head! I read an article, in a renowned, serious newspaper, that 4% of the population that goes to doctors' offices and hospitals in the United States suffers from this. And 2% of the Internauts are "cyberchondriacs," using the web to research diseases or exchange medical experiences and discuss symptoms. I heard the total reaches 1% of the world's population. And if someone out there has any problem capturing percentages and thinks 1% is nothing, I repeat: 1% of the world's population finds nothing unusual in relating a mosquito bite to hepatitis B! "Isn't the disease transmitted by blood? Well? What's so absurd about thinking a filthy mosquito that feeds off people's blood could be a bioterrorist?). Those same people think they are going to die in the next 60 seconds! Just like me!

4

It had all the ingredients to be a simple Tuesday, with plenty of sun outside the office, while I was stuck inside with the air conditioning blasting away against the back of my neck. I have always hated air conditioning. First, for the obvious reasons: it propagates potential respiratory diseases. Second, because I hate feeling cold. Also, the central air at the office was programmed by someone who must live in the North Pole, in some igloo with no heat. The person in question has no idea that thin women (and thank God I'm thin) feel colder than men do. Biology explains this: thin women have less fat, consequently less resistance to cold. Besides being more full-bodied, men have more muscle mass. The more heavy set ones, like those around here, have more body fat, thus more resistance, and don't feel much cold. Not like me. I feel cold, and a lot! And if I didn't take my sacred dose of vitamin C every day, I would always be coming down with a cold, even in the peak of summer.

When Julia called, it was already a little after 2 p.m. and I had just returned from lunch. I had lots of work waiting for me, and not the slightest desire to do anything, except shoot the shit. So, at that moment, Julia was given my most undivided and sincere attention.

- "New what? Beautician? I asked as I checked my emails.

- "Yes, Amanda. I think you are the only girl on this island who hasn't heard of her." *she continued:* "She's Brazilian and she does artistic waxing."

"What's that? Does she dye our pubic hair bright colors or something like that?" *I asked, though still not very interested in the subject.*

A loud chuckle burst from my iPhone, leaving me nearly deaf.

"No. Amanda, when the subject isn't medication, directions for taking medication and new diagnosis technologies, you are the most uninformed person I know." *She taunted.* "She uses wax, the famous Brazilian hair removal system. Nothing new so far. But she is able to make incredible designs. It's really interesting. A friend of mine went there a few weeks ago and was really pleased with the flower she made, and it kept its shape for days."

"A flower. Wow!" I exclaimed sarcastically. I couldn't believe that crazy talk. I tried to remember why I was paying attention to the conversation. And then I did. Just because of my total lack of desire to get back to work, which consists of nothing more than trying to save the world from its predators. But instead of that, Julia was trying to convince me to go to a hair remover who used a millenary torture technique, in my opinion, so I could have a flower designed on my intimate parts. Did anyone happen to see my mental sanity lying about somewhere?

"I already made my appointment. I'm going on Thursday. And I'm already thinking about the design I want. Maybe a star. I don't know..." *She said all excited.*

"Why should I participate in something like that? I don't have a boyfriend, and I'm not planning on going to a pool and I think... Honestly, it's absurd to pay $70 plus tip for a horrendous experience like that."

"Amanda, think of it this way. You're walking down the street and suddenly feel bad. (She knew she'd get me with that one, and then continued.) You are rushed to a hospital and when you get there, there's this big, ugly nurse. She pulls down your pants without worrying about the content she's going to find. She doesn't even wonder if everything will be in order or not. (She paused for dramatic effect.) Then, she doesn't even worry about covering you with a sheet or towel. After all, it's more important to find out what's wrong with you. And then..." (I was forced to interrupt her.)

"I get it. My hairy intimate parts will be exposed for all to see."

"Besides, you'll feel 20 pounds lighter once you get rid of all that hair down there." (I could detect muffled laughter).

"Wow! Twenty pounds, I must really be in need of a diet. 20 pounds in one day sounds like a great start." *I replied, participating in on the joke.*

"Isn't it great?" *She was excited again.* "Can I make an appointment for you too, on Thursday?" *She asked.*

"No can do on Thursday. But give me your find of the century's phone number and I'll call her myself to make an appointment."

"Amanda, really try it. You'll look beautiful and you could ask her to design a heart. Who knows? Maybe it'll bring you some luck on your next conquest." (She laughed uncontrollably. I hate when she does that.)

I took down the address, hung up, and went back to work (at least I was trying to get back). But, besides my imaginary health problems, I'm also known for being extremely curious. And, I couldn't get the story of artistic pelvic hair removal out of my head. So I decided, after Julia's free and spontaneous pressure, that I should give it a try. And I even thought: "Why not? Who knows? Maybe I'll enjoy it. Who knows? Maybe after the first time, I may want to try something else. So, I called.

"Lucinda's beauty salon, Marcia speaking." "Hi, how are you, Marcia?" "Fine, thanks. Would you like to make an appointment?" "Yes, please." "Hair, skin cleansing or hair removal?" "Artistic waxing." (I felt ridiculous pronouncing the word "artistic".) "What hair are you going to remove? Groin, underarms, legs or full package?" "What's the full package?"

"Full package is the artistic groin, underarms, half legs and upper lip. When you get the package, you get a special discount, and you also get a refreshing gel to use the first days after waxing. What would you like?"

"Complete package... I think..." (I hesitated a moment, I don't know what this complete package is. I didn't know if I'd be sorry about my choice, but I decided to risk it.)

"Name and phone number, please?" *I informed it to her.* "Is Monday, 5:00 p.m., good for you, Amanda?" "Yes, yes. That's great."

"All set. Lucinda will take care of you on Monday at 5 p.m. sharp. Thank you." (And she hung up as quickly as a delivery restaurant clerk who needs to hurry to take the next call before the customer gives up.)

***

The weekend went smoothly. I didn't have a heart attack so, no threat of an aneurism. The thought of convulsions was another thing I didn't have. I didn't even have to turn on the computer to get information about any new disease. *The New York Times* obituaries only had about a half dozen deceased, most of who had died of old age, purely and simply. The others had died in a car accident, four from the same family. A tragedy, no doubt, but no report of serious disease. Endemics, epidemics, or pandemics were also discarded for now. The world was a safe place for the time being. And that's a relief. There were also many announcements for Seventh-Day Masses and Ceremonies at synagogues. Nothing that really caught my attention.

I went to the movies with Lauren. She was able to get a day off from her domestic marathon. Eric had agreed, with a little "arm-twisting," that she needed a day off. Sophia's a doll, but to be a full-time mother is not an easy mission. So, he stayed with her so we could go to the movies and have a "sisters' day out." Like in the old days. Ever since Lauren got married, our moments together have grown few and far between. It's a shame. We used to be so close. We'd spend hours on end trying to be rebels or to save the world. We watched a romantic comedy, one of those that make you sick to your stomach it's so sweet, with a predictable ending and moments when we almost cry, but a good movie. We ate lots of popcorn. I hadn't done that in ages. I was even able to get Lauren to drop her eternal salad, vegetable and chicken diet to try my buttery popcorn and a little of my ice cream with caramel topping. She made a "yuck" face, but then asked for a little more. It was great. Great being with her. Great not thinking of anything but fun and good times. Great spending a little of my time with someone I love so dearly.

I returned home at 9 p.m., took a warm shower and put on my red pajamas with the white polka-dots. I brushed my teeth and put rollers in my hair so it would be curly the next day. I like my straight, naturally straight, hair, but sometimes I feel like a change. I had a salad for dinner; ate light. After all, I had already eaten a lot of junk when I was out and I didn't need indigestion. But, just to be sure, I took an antacid before going to sleep.

As I got ready for bed Sunday night, I remembered I had made that appointment with Lucinda for Monday, the most famous Brazilian in New York after Gisele Bündchen. She was the miracle woman who would make me lose twenty pounds in pubic hair alone. And, besides that, she would help me conquer the heart of some "handsome bachelor" running loose about town, if such a thing truly exists.

I remembered to put on brand-new lingerie to make a good impression. That was my second mistake. The first was to have chosen the complete package without any right to reimbursement should I back out. The second mistake cost me a pair of Victoria's Secret panties. In the end, the first mistake I found out much too late and it cost me a lot more than that. After all, there is no price for pain and despair.

It was finally time for me to meet Lucinda and her rewarding form of torture, which had made my friends line up just to give her big, fat tips on top of her pricey services. I had a very light lunch, a salad, vegetable mix, and tuna. I didn't know what was waiting for me so I chose to avoid foods that might have undesirable side effects, like gas, for example. I'm a hypochondriac, but I don't have to go about giving out free samples of all the gases that inhabit my body.

At 4:30, I finished things at work and left a note for my boss. I lied, like everyone else at the office. I said I had an appointment with a former revolutionary from Colombia. A really important guy who had precious information that could help me win a lawsuit I had filed against illegal deforestation in the Amazon. The guy had lived in the forest for several years and knew the region's problems well. *That was the story I made up.* At the end of the note, just: "Back in two hours." And, I left.

I grabbed a cab on the corner of 3rd and 72nd. The cabbie was a nice Indian man, with an enormous red turban. We were there in no time. The salon was Downtown, on 14th Street, between 6th and 5th. I didn't even have to look very hard. It was clearly signed and the movement of women going in and out was impressive.

When I entered, I immediately ran into Marcia, the girl from the Dial-a-Torture delivery service. She gave me a sweet smile, yet on her face I could read: "Are you the next victim? Come on in and relax. Lucinda will torture you in a minute."

"Good afternoon. Do you have an appointment? What's your name?" "Amanda. I have a 5 p.m. appointment with Lucinda. I think I'm a bit early." "Yes, sit down and wait. Lucinda's with another client."

Her voice was incredibly powerful in person, and she had an arrogant and bossy attitude. She was that kind of girl who loves looking you up and down, head to toe. She wiggles her nose from one side to the other as she talks, as if she smelled something foul.

Less than ten minutes later, Lucinda appeared at the top of the stairs. The salon was large and it covered two floors. The hairdressers and manicurists stayed on the bottom floor, while the beauticians were on the second floor. The lady at the top of the stairs was tall and blonde, but, although I am no specialist, I could see the dye job was of poor quality. Always smiling and very pleasant, but what you deserve at those prices. She had to make up for it somehow, going beyond her talent of creating designs on her clients' well-groomed pelvises.

I have to trust her. I thought. But, on the other hand, it is just hair. It will grow back. If I don't like it, it's quite simple. I've already gone more than a month without sex. I'll just go another two weeks until the hair grows back again, that's all. No one will have any knowledge of this episode if I don't say anything.

She made a signal. I thought it was for me, so I stood up. Then, she asked me to go on up and to follow her. And, so I did, following her to the room where I would be scalped. After climbing the stairs, I entered a spacious corridor. There were very tiny rooms on both sides, cubicles with semi-transparent glass doors. You could see nothing but shadows moving about. But, from behind the low doors, I could hear groans, cries for help (I think that was my imagination), excited conversations and feigning laughter. The film "Hostel" quickly haunted my mind. With each step I took towards my voluntary torture room, the butterflies in my stomach increased in number. Already nervous, I began to fear the worst. A crisis, right then and there, a nervous attack, a hysterical scene worthy of *The Exorcist*. I tried to control my mind. *"Take it easy Amanda. It's just a rite of passage into the world of mature, well-resolved women, hairless."* I thought. It worked. I was able to calm down and find out where all that was going to take me.

We arrived at one of the boxes. There was a cot, and some items, which were probably part of the ritual and indispensable for Lucinda. There were some hooks on the wall where I could hang my handbag and clothes. That's right, all my clothes. As soon as I entered the minuscule space fit only for two, me on the cot and her standing, Lucinda started giving me instructions and left the room, perhaps for me to feel more at ease. Since it was the complete package, I was to remain only in my lingerie. After being ordered what to do, I timidly took off my clothes. I arranged them neatly on the hooks and lay down on the cot.

Lucinda returned a second later. She had some wooden spatulas in her hands and a small jar with some sticky, brownish caramel goo (with some ridiculously over styled name), I later learned was the famous hair-removal wax.

Without even looking me in the eye, she began her job, stirring the wax and asking: "Do you want a Bikini wax or normal?"

A thousand thoughts ran through my mind, but none that justified the question. I had no idea what she was talking about and in a purely arrogant act, because I didn't want to look stupid, I guessed: "Bikini." That was my third mistake. Right then I learned a very important lesson. Never answer a strange question, in a strange environment, unless you do so with another question!

"I'm going to begin with the pelvis, and as I do my job, you can concentrate on choosing a design. Have you thought of anything?"

"You can choose a design?" What's she talking about? Does she have some sort of obscene catalogue with several designs, sizes, and hair colors? Is this a salon or a Sex Shop? I thought. And she did. Right under the cot, there was a small cabinet where she kept her work tools. She opened one of the drawers and pulled out two enormous photo albums with several models, probably clients, exhibiting her "art."

"Open your legs wide." *She ordered.*

"Hmm..." I consented although I didn't understand a thing.

There I was, completely vulnerable, wearing only panties and a bra, my legs in the lotus position, and here she comes wearing a surgeon's mask on her face and twine in her hands. I couldn't contain my thoughts and the images flashed through my mind again, as if I were watching a trailer for the film "Hostel" in my head. *Oh my God! What does that woman intend to do with the twine? Tie up my arms and legs so I can't run away?* As I went nuts and watched, my eyes popping out of my head in fear, she ran the twine along the sides of my panties, holding the front part down very firmly so it wouldn't interfere with her work, out damaging my panties beyond repair. Whew! I sighed in relief. There was no reason for concern except for the pair of new, beautiful and expensive underwear, which I would have to throw in the trash.

I skimmed the photo albums nervously, but without taking my eyes off her every move. She seemed not to notice my tension. And if she had, she showed no signs of caring. She went about organizing her supplies on the table that was there to help her. A warm pan with the brownish goo inside (the so-called wax that I had already ensured was disposable). Electric hair clippers, some new, wooden spatulas, in several sizes, an eyeliner pencil, and sterilized tweezers were all I could see. So far, nothing my other ego, Amanda the Hypochondriac, had to worry about.

I pretended I was familiar with everything and made sure to choose the design quickly. That wasn't hard. My choice was the Playboy logo, which between you and me, I doubt she pays copyrights to use. However, I decided to forget the fact I was a lawyer and as such I should do everything within the law. After all, it would be a privilege for Playboy to have its logo designed on my intimate parts. And that would not imply, could not be considered misuse of image. (I imagined myself in a courtroom, defending this version to some cranky judge).

"Your hair is too long. I'll need to trim it a little before starting. That way it hurts less."

Hurts less? Why? Does it hurt a lot? No one told me this was going to hurt. A little, insignificant pain okay, but really hurt? I think I want to call my mom.

"Oh! Sure." I agreed, thinking... *Relax, make yourself at home.*

She carefully trimmed the long hairs. I remember thinking how deft she was and how meticulously she treated my privates.

Then, she pulled out the larger wooden spatula and began to spread that hot cream over my pelvis. I felt it burn. The smoke rose and the faint smell of burnt hair reached my nose. But, up until that moment, the feelings had all been good. Warm, relaxing, even pleasant. That's when she pulled for the first time and with every fiber in my being I pleaded: God kill me!

It was so fast and yet so fatal. I thought every inch of skin on my body had been ripped off with it. I imagined my pelvic muscle, visible, with blood shooting towards the ceiling. I tried to look through my half-closed eyes, but I didn't have the guts.

That's when Lucinda became aware I was new at this. I was white as a sheet and my breathing resembled the panting of a tired dog. She stopped for a few seconds to ask if I needed water, or if I would be able to hang in there until the end.

"Are you okay?" She asked with a maternal look.

"I'm fine. How about you?" I answered, out of it.

She laughed and went on with her business. I could only think that Julia's recommendation had been a provocation. She didn't want to go through this traumatic event alone. Therefore, she had included her so-called best friend in the little package. And I'm sure she said horrible things about me to Lucinda, because I am certain this woman hates me.

I felt so much pain at times I wanted to give up. However, the relief of a few painless minutes was sufficient for me to create courage and allow her to begin her medieval process all over again. Other thoughts came to mind, bewildered by such immense pain. I thought of the worst exams I had already taken in my short lifespan, and thus I was able to relax. After all, what is Lucinda's "art" compared to a lumbar puncture or an endoscopy?

"Girl, it's looking great." She said in her attempts to console me. "It is, isn't it?" I answered moaning, almost crying. Trying not to make it too obvious, so she wouldn't think I was some sort of nutcase.

During a short moment of distraction, mine of course, Lucinda, demonstrating incredible strength, spun me around 180 degrees, using a really fast "ninja" maneuver. By the time I realized what was going on she was already waxing my perianal and labia area. Only God and I know how much that hurt. I felt a stubborn tear trickle down my face but quickly wiped it away so she wouldn't notice.

"I'm almost done here." She said with her face between my legs.

"Uh-huh..." What else could I reply, I thought.

A new mantra popped in my head and I began to pray, or better, to beg for this to be over soon. And when

I thought the worst was over, she appeared with the damn tweezers in her hands.

"I need to use the tweezers here because a few hairs always hang in there, okay?"

"No! No! No! Of course, it's not okay! My soul is nothing but blood, and I can't begin to describe my skin. You are a crazy, unloved sadist and I'm an insane masochist who pays you to torture me! I don't think so! Nothing is okay in this godforsaken room!" I shouted, in thought.

"No problem, Lucinda. Go right ahead." And I smiled sheepishly because I knew I was lying and I knew she knew it too.

"There. Hurt much?" She asked, smiling.

Does this "crazy lady" actually think this is funny? I wanted to tie her to the cot and remove every hair from her body just using the tweezers. Very slowly, plucking every inch of her arms, legs, face, anywhere I could find even a single hair. From her big toe to the last hair in her nose. Her entire skinny body. Look her in her eyes and smile warmly, as if saying: "welcome my friend." I vented my anger again, once more to myself.

"No, honey. Not at all." I said trying to convince myself.

I didn't even want to look at the result. I felt too exhausted from all the mental effort to take off running. Trying to convince myself the sacrifice would be worthwhile.

"Let's do the rest?"

Rest? What rest? The truth cruelly filled my ears. I had agreed to the complete package, which included half-legs, upper lip and underarms. I looked from one side to the other of the tiny room trying to find the most dignified exit. Jump through the small window? I don't think so. Surely, my hips would never fit through it. Or grab my handbag when Lucinda was distracted and take off through the door? Neither of the two seemed dignified enough. So, I decided to face it with an open chest, or better, open arms. It was time for the underarms.

I had already paid, suffered, and cried. What could be worse? And it was. Although my legs are longer and have thicker hair, the pain was relatively less than in the tiny underarm area, which didn't come close to reminding me of how badly I suffered with the groin. Hang in there quietly for another thirty minutes. When I was just or the verge of screaming: God take me away from here! Or Enterprise, teletransport me! I heard the news of my release: *"We're all done for today,"* she said triumphantly after another job well done. *"For today? For the rest of my life! I'm not coming back here ever again."* I thought with assurance. Suffering because I'm sick and need medical care and exams is one thing, but to suffer in the name of vanity, of futility, is something I don't believe in at all. It's against my principles. Honestly now. Some women do it every fifteen days. And, *I'm* the one who's nuts! Hah!

"I'm going to sprinkle some talcum powder down there and then leave the room for you to get dressed, okay?"

"Yes." By then I was basically monosyllabic.

As soon as she left the room, I jumped into my pants and put on my shoes at lighting speed. I grabbed my blouse and handbag, running towards the exit as I was still getting ready. Before breathing fresh air again, I paid and left a generous tip for Lucinda with the implicit promise to never set foot in there again.

When I was already on the outside, Marcia the arrogant called out my name three times, and on the fourth attempt I could no longer ignore her. She was less than three feet away.

"Amanda, you forgot your refreshing gel." *She yelled.*

"Oh! The gel. Thanks Marcia. How could I ever live without it?" *I joked.*

I threw myself into the first cab that stopped in front of me. I shouted the address to the cabbie who looked at me in fear.

I want two things during my next incarnation: to be a man and to be ignorant. I must say ignorance truly bliss. Those who are have no idea how wonderful it is. Look at me for example. Up until today, I had no idea a woman had to suffer so much just to keep things smooth and pretty. And, now that I know, I would have preferred dying rather than knowing.

***

I went back to work, walking with some difficulty. When I opened the door to my office and finally thought of sitting, I turned and saw my boss standing right in front of me with a silly smile on his face.

"So then? How did it go with the Colombian revolutionary?"

"Well. To begin with, he wasn't Colombian, but Brazilian. And furthermore, he wasn't a revolutionary, but a terrorist. I don't think he'll be much help. I didn't believe in his stories and to be honest I hope to never see him again.

He left the office clearly disappointed. *I felt to blame for having exaggerated so much.* I locked my office door so no one could disturb me and went about spreading that tedious, refreshing gel on my red legs. It burnt more than hot chili pepper in the eyes. I was dying to call Julia and unleash my anger. But then I looked at my bunny again, and this time I took a good look. "You know what, it actually does look good." I thought, now proud of myself. "Now, I just need a magician to pull it out of his hat! Who knows? Maybe that will solve my frigidity problem."

5

I had always gotten along very well with animals, until today, until this ill-fated Saturday morning. Utopically, it was to be my day off. Relax, take a walk, see people, take my clothes to the dry-cleaners, and buy fat-packed foods, guiltlessly, to stuff myself with over the weekend. That was the plan! Nothing special. Just a weekend of laziness. No concerns or commitments with work. Nevertheless, my castle of cards came crashing down and my plans unexpectedly interrupted by an unruly pit bull. It is now eleven-thirty in the morning, and here I am in the emergency room. With a very young and inexperienced resident stitching a "prêt-à-porter" with two bands on my leg.

When I woke up, I could never have imagined what was about to happen. My day started off like every other day. I woke up early, had my five minutes of paranoia after gazing into the mirror and realizing my skin was dry with small red blotches spread about my face. They didn't exist up until yesterday. It didn't take long for me to associate that with *Sjögren Syndrome* (a disease that causes extremely dry skin). Of course, I was convinced that was the first symptom of early aging. My skin could be suffering a terrible process of acute dehydration. In a few months, I would be unable to cry, I would have no more saliva in my mouth, which would be full of cavities, and I would feel horrible pain in my joints. Soon after, I would be in a wheelchair due to a worsening of arthritis. Oh my God! That's how it happens. I know it! *I could see myself in total agony.* Five full minutes with my thoughts spinning about that unfounded theory. But, since both the dryness and blotches disappeared ten minutes after washing my face and using a powerful moisturizing cream, I rid my mother of another one of my morning crises.

I brushed my teeth and organized my clothes to take to the dry cleaners. Everything was great. I had planned to have breakfast at Viand, on 61st and Madison. I always go there on Saturday mornings for my morning meal and to chat with Fernando. He's a very friendly waiter who shouts out my name, announcing my arrival to the entire restaurant as soon as I appear on the outside of the glass door. I grabbed my bag of clothes and my handbag. I was just about to open the door when I realized I wasn't carrying my keys. So, I went back to get them from the dinner table, probably taking less than a minute. A precious minute that could have saved my day and my leg. When I finally exited the apartment, I ran right into the attack. Yup, directly into it. I opened the door, and there they were: the delivery guy, the dog, and the dog's owner. Up until then, I hadn't exactly understood what was going on. But, it didn't take long to understand that the dog was attacking the delivery guy. And the dog's owner was attacking the dog, or something like that, and that I would be the next to be attacked. Lack of luck on my part? You can say that again.

Ever since I moved into this building, I have always had a peaceful coexistence with my front neighbor and his pit bull. Both are gorgeous, I must admit. But, if the dog's owner is as aggressive as his PET, I intend to keep my distance. The lovely dog was assaulting the FedEx delivery guy. It had already bitten his boot and was about to go for his jugular. That's when I showed up. I saved his life, and instead of thanking me, he didn't say one word and ran off. I didn't hear one thank you! He just left his packages behind, and me, at the mercy of the bloodthirsty dog. The guy just disappeared down the stairs. Result: as soon as I heard the slam of my apartment door closing behind me, the *monster* had already taken possession of my thigh. With its sharp teeth, it clamped down on a large piece of my leg between my hip and knee. It enjoyed my femur as if it were a juicy piece of meat. I didn't have time to understand the situation. Much less think of reacting! That hairy thing charged at me, its mouth salivating. I felt like fresh tenderloin hanging from a butcher's hook. The laceration was the size of the Great Fissure, in other words, impossible to calculate. And it wasn't even 10 in the morning!

While one mammal was trying to control its other mammal, which had already ripped off half my leg, the latter began to enjoy tearing apart my clothes. My Pink dry cleaner's bag, which I had just bought less than two weeks ago, was ripped to shreds. The bag had three pairs of jeans (two were Diesel), several quality and expensive sets of lingerie, nylon stockings, two Chanel suits with their respective skirts and a pair of Dolce & Gabbana slacks, some Abercrombie & Fitch T-shirts, a pair of GAP pajamas and sheets made of pure Egyptian yarn.

Just like the animal, it became impossible to control my "rebellious" side. No matter how hard I tried, I couldn't contain myself. Words poured out of my mouth, ordering things that made perfect sense to me. In reality, they were part of my instinctive plan to save myself.

"Do you know how much bacteria that beast's mouth has? I'm bleeding a lot. Do you think it hit my artery?" *I rehearsed a faint, but went on:* "I don't have a chance. I have to get to a hospital in five minutes or it will be too late." *I was shouting.*

"Calm down! Let me control him and I'll call an ambulance."

"Let that monster eat my dirty La Perla lingerie! I hope it dies of indigestion. And go call 911, now! Call Animal Control Services, the Secret Service, police, FBI and CIA. *I shouted, throwing my cell phone at his head.* "Let go of that animal and call now! If not... I'm going to bite *you!*"

He hesitated for a second, but decided to listen to me. By that time, he didn't know which was the real danger, the pit bull, or I. As the dog continued to tear into my Diesel jeans, the annoying guy finished calling and announced: "They'll be here in ten minutes. Try to remain calm."

Remain calm? Remain... huh..? What does he have in that hollow head of his? Rocks? Didn't he get it that in a few minutes all the blood that keeps me alive may be on the floor and my spirit in another solar system? Doesn't he realize that his beautiful puppy has just ripped off my leg? And looking at my lacerated leg, I still had to remain calm! I was thinking, wanting to poke his eyes out with the heel of my shoe.

"Ten minutes!" *I shouted at the top of my lungs.* "I could be dead in ten minutes. You're an imbecile. Didn't you tell them your little mutt mortally wounded me? When I die, because I know I'm going to die, you'll be indicted for murder! I'll go to hell, but you'll soon be joining me! You and your murderous mutt!"

Although I was nearly unconscious and fighting off fainting, I could hear the sirens from afar. I could recognize different ones. One was the police and the other an ambulance.

"I can already hear the ambulance. But what about the helicopter? I can't hear the helicopter? Didn't you call a helicopter rescue team? You're a dumb! I swear! I've never seen anyone as stupid as you in all my life!"

After that, I swear I can't remember a thing. The last thing I recall as I passed out were my hands sliding down the hall's beige wall, leaving a trail of blood as evidence to my suffering.

There are several speculative theories and poorly told stories. Someone not very trustworthy and gorgeous, like the dog's owner, says I flipped out completely. He says I was shouting unintelligible things, like: "get the defibrillator, my heart is failing." Or "I need my computer. I have to check if this breed of animal transmits any specific disease!" Or else "I didn't update my will this week. I can't die like this, not in such a stupid manner.

Why not a generalized infection? At least I would have time to redo my will." He also mentioned something like: "Julia was right. She had a feeling something bad was going to happen to me. Thank God I had my little bunny made. I won't be embarrassed at the hospital!" I honestly do not believe that version. Or the other, that says I started a medical monologue. One of the paramedics asked Brian, my neighbor, the dog's owner, if I was a doctor or a screenplay writer for the TV series *House*. I demanded exams, medications, and vaccines from the paramedics. Full of reason and scientific terms he says he can't recall, given the circumstances, nervousness, and tension. Others say I fainted. I fainted right there, by the stairs, as I was trying to control myself. I was breathing with difficulty, faster and faster, until I fainted. A guy from the ambulance, the first one to arrive, said I was already blue in the face, and that just before passing out I had told him, "I'm AB negative. The rarest type, don't forget, don't forget." And out I went, he says.

As always, my mom thinks all the theories are true. I think it's all a bunch of scheming and gossip made by curious people who have nothing better to do.

***

I've finally been allowed to go back home. Despite the trauma, I'm anxious to get back to my place. Not that I don't like hospitals mind you. In reality, I love them. But staying in a private room is one thing. Staying in the emergency room with a bunch of sick people is a whole other story.

I've always made a point of paying for a good health plan. I have Medicare Top, the type that covers private rooms in five-star hotel type hospitals. Big rooms with curtains, wide beds, and all that fancy equipment. They have all the cable channels. A large closet and an extra, and comfortable bed for a companion. And the bathroom? There's even a bathtub. Wonderful. It's like a vacation at a spa.

I tried to convince the doctors it would be best if I spent 48 hours under observation. But, since my wound, according to them, was minor and superficial, I could already go home.

"Amanda, your cell phone's vibrating. Want to answer it?" My mom asked as she stretched out her arm to hand me the phone.

It was Lauren, my kid sister, asking me if I was okay or if I would be in an induced coma for a few weeks. Of course, she was just joking as usual.

"Hi, Lauren. Yeah, I'm fine now. Thanks for your concern. Yes, huge. The monster ripped half of my right leg off. I swear. Ask mom." *My mother just kept shaking her head as she listened to the dialogue, astounded.* "Thanks for calling. Love you too." *And I hung up.*

The second I hung up, a doctor stuck his head in the door. He was one of the doctors taking care of my case. He was experienced and he wanted to give the final instructions before releasing me. He approached to talk, a bit tongue-tied and walking in a slightly funny manner but, all that mattered was that he was competent. He seemed concerned, wanted to provide the necessary explanations about my debilitated health, prescribe the medications and set up my return visit.

"Amanda's fine. It was a superficial bite and only four stitches were needed. No nerve was affected. She'll take the stitches out in a week, but she can already go back to work on Monday." Just like that? A beast attacked me on my day off. I needed several stitches on my once perfect leg. I'll spend my entire weekend in bed. I had more than five shots. And I'm not going to spend a single day in the hospital.

I saw the relief on my mother's face. After all, this was my first real occurrence in years. She was shaken up and visibly concerned. Maybe because she knew, even before I did, that this episode would not end there.

After all, an animal bite can transmit a fatal disease, popularly known as rabies, or hydrophobia. The disease is transmitted by the animal's saliva, if it is contaminated. The symptoms generally appear two years after contamination. It's called rabies because the person or animal tends to have terrible fits of violence, get very irritated, and lose control. My mother was informed by the doctors and instructed to ask for the dog that had bitten me to be tested. She already knew I'd go nuts and would spend the next two years just waiting for the disease to appear. I was given the preventive medication, a vaccine with the disease's antibodies and a tetanus shot. But, they were just preventive. If I had really been contaminated, nothing could be done. Certain death was definite!

I went back home and my mother insisted on staying with me over the weekend. She kept me away from the computer. She needs to ensure I wouldn't research anything about diseases related to dog bites. She talked to my neighbor who paid a friendly visit with flowers and apologies.

I asked her to answer the door and to tell him I was in a coma. As such, I couldn't accept his apologies, much less see him again.

"Good afternoon, I'm Brian. My... it was my dog... Attacked Amanda... Well, I... I'm really sorry. *He said, embarrassed about what had happened, handing my mother the flowers.*

"Mom, don't forget to tell him to take those flowers back. One murder attempt per day is sufficient." *I shouted so he would hear me.*

"Sorry, Brian. Amanda's not in a good mood. She's a little upset about what happened. You understand, don't you?" *She said kindly.* "But thanks for the flowers. The doctor said she's fine. She needed four stitches in her leg, but she's fine. Don't worry." *Trying to console him. As if he was the one needing consolation.*

"I understand. I'm going to work now, but if you need anything just give me a call. Here's my card. I mean it, if you need anything, just call." *Feigning concern.*

"Brian Marshall. Le Antique Restaurant. In Soho? I think I've heard about that place. Are you the manager?" *She asked out of curiosity.*

"That too. It's my restaurant. I'm the owner. But I can guarantee the food's good. The Chef is from Turkey, but he studied gastronomy in Paris. He has some incredible recipes. You should try it someday." He said, bragging.

"Who knows, maybe one day?" *She said and then smiled.*

"You are my guests. Accept that as my apology, since the flowers didn't have the expected effect." He was disappointed. I think he thought, what type of woman doesn't like flowers? Simple answer: the allergic ones.

He said goodbye and left, taking the flowers with him. Then I had to listen to my mother defend, and even worse, praise the guy, asking me if I had noticed how cute he was. Single, intelligent, loves animals, good heart. Full of predicates. The guy suddenly became the best catch in town. "I think not! Thanks," *I thought.*

"It wasn't his fault Amanda. The dog got restless because of the delivery guy. That happens. That's life." *She argued.*

"How do you know all that after a five-minute talk with him?" *I asked impatiently.*

"I saw it in his eyes." *She said smiling.*

Saw it in his eyes! Right. My mom's like that. She has this habit of thinking everyone's good. She looks someone in the eyes and if they aren't yellow (hepatitis) or red (pot), she immediately thinks they're a good person. If he has sheepish or "poor me" eyes, well... She quickly labels him a "good son-in-law." I can't take it!

I spent what was left of my Saturday in bed being babied by my family. Lauren, Sophia, and Julia also came over to care for me. On Sunday, I could feel my strength slowly returning to my body.

I got up at 10, which is very rare. I love to sleep, but I'm always out of bed by nine. I took a shower and when I had finished, Julia, who was at my apartment bright and early, helped me change the bandage. But, don't think Julia was interested in my health. She was dying to hear about Brian. She wanted details about the visit he had made. So, she and my mom delighted in romantically fantasizing with all of the details of my tragedy.

We went out for brunch, the three of us. We went to Café Dari, in Soho. The line was huge, but I was able to convince the manager that I couldn't stand around waiting for a table for more than 30 minutes. He kindly offered us the first table available. I was actually thankful for yesterday's incident for a moment. Spending hours in line at a restaurant stresses me out. On our way back, we grabbed a cab to the entrance to Central Park at 61st and 5th. We walked a little and sat in the green grass to rest.

I got back home while the sun was still shining. I got my work clothes ready for the next day and went to bed early. I slept like an angel, no memories, and no nightmares about what had happened. I had apparently gotten over the episode.

6

"To be honest, I don't recall how long it's been," I say, trying to minimize the issue and pretending it was of no importance. "Maybe eight weeks, or more... I don't remember." "Eight weeks without sex!" she screamed into the phone. "Julia, I really hope no one is near you at work right now, because you have just announced to your entire company, perhaps the entire block on which it is located, or maybe even the whole city, that your best friend hasn't had sex in eight weeks." I could not believe she did that! Julia's impossible. So much indiscretion regarding other's sexuality! "This is an intimate, that is, private matter, and I am only sharing it with you because... because... I don't know... I don't even know why", I was already irritated by her thoughtlessness, "maybe because I can't keep my big, fat mouth shut," I added, upset and mad at myself.

"Amanda, it's been five weeks since Diego, do you realize that? I'm already organizing my next birthday party and you're still trying to get over the consequences of the last? Is that right, eight weeks? I don't know how you can go so long without sex with so many wonderful men in this city," she laughed. "You have to agree with me. It may be difficult to find a stable and long-lasting relationship in New York, with a sensible, mature man, who has a good sense of humor and responsibility; who thinks about the future and has a good job. But sex? Amanda, come on…"

"First, take all the married men off your list of wonderful. At least 50% of the men in this city are already in committed relationship. Then, of the remaining 50%, you can exclude gay men and those guys who are scared to death of a relationship. And artists too, and those who think they are artists. And those with three jobs (they are too busy to even think of sex) and have no time for a relationship. The workaholics, who I have no interest in, and the unemployed, who I also have no interest in. And then you get to the mind-boggling conclusion that less than 2% of the men who live in New York are available and willing to have a relationship", I concluded my analysis, exhausted. "And even then, you have to be careful, because that 2% has just come out of some sort of relationship and they are frustrated, hurt or just want a one-night stand with a beautiful woman."

"But who's talking about a relationship, Amanda? I think what you need is some fun. Hot and exciting fun. Who knows, maybe an affair, maybe even with some married guy, to break the routine? Hmm, they're the best," she roared, laughing loudly. Of course, Julia wasn't serious. Ever since I have known her, not once have I seen her go overboard. Her taste in men may be questionable and even a little problematic, like the time she ended up at the police station because her then boyfriend was carrying enough marijuana to supply the entire city. But, she had not known the guy was a dealer. She only found out after the police officer showed her his criminal record. Even today she swears the guy is a sweetheart and was only holding onto the package for a friend. Yeah, I know, my friend's pretty naïve.

"Julia, you've known me for so long... Haven't you realized yet that I don't take any chances with casual sex? Do you have any idea how many people in New York have STDs? Besides..." she interrupted me. "I know, I know... But how are you going to solve this problem then? Because, let's face it, your situation can now be considered a problem. We could over categorize it as an emergency."

"It's not my fault I have such highly selective radar. I can't just go out with anyone. Or hop in bed with some guy on the second or third date. I just can't do it!" "Second or third date? Amanda. Wake up girl! I know, you took one of those anti-whatchamacallits that make you all drowsy, right? Huh? Third date? Yeah, right... that's why you've been so long without any carnal comfort."

"I'm just waiting for a decent guy who has a job and reasonable hygiene. Of course, if he knows the Heimlich maneuver, I will have found my soul mate." "Reasonable according to whose parameters? Yours or mine? For me, if the guy's feet stink a little or he arrives at my place a little sweaty after a tennis or volleyball match in Central Park, I'm cool. It's even acceptable if he skips a shower once a week. And whose maneuver? What's that Amanda? A new S-M technique?" she let out another burst of laughter. "Oh, I know, I am just kidding. The guy's feet can't stink, nor his breath; he has to be thin and have hair, and now he has to know that." "You'll never get it. How horrible... That's why you only date rock band vocalists with long, dirty hair and jeans. My God, pants that go straight from the store to his body and from his body straight to the trash can. Not to mention that happens without the jeans ever seeing the inside of a washing machine. No doubt, my friend, your parameters have way too many formulation breakdowns," I taunted. "I know, call Diego. You never know, right?" she suggested, knowing I couldn't do that. "You know I've already thought about that. But the chances of hearing a loud "no" are enormous. And since I'm used to working with realistic data and good odds of winning, I prefer not to put all my chips in with such a high rate of failure." "You need help in this search of yours from Mr. Reasonable Hygiene," she said. "I think I can help you with that." "How? Don't start with one of your exes from college. Those frat guys who sit around drinking and burping while watching football at some Irish pub in the city. And then they call us "my pretty lady". No way! Or one of the guys from your "rock star" boyfriend's band. What's his name again? That guy full of piercings? Please, heavy use of Benadryl really upset my stomach. Then, I'll need medication to control gastritis and...". "Amanda, I think the solution to your problems is 6 foot 5 inches tall and standing right in front of me," she interrupted me, not interested in the end of the story. "Who?" I asked, not knowing whether the answer would please me. Actually, I was almost sure it wouldn't. Julia had been my friend for years and she could never understand what it was that

I was looking for in a boyfriend. Well, I can't blame her. I am a truly complicated person. Things like kindness, cleanliness and tolerance are not part of those indispensable characteristics for what she calls the "perfect man kit".

"My boss!" she said, excitedly. "Whoaaaa! Calm down there. You must be nuts. That bald guy with serious bad breath? No way..." "No, Amanda, not that boss. The other one, Peter." "But wasn't he engaged, at the door of the Church?" I asked, this time anxious to hear a negative answer. "They broke up. That's all everyone has been talking about here at the office. People even made a pool to guess the reason for the "perfect couple's" break up. Remember how interested I was in him when I first started here? Remember how he treated me when..." Julia now went on and on about Peter, the wonderful, not showing any interest in her. Obviously, it was because he had had a beautiful fiancée who speaks four languages, works at a travel magazine and has all the makings of the perfect wife. Everyone admired (or was jealous) of the couple and made plans for the two to stay together and soon have a beautiful child. Yes, beautiful, since both were, of course, beautiful. The perfect genetic combination. While Julia rambled on, I thought: just a few weeks ago that guy was off limits. I sighed. Now, he could be the charitable soul who would help me cure my frigidity. Could that be so? I tried not to get too excited about the whole thing. If they broke up, it could have been for several reasons. And, some of them could make room for reconciliation. And, the last thing I needed was more headaches. Other things were going through my mind.

Maybe he had cheated on her, and I wouldn't like having that sort of man in my life. If he had the balls to cheat on a woman like her, what wouldn't he do with me? I tried not to think about it. It was all delirium in Julia's mind. Peter was still unreachable. "Julia, I have to get back to work. We'll talk later." I hung up before she could begin making plans for my wedding with Peter. Four days went by, and to be honest, I no longer remembered that crazy phone conversation I had with Julia. She didn't mention "Peter, the Perfect" either. It was Thursday, a hard day at the office. We had just irrevocably lost a lawsuit against a fishing outfit that won the right in court to continue fishing for lobster during spawning season. An unbelievable and totally incoherent verdict. But, it's like I always say: no one knows what goes on in the mind of a judge. I guess this one just loved lobster and couldn't live without it, even if that meant the extinction of the species in a few decades. Carl, the attorney who coordinated the lawsuit, was visibly crestfallen, crushed. I even thought about offering him one of my pharmaceutical cure-alls. I think it would have done him good to sleep three days straight. My boss was not in the friendliest of moods either. They expected to use this lawsuit as a sort of banner to lead a new campaign around the world to make small fishermen aware of the damage this does to the environment. I wasn't directly involved, but working at an organization such as ours (where you are extremely loyal and literally try to save the world) is like playing on the Yankees. Winning is all that matters and the only thing that makes everyone happy.

I get an average of about 30 text messages per day on my cell phone. Most are from work colleagues. Some are from my mother, or Lauren, a few from Julia, Marc and one friend or another. So, I wasn't surprised when I received a message from Peter on my iPhone. He works at an advertising agency and maybe he wanted some advice about some legal matter. I know. Not probable, but what ensued was even more improbable.

Peter Thompson: "Are you free tonight?" Wow, straight to the point. He obviously got my number from Julia, who must have laid it on real thick. I can even see her telling him how I need affection and a friendly shoulder, or something of the sort. Me: "Depends, what's your idea?" Peter: "Just dinner, wine and some pleasant conversation." Perfect! I loved it! Julia really had done her homework. As promised, she had arranged a date between Peter and me. That girl is awesome. I first met Peter a few months before, when Julia practically dragged me to a company party. They worked at an advertising agency that has an account with almost all the big fashion companies in the market. Julia insisted a lot. As I argued and invented excuses not to go, she practically begged. But I wasn't feeling very well that day. Trying to make her understand, I claimed in scientific terms what could be summarized as: *Julia, I can't. You don't understand, but I AM SICK.* There was no way out. Less than 40 minutes later, there I was, dressed and made up like some drag queen, at Julia's party. Bustling party, cool people, colorful drinks and a bunch of strange advertising people. Dressed up like new grads. Cheerfulness, surrounded by beautiful and incredibly thin and tall girls, all possibly models. The music was so loud it affected my auditory nerve. I still don't know how I didn't go deaf. Perhaps someday, I'll still feel the (delayed) results of that night and need to wear one of those hearing devices.

It all took place at one of those wonderful Manhattan penthouses, on the corner of 5th and 27th. What a beautiful place! I could see a great part of the illuminated city from up there. The Chrysler building, the lighting of the Empire State Building (which that night was paying tribute to the French flag). It probably referred to some celebration or holiday in the land of gastronomy, champagne, cheese and wine. *Man, I'm hungry!* These parties are usually fantastic. And it was in such a seductive ambiance that my eyes first gazed upon Peter Thompson.

He was wearing a blue and white striped shirt, rolled up sleeves, new jeans and new shoes. His wavy hair needed a new cut, but nothing that could make someone think he was sloppy with his appearance. Well-shaven, smooth and light-colored skin. He didn't have those scars or irritations most men have. His hazel eyes were a mix of different colors, ranging between dark green and light brown, almost yellow. He resembled a little boy, but with strong arms. Beautiful arms, and a carefully chiseled body, no doubt from a fitness center. But, it wasn't just his beauty that impressed me. It could have been his size, attitude, his expressive eyes. An attentive, daring look. He circulated among the guests with ease. He would make sarcastic, yet funny comments. Say intelligent things. He would arrive, leave his mark and disappear into the crowd. It seemed like part of a plan to structure the image people made of him. We were introduced during one of those appearances, in a group I was trying to befriend. He smiled, shook my hand and said something nice. But even before I could even get excited, I also met Barbara, his fiancée at the time.

I became silent and pensive. My fingers were glued to my cell phone keyboard. I thought of several words and tried to organize them into a sentence that would make some sense since the euphoria of the situation did not allow me to act naturally. I was flustered, I admit. It is not an everyday occurrence to be invited to dinner by a man like that. A guy like Peter, my mother's dream son-in-law, apparently satisfied all my demands. The only thing more difficult to do than find a man like Peter available is to find a free cab on a rainy day. So, I had to be careful with my answer. If I said yes, I could look too easy. If I said no, I may never get another chance to say yes. I thought about it, decided not to take any chances, and accepted. There are a million girls in this city after a guy like Peter. That was already reason enough for me to accept. When considering my sexual situation, the invitation could just not be refused. What do I have to lose? Nothing. So...

Me: When and where? Peter: This evening at 7:45. Is that good for you? It's funny how people react to certain situations. When he mentioned an exact time like 7:45, I actually doubted his mental sanity. And hey, coming from me, the strangest person I know, that's kind of hilarious. Could he have obsessive-compulsive disorder? I didn't have the courage to ask. But let's face it, it's pretty strange for someone to set an informal appointment like that: *Let's meet for coffee tomorrow at 3:28.* Me: Perfect. Where? Peter: 56th and Broadway. Don't be late. I'll meet you in the lobby of the Summer Hotel. I want to show you something there. But I'll make reservations at a restaurant nearby. We won't be staying at the hotel bar. Me: Sounds great to me. How do I find you there? Peter: Don't worry, I'll find you! (That sounded so powerful! Perhaps a little authoritarian, but I must confess I enjoyed it.) I hadn't been this excited in a long time. My stomach was aflutter, and it wasn't the usual gas. I wanted to dance about the office, tell everyone that a wonderful man was interested in me. And that I finally had a date with someone worthwhile. I opened the door and asked Sarah, my assistant, to bring me a cup of chamomile tea. I took two anxiolytics, a cup of tea and did some breathing exercises to keep myself in control of the situation. I only had three hours to finish my work at the office, which would take two hours and forty minutes, go home, another 15 minutes on foot, plus three minutes in the elevator to my apartment on the fourth floor. Take a bath, another 20 minutes, think of which clothes to wear (times like this are the worst for me!), make-up and perfume, another 15 minutes. Calculating the time, it would take for the taxi to cross town from the East side, where I live, to the West Side, where I would meet him, I thought: I think I can be there by 7:45, as he expects.

I didn't spend more than five minutes of my precious time calling Julia and telling her everything that happened. I had to hang up, making her furious and with a touch of envy and curiosity, waiting for the details I promised to tell as soon as the date was over. As I rushed about to avoid being late, I mentally asked my body to obey me and for my mind to not stop functioning unexpectedly. A breakdown now would be unacceptable. Heart and lungs, although accelerated, were also functioning in an acceptable manner.

Bath taken, make-up on – light make-up this time, almost imperceptible. And the clothes? I had to choose something that stood out. Not too sensual, yet not too sober, something elegant and discrete. Pretty enough to make a good impression and daring enough for Peter to want to find out what was underneath. *Not this one. This one either... oh my, I still have this dress? This one... maybe. I think this one will do.* I chose a black and white plaid dress, with a knee-length, flared skirt. An average- sized, black camellia (according to Marc, one of my gay friends, men don't like women who wear huge flowers on their clothes or in their hair. So, I'm going to wear a discrete camellia and if the date is a fiasco, I already know what to blame: the camellia!). Small silver purse and very high heeled, silver sandals. At first, I thought it was perfect. When I got in the elevator and saw myself in the full-length mirror I felt insecure and the insecurity grabbed hold of my soul and created a huge lump in my throat. Time to take another tranquilizer. This time I opted for homeopathy; they are not as strong, and I couldn't take the chance of looking all drugged up on my date with Peter.

When my watch read 7:35 I was already in the cab. The driver was quick. Despite his poor English, he seemed smart enough to avoid getting me stuck in the middle of Times Square at rush hour. At that hour, I'd be stuck there for an eternity and no doubt be late, ruining not only the date, since Peter was very clear about "Don't be late!", but my health as well, because I would have to take huge doses of Prozac to get over the trauma. As I observed the city lights at the end of a warm, but pleasant, summer night, I tried to guess where Peter would take me. I prayed it wouldn't be some Italian cantina, where my dress would be motive for plenty of snickering, since it resembled a checkered tablecloth. It wasn't red and white, but nevertheless, it would not make me feel less ridiculous. Another disastrous option would be one of those Korean restaurants with the grill in the center of the table. The smoke those things emitted would attack my throat and I'd spend the whole night coughing. What a complete disaster that could be! When the cab driver pulled up six feet from the hotel door, my watch read 7:41. I still had four precious minutes to go in, cross the lobby and make myself visible so Peter, like he had said, could find me. I ran elegantly to the entrance where the doorman was waiting for me with the door half opened. As I approached, I asked him where the aquarium was – the only hint Peter had given me. The young man kindly crossed the hall with me, leaving me in front of a huge aquarium in the middle of the lobby decorated in Chinese motifs. Fish of many sizes, types and colors swam about in harmony under glorious blue and green lighting. An obvious simulation of the ocean's colors. It was a beautiful place. I was distracted by the beauty of the fish when Peter approached. I didn't notice his arrival, but I saw his reflection in the aquarium's glass wall. His cologne was alluring. I turned quickly, giving him the chance to greet me with a kiss on the cheek. "You look beautiful. Love the flower." Either Marc was wrong or Peter was a natural seducer. Either way, one point for the camellia. "Where are we going?" and before he could reply, "May I ask you a question?" "We're going to a French restaurant nearby. I arranged to meet you here, because I love this place. This aquarium is fascinating. Don't you think?" "It's truly beautiful" "What's the question?" Question? What question? Trying to remember after being swept away by his smile. "Why 7:45?" I found it strange to be so precise with the minutes and smiled kindly. "I leave the gym at 7:20. I calculated enough time to get home, shower and change. I thought we would take about 15 minutes here, so I made the reservation for eight. The restaurant does good business and reservations are a must." "Well then... We had better get going or we'll miss our reservation." The restaurant was truly fantastic. The food was divine, dessert exquisite and coffee delicious. Peter enjoyed the fact I was a girl who likes to eat. I'm not some diet nut like most women. I really eat. Most women don't eat on first dates, he said. Some never eat. And that's horrible, because then HE feels inadequate. Unfortunately, the night ended early. Peter interrupted my romantic deliriums saying he had a morning meeting and had to get up early. But not before solemnly promising to call me back for another date. As we left the restaurant, he put me in a cab on my way home. He said goodbye, giving me a tender kiss on my forehead. As I went on my way in my cab, he turned the corner on foot towards his place, four blocks away. While still in the cab, I remembered I couldn't leave Julia hanging without any news. She would probably be kept awake thinking about it. And worse, she may ask Peter about our date. I couldn't allow that. "Tell me everything!" she answered her cell phone anxiously. "There's not much to tell." "What do you mean? Don't start, Amanda. Don't start with this Miss Discretion business. Cut straight to the details." "Well, we met at the hotel..." "Hotel, just like that, straight to the hotel room? But doesn't he have an apartment in Manhattan?" "Julia, we met at the door of the hotel because he wanted to show me an aquarium. That's all." "Oh... okay, go on." "We went to a wonderful French restaurant. The conversation was great. We talked about lots of things and found out we have a lot in common." "Like what? Does he also eat medication like candy?" "Very funny. Look, I've got to hang up. The cab is already pulling up to my building. We'll talk tomorrow, okay?" "No!" she let out a deafening scream. "Pay the cab and keep on talking. I want to know all the details." I paid the cab and continued. "There's not much more to say. He was a gentleman. Kind and sweet, as you are already tired of knowing. We had dinner, and he said he had to get up early. He called me a cab, said goodbye and left. That's all." "And the kiss? Wasn't there a kiss?" "In reality yes, and it was very tender." "Does he kiss well?" "I don't know, Julia." "What do you mean? You kiss the guy and don't know? If you don't know, who does? Me?" "Julia, he kissed me on my forehead." "Your forehead? You must be joking. You want to kill me! My grandfather kisses me on the forehead! I don't believe you spent an entire evening next to that Greek god and only got a kiss on the forehead, Amanda!" she grumbled, incensed. I talked to her for another ten minutes, trying to show I was enchanted by his behavior. And that I would be very happy if he asked me out again. I hung up, entered my apartment, took a bath, and as I got ready for bed, I received a message on my cell phone. *I had a lot of fun this evening. Let's do it again. Pleasant dreams.*

7

One mocha Frappuccino, please. And a slice of pecan pie, too. I gave the girl with the unusual red hair my order at Starbucks while I waited for Julia. I was hoping she wouldn't be too long. Otherwise, my anxiety would force my ingestion of carbohydrates to reach the maximum limit I allowed myself on weekends. I was so hungry that my mouth was watering while my eyes scanned the coffee shop's showcase of delicacies. I got so busy with my weekend chores that I simply didn't have time to stop for lunch. Julia and I had agreed to meet there at about two in the afternoon. Since it was Saturday, I first had to finish my start of the weekend routine. A few items on my list of duties had already been scratched off: Take my clothes to the dry cleaners, ok. Get a manicure, pedicure, and skin cleansing, ok. Clean and organize my closet, a chore that only gets on my list every 15 days, but it was there this Saturday. I would do that when I got back. It was just past noon and I had already finished my list, except for my closet. But, since I had a couple more hours, I decided to do a little shopping.

I took a short route that included the new Victoria's Secret on Lexington to buy some lightweight pajamas. Then, off to the Chanel store to buy perfume, Mademoiselle Chanel, my favorite, which was almost gone. I also decided to stop by Bloomingdale's to buy a set of Ralph Lauren sheets for my bed, which, as you know, is rarely visited by a man, but you never know. And when that happens again, I intend to have new sheets. It would soon be Sophia's birthday, so I thought of seizing the opportunity to buy her a beautiful present. Maybe one of those *American Girls* dolls, with their white skin and long, black hair, big eyes and long eyelashes, like hers, and a complete wardrobe for her and the doll.

I used my credit card for the first time that day at *Victoria's Secret*. I walked through the ground floor, among the lingerie, creams, and corsets, in search of comfortable flannel pajamas. After all, the last thing on my mind was to impress some guy. Actually, my frigidity, which could be an acute and temporary case, was becoming chronic, due to the pure lack of enthusiasm in someone to help me solve the problem. I found what I was looking for on the third floor among the cute *Pink* stuff. I bought a pair of pink, flannel pajamas with colorful hearts and another pair that was blue with tiny and colorful stripes. And a pair of big fat and very comfortable slippers. Two T-shirts and six pairs of socks, some lingerie to replace those I had lost during my attack. I'm actually thinking of sending the bill for those to Brian, which only seems fair. I bought everything I needed. Perfect apparel for a single girl to have fun at home alone, with plenty of popcorn, good movies and several novels and self-help, medical and a few esoteric books to read (yes, I'm very eclectic).

I left the store and ran across the street while the cars were still stopped at the traffic light on 60th and Lexington, on my way to *Bloomingdale's*. The store was crowded, as usual, on Saturdays and at this time of day. I was walking through the store in search of an elevator that could take me to my sheets as fast as possible, since I didn't have much time to spare. I spun around 180 degrees and finally caught sight of the transportation I wanted. I ran to the door as several people were trying to accommodate themselves in it. When I was fewer than three steps from the door, I had a moment of hesitation. Even before I could control myself, I was the victim of a terrible incident. I felt this intestinal discomfort at the door of the elevator. So far, no problem, it happens to everyone. But what happened next left me hysterical and horribly ashamed. I felt this uprising in my stomach and when I thought about holding it back, I just made matters worse. An evil smelling stench engulfed the environment as soon as the elevator door had closed quickly behind me. I feigned total ignorance and looked for a corner to lean against. But as I moved, the odor spread about the elevator, making me look even more suspicious. The bed & bath department was on the sixth floor, but I was so embarrassed I abandoned the tiny, crowded cubicle on the first stop, which was the third floor, feeling the critical and outraged eyes of all the other occupants. I preferred to take the stairs and thus have the freedom to release a few more minor pops without bothering anyone or further embarrassing myself. I was unable to count precisely how many, but that day my daily production was much higher than the national average of 15 farts per day.

Some days I feel like that, a bottle of champagne ready to burst. I don't know if it happens to everyone, but I get the feeling I produce more gas than the average person. I have always been able to hide this, keeping a degree of normalcy during each situation. But things have gotten a little out of control lately. I can't take elevators with other people anymore. Taxis have become a scary experience as well. I've created embarrassing situations in lines at the post office, bank, supermarket, and drugstore. If I see a line with more than 10 people, I try to avoid it. No doubt the wait would lead to a disastrous episode.

I went to the gastroenterologist about four weeks ago. He explained that a normal person releases on average one to one and a half quarts of gas per day including burps and flatulence. But even though I swore my daily production was much greater, he was not convinced and said it wasn't serious.

"Amanda, this is normal. Everyone releases gases. More on some days and less on others. But it's normal." He said, not too patiently.

He's one of the doctors I have the displeasure of running into on a weekly basis at the Lenox Hospital ambulatory center. Dr. Hanson is a big man, and one whom I'm actually a little afraid of. His deep voice takes me back to my pre-school classes. I feel like a little girl being scolded for peeing my pants involuntarily. And he, just like my evil teacher, does nothing to make my life easier.

"I know my bowels are lazy and I need some additional incentives for them to work. It's probably because I have some sort of genetic defect. I should be admitted for more detailed exams." *I ordered desperately.*

"Amanda, I can't do it. You're not sick. You just feel something that is normal for any human being. Maybe we should change your diet? How about that?"

"That's it? Sorry, but I don't think you get the picture. Some days I feel like a personal sanitary landfill. What is a change in my diet going to do? My case is surgical, I know it." I responded angrily. Since when is a change in diet a solution for a problem as serious as mine. I thought.

He laughed and insisted on the diet.

"Are you on any sort of diet? Anything different you may be eating every day that could be causing this discomfort?"

"I'm on the blood type diet. I'm AB. I bought the book on that diet a few years ago and I really feel better with it than my previous vegetarian diet. I eat a lot of fruit, fiber, lamb, and turkey. I love codfish, tuna, cheeses, and dairy products. I drink water all day long. I'm not a full-fledged smoker, but I do smoke occasionally, and I'm a social drinker as well. I mean, sometimes I get home completely drunk. The other day the cabbie had to open the door to the building for me, but that doesn't mean I'm an alcoholic. Or does it?"

"Smoking and drinking are not healthy, you know. But that has nothing to do with your case. But, the diet you described seems balanced. I'm going to forward you to a nutritionist. If there is any problem with your diet, she'll help you solve it. That's the most I can do here," he said, getting rid of me before I could say another word.

That's all. Visit a nutritionist? I was outraged. For a hypochondriac like myself, leaving there with an indication to see a nutritionist didn't seem to be a very serious option. But he didn't seem to care about the disappointed look on my face. When I begged him for some medication, he practically kicked me out of his office.

***

I finished my shopping at Bloomingdale's, but didn't have time to get Sophia's present. It was almost time for me to meet Julia, so I went straight to Starbuck's. When I arrived, Julia wasn't there yet, so I had time to arrange my packages on a table in the corner near the window. That way I could see the activity on the street. I placed my order, sat down, and began to wait.

Julia and I are very different. But, there are some special things about our friendship. We met as soon as I arrived in New York and immediately became friends. She found it cute how I theorized about diseases and how I faced my fragile health. And I love her happiness. She's one of those unique people with huge hearts who cares about others. She's always happy and positive. It doesn't matter what happens, she always finds a way to positively justify the unjustifiable. Julia has incredible qualities and an outstanding capacity to make people like her. Maybe it's her huge, white smile, with those borderline perfect teeth. But, the fact is Julia has charisma and charm.

As I was sitting there enjoying my Mocha Frappuccino and reading an article (Anatomy of a Meltdown – by John Cassidy) in *The New Yorker*, Julia appeared on the other side of the window. She looked overjoyed, almost in ecstasy. And me? Curious, of course, to learn of the reason behind such euphoria.

The reason had a first and last name. Lucas Stone, a gorgeous and perfect guy Julia had met a few months back. She had been dating him for some time now, and he had finally officialized things. She had just been given the keys to his apartment. For those who don't know, that means two things: first, you are not a nut and the guy trusts you. Second, that you are now the only woman who will circulate about his apartment, in other words, you are official.

"Congratulations! I think he really does like you!"

"Isn't that great? I'm ecstatic. I think I'm going to cry tears of joy. He loves me!"

"Oops... Calm down! Julia wake up or you're going to get hurt. I don't want to be a party- pooper, but I don't know... He didn't say he loves you, did he?"

"No, but this is an act of love."

"No. Listen, Julia. I know I'm not a specialist on love or relationships. In reality, far from it, but let's take things slowly. Men are practical. They think practically. He didn't metaphorically come out and say he loves you. Men don't say things metaphorically. They don't even know what that is. He just said here are my keys to make your comings and goings to and from my apartment easier. That's the message. Men love with reason. They show what they are thinking or feeling with attitude. If a guy really loves you, he'll try to make you happy. That's all. His behavior will say what he feels, and every once in a while, he'll say: I love you!"

"I know, but it means things are going well between us. He likes me. I feel like it's going to be different this time." *She said, still overjoyed.*

"You are his girlfriend, no doubt. But be careful, OK? Men say exactly what they mean. We have to learn to listen. They always say what they want and how they feel, yes, timidly at times. They don't open up like we do, but, they say them."

"Amanda, I know I'm getting involved again, and maybe I'll get hurt again. But I'm so happy. Couldn't you be happy for me too?"

I just smiled. After all, she was right. Sometimes it's better to run the risk and give your all for love - come what may. Better than sitting at the window waiting for love to pass by and ask if it can come in. That may or may not happen and the pain and frustration of being alone may not be less than that of losing someone. Could that be so?

I left Julia and her huge smile on the corner of 57th and 3rd and decided to grab a cab even though I was so close to home. I was exhausted, hungry and in need of a hot bath.

As I was on my way back home at around 5, I remembered I had to make a stop at CVS to pick up some medications that were lacking in my medicine cabinet. Things like Tylenol, Band-aids, Neosporin, and pads. I hopped out of the cab in front of the store and went straight to the light medication aisle. I also stopped by the vitamin department to check if there were any novelties, but it seems like pharmacists are lacking imagination right now. No big scientific discovery either. There was nothing for my gas problem. I guess I am doomed to die or be killed *farting* away.

A half hour later, and I was back at home, exhausted, with my purchases and mail in my hands. I wanted nothing else but a nice, warm bath, a tasty meal and my sofa.

The elevator door opened and I got out with my many handbags. I turned left, walked down the corridor, first in front of the door to apartment 4A, where a disgusting neighbor lives. One of those old, lonely, and boring types who complain about everything, you know? Then, in front of the door to apartment 4C, where a mad assassin of a dog I refuse to comment about, lives. I turned my body a little more and there was my door, 4B. I thought of putting the bags on the floor to look for my keys, but I hesitated, remembering the number of worms and bacteria there are in an inhospitable environment like a building's corridor. I balanced my shopping bags and shook my handbag in search of my keys, which fell on the floor. I bent down very slowly, trying not to spill any of the content of my still open handbag and to my surprise I saw a vase and a card, right there, at the foot of my door.

There was a small cactus, delicate and intriguing in the vase. It was no more than 5 inches tall, light green in color, and covered with inoffensive, firm needles. There was a piece of transparent and shiny cellophane wrapped around the tiny vase. I opened the door and put my shopping bags on the table. I went back to the door, now very curious and anxious to get the vase and card. I put the cactus on the window-sill and began to read the letter...

Our most sincere apologies for what happened. I hope you are well. I think this plant is a better match than the wild flowers. I checked on the Internet and there is no record of people allergic to cactuses, so you are safe. If you need anything, just knock. Take care Little Cactus, Brian and Ali.

I must confess I was moved. But I saw that as a provocation. Not because of the present itself, but because Brian had taken the time to find a way for me to feel better. Why does he care? His dog bit me, but my mother already told him I wasn't going to sue. So why go through all the work? Why be so kind? It could only be provocation. *I must set this straight. I thought.*

My thoughts were at a thousand miles per hour, seeking an answer to Brian's deed, when the phone rang and interrupted everything.

"Hello! Amanda speaking." I answered, confused and tired, like I was at the office.

"Amanda, it's me, I need your help." Said Robert breathing heavily.

"Hi Robert, good afternoon to you, too, how have you been...?" *Trying to be sarcastic because he's always so rude!*

"Amanda, sorry, but I don't have the time, or frame of mind for niceties right now. I have a serious problem and I need your help, now."

Robert is one of the attorneys who works with me. He's a master killjoy. He's always interrupting my weekends. He has this gift of guessing the moments when I'm most tired and dying for a warm bath. The kind of bath that strips us from every thought, you know what I mean? The other day I had just prepared one of those. Perfectly warm water, my *Fresh* bath salts, which are just marvelous. Perfumed candles lit around the bathroom, creating that soft, gentle light. And me, completely naked, with my feet one inch from the water, ready to be delighted. And precisely at that moment, he calls me (as always!) asking for help. And as usual, I blow out the candles, throw on my clothes, and run to give him a hand. Today at least I had just walked in and was still dressed.

"What is it this time? Is it really urgent and important, or is it like last time?" *Being ironic.*

"Amanda, please, let's not start." *He cried almost begging.*

Last time Robert called me with a legal emergency, he had been trying, unsuccessfully, to get one of his client friends out of jail. Robert is an incorrigible womanizer even though he is on his fourth, and in his words, definitive marriage. He's been married three times before, to completely different women in terms of style, way of life or make-up (the last one resembled a cabaret dancer, if I may say so!). But none of them is able to tame him. So, he keeps getting into messes with women you'd never bring home to mama, understand? The kind who are prohibited from entering family hotels or those with 4 or more stars. Not that he's gorgeous or has any sort of attraction we can observe with his clothes on. After all,

I've never seen him without clothes and I'm definitely not interested, but that may be the answer. But I repeat, I'm not interested. The fact is that for a silverish-blonde, green-eyed man, about 5'6", which we cannot consider tall, and in my opinion, resembling every other blonde man from the state of Maine, where he was born, he's completely normal.

He loves to party, has no respect for women, and I honestly cannot understand the reason for his success. Nevertheless, on his clubbing adventures or orgies and drinking sessions, one of them always ends up in jail. Either because they hit someone at one of the city's thousands of clubs or because of drugs or DUIs. And then, as usual, although I REALLY WISH IT WEREN'T SO, he calls me. Hoping I can discreetly help him set his clients free. After all, that sort of behavior is not well-accepted by the New York State Bar Association of which he is a respected member and considered an attorney with a brilliant career, as he himself enjoys bragging about. Robert is a sort of spokesperson for the firm. Every time someone needs to go to the media to give an explanation or demand measures, he's the one. And I must admit that his Ermenegildo Zegna suit, added to his intelligence and eloquence, forms a competent and successful attorney. A boring, arrogant, snobbish and pretentious one as well. But, he's good at what he does, I must admit. And since the firm needs him and my work often depends on his performance, I try to help him whenever he calls.

"Amanda, this is really serious, and I need your help and total discretion. I don't know what to do." *He sounded desperate.*

"Big news. Which of your little hussies is in jail this time? Ashley? Margo? What's that Thai girl's name, the one who promised to teach me some *vaginal muscle tricks* – I whispered that part – so I could please my boyfriend?" (*That is, the day I have a boyfriend, because I'm still frigid and without any perspective of reversing the situation*). "Have you seen her lately? Please, tell her I'm still waiting for my lessons... *He interrupted me abruptly.*

"It isn't about a friend this time. Now the problem is with Jocelyn. You remember her, don't you?"

Of course, I do. Jocelyn is Robert's current wife. She's a descendant of Argentine's, but born in the United States. She is truly beautiful. Long, black hair and big, black eyes. White skin and meaty lips. She has a wonderful body. She does not look a day over 38, but Robert told me she's already a little past 45. But, that honestly doesn't matter. She's truly beautiful. And kind. She's practically a *saint*, with so much vigor and courage. She deserves a medal for putting up with him for so long. I think it's been three or four years, if my memory serves me right. Long years for her. It must be bitter medicine to be with Robert and his little hussies that long. She really deserves an award.

"Yes, of course, your wife Jocelyn. What happened? Is she all right? Is she well, I mean... Is she sick? Something like that?" *When dealing with families everything always gets serious and cases involving family and health always move me.*

"That's right. She's fine, I think." *He seems really confused.*

"What do you mean, you think? Where is your wife now, Robert?"

"That's precisely the problem, Amanda. She's at the hospital now." *It sounded like he was about to cry.*

I was speechless. I felt tremendously guilty after joking with him, and suddenly the matter had become really serious. His voice was tense, choked and I thought he would cry at any moment. So, I immediately tried to reassure him. "Don't worry. I'll do everything I can to help you and her. I promise. Now, tell me everything. I need to understand. What happened? What does she have?" *I asked with a sweet and calm voice, trying to comfort him.*

8

Everyone knows I'm a hypochondriac and I don't need any self-examination or prevention campaign to remind me I have to check myself from time to time – please! In reality, I check myself daily! Just to see if my body is going through any sort of anomaly or deformity. It's part of my daily routine, like brushing my teeth. But unfortunately, not everyone takes the time to do a self-examination. Often, they don't even take the time to have their annual checkups... Then, when they go to the doctor because they don't feel well, surprise!

That's exactly what happened to Jocelyn. She's the type of woman who goes to the gym five times a week. She works out for two hours and even takes water polo lessons. "I'm as strong as an ox!" she used to say, and never took the time for routine exams. And then one day her world fell apart. After reading a story in *Glamour Magazine* about an actress who was diagnosed with breast cancer, she finally decided to give in to media appeals.

That same day, as she was taking a long bath, the kind that relaxes one's soul, she examined her breasts. She began the process calmly, feeling her breasts with circular movements from the base to the nipple. Then, she went on to her armpits, just like the Internet pamphlet taught. On the left side, all normal. But to her utter despair, she found a lump on the right side. Jocelyn repeated the process several times, trying to keep cool. She took deep breaths and repeated to herself that it was probably all in her head since she was so moved by the story of the actress. But, it was really happening. It was true. There it was; firm, ovular in shape. She could feel it and squeeze it (which caused some discomfort, slight but bearable pain – as she described it to me). She was able to remain calm for ten long minutes, but then there was no way out: she lost control and began to cry. She was just a month away from her forty- sixth birthday (between us, just that fact is disturbing enough!) and this was her present: breast cancer.

As Jocelyn told me her story, I began to think of all the problems the disease would cause me if I were the victim. And putting myself in the shoes of a victim of some fatal disease is child's play to me. Biopsy, mastectomy (surgery to remove part or the entire breast), lose half or even the whole breast, place a silicon prosthesis (that actually seemed to be something good; increasing one's bra size a couple of numbers could not do any harm to my monotonous love life). Not to mention radiotherapy, chemotherapy, hair loss, feeling miserably hot. Depression and all those other side effects a disease of that magnitude could bring on. But, of course, I spared Jocelyn of my musing and insane thoughts. I know it may not seem that way, but I do have good sense! And poor Jocelyn already had enough problems.

When Robert told me, Jocelyn was having health problems, I never thought they would be so serious. But, when he said the word "cancer", I dropped my shopping bags, threw on the first clothes I found in the closet, grabbed my handbag, making sure my daily planner with all my specialists was inside, and ran off to the hospital. This time I didn't want to waste time checking symptoms or medical references. I knew exactly what it was. Because any hypochondriac worth its weight in gold knows everything about diseases. And in moments of crisis, that turns against us. Believe me: ignorance is a blessing I cannot share. On the other hand, when you need to help someone with your knowledge, it becomes something good. And I was happy to be able to help.

I arrived at the Manhattan emergency room and was helped by a very considerate girl behind the counter. She realized my affliction was sincere and in fewer than five minutes I was standing in front of Jocelyn, who was still waiting for care. Forty-five minutes later, a doctor finally arrived and called her by name. He looked like a resident, young and insecure (among the worst, in my not too humble opinion). He practically turned her upside-down during her check-up. As he carefully and delicately examined her breasts, she told him her family history of disease – and I checked his references, suspicious that a post- adolescent doctor with pimples on his face would never be good enough to treat Robert's wife. And I ensured him I would make sure of everything for her to have the best.

I never thought I would ever say this day, but I was relieved and began to think: *thank God I wasn't the one in need of treatment.* I had such misgivings about the young man's competence I called Dr. Richard Ember, my friend the hepatologist, who by chance also worked at Manhattan Hospital. He ensured me the *recently graduated* Dr. Matthew H. Craig had, indeed, plenty of experience and had passed his residency period with flying colors. However, he advised me to omit the information about my hypochondria, because he could get nervous that my knowledge of diseases went beyond pure and simple curiosity. As I had expected, he followed all the projected steps necessary in these cases. He forwarded her to an ultrasound, mammogram and other exams. Just like that.

I recalled one time I ended up in hospital suspicious of having something similar to Jocelyn now. I begged for a mammogram, but the doctor on duty told me that it could only be unnecessary at my age. *"Girls under 30 are commonly affected by benign nodules or inflamed exocrine glands. Benign nodules are like tiny masses with a soft, rubbery consistency, and do not represent any danger,"* he explained frowning, perhaps believing it would be better understood that way. It's true I know more about medicine than the average person, but I am not some science genius. Please!

We returned to Dr. Craig's office, terrified, 1:50 later, with all the exams in hand. I had already tortured the doctor who did the ultrasound, making him give me details of every dark point that I, as well as he and Jocelyn, observed on the screen. *"Yes, Amanda, she has a nodule (Jocelyn's face hardened; her eyes welled up with tears). It's right here, very visible. It measures about a half centimeter. We have no way of knowing if it's malignant or not just by looking at it. We'll need to do a biopsy. But Dr. Matthew will be the one to decide that."*

Now, I was in shock. Poor Jocelyn. She had truly found the disease that could kill her. I have been trying to convince doctors, my family and friends that I have a disease like that for some 20 years now. I always swore something like this would consume me. But no one believes me. Now, for the first time, I am face to face with a real diagnosis. And I feel comfortable in saying I am very happy not to be the victim.

The nodule is there, on the right side of Jocelyn's breast. The creature had size, a name and last name: Lymph Node. Jocelyn and I were introduced to it with great displeasure. She had her first fit of crying and hysteria right there, in my arms, in one of the hospital's corridors, among sick people who were dying and family members who could not believe her reaction. She cried compulsively, and when someone approached to help me comfort her, she simply said: "Let me die in peace" or "Can't you see I'm near the end?" And they would immediately back off. I understood her pain perfectly. Nevertheless, I was confused. Her reaction was disproportionate and unbalanced. Probably the same as I would have had in her place. But, Jocelyn is considered normal by everyone. Normal? All right, lesson learned; normal people also do crazy things and behave oddly. Funny, I used to think only hypochondriacs were consumed by such fits.

I considered calling Robert, but I thought, if he had asked for help and wasn't there at that moment, it was obviously because he wasn't prepared for this. I hesitated to ask if she wanted me to call him, but I preferred having her remember to ask me to call him, which never happened.

My hypochondriacal thoughts haunted me once again. The obsessive idea of having breast cancer was driving me nuts. I was already imagining myself at the age of 29, bald, sitting in a wheelchair, with just a few months of life ahead of me. Yes, a few months. If it had been me, I'm sure they would have only found the tumor too late. And since I have insisted on this since I was 18 years old, it would be a tremendous lack of luck to find a tumor in its terminal phase. I thought: What if that were me? Who would I like beside me now? My mother, of course. Who else? Julia, maybe, or Lauren? Lauren? No way. I can't count on that one. She's always too busy. One of Sophia's school events, or going nuts trying to make a butterfly costume for the girl that won't embarrass her at some stupid party. For a moment, I felt sorry for Jocelyn for being so alone. I was there with her, but who am I to comfort her? I'm not family. I'm not her friend or even a colleague. I looked around and saw only suffering. Sad faces, filled with pain.

"Amanda! A voice whispered in my ears. We both looked towards the voice. Jocelyn stopped sobbing and seemed to feel better for an instant. That soft and sexy voice belonged to Brian. "What are you doing here?" he asked, reading my mind, as I was asking myself the same question. *"What is he doing here?"*

"Routine exams," I preferred to lie. I didn't want him to find out Jocelyn was on her death bed. It wasn't my place to spread such news! "And you? What are you doing here? Are you sick?" I asked quickly to distract his attention from Jocelyn's own private Calvary.

"No. No. I just brought in a restaurant employee who hurt himself today." "Is he, all right?" I think I sounded sincerely concerned, because I could tell he was moved. "Yes. He burned himself in a moment of distraction, but he'll be okay," he stopped and stared at me, as if leaving behind that *irrelevant* matter and thinking of something more important. Then he continued: "I'm waiting for your visit, to the restaurant, I mean," and he winked. "You said you wanted to get to know the best *crème brûlée* in town, but you never showed up. I'm anxious to show it to you," he added enthusiastically. The last time we had met in the elevator, just before sending me the vase with the cactus I told him, don't ask me why, my favorite dessert. That was when he had invited me for the thousandth time to go to his restaurant. I just smiled as I tried to concentrate on the conversation and not give some stupid answer. As I gazed into his eyes, I heard another voice abruptly cutting the mood between us, shouting out Jocelyn's name in a far from soft tone.

"Amanda..." five seconds later, Jocelyn was catching my attention, calling me to go with her to the room where Dr. Craig was waiting. "Of course, let's go!" I replied, still gazing into his eyes. "I need to go," I said. "But don't worry. I really want to try that *crème brûlée*." I smiled again and moved away, heading towards the office where the doctor and Jocelyn were waiting for me. As I moved away, I shouted: "Thanks for the cactus! That was very creative!"

I went through the door, and as it slowly closed, I noticed he was still there. Standing in the hall, with his hands in the pockets of his slightly worn jeans, watching me until the door closed sharply. At that moment, the reality of Jocelyn's condition hit me in the head as if a piece of the ceiling had fallen on it. I felt a huge "weight" fall upon my shoulders.

The doctor analyzed the exams and got straight to the point without hesitation. He just reinforced what we already knew: she did indeed have a node. Only a biopsy would say whether it was malignant or not. But I, as always, was overtaken by peculiar pessimism when it came to diseases. I could already imagine myself holding a handle of Jocelyn's coffin, and I was rehearsing my eulogy: *Here rests my great friend Jocelyn. We were so close, friends almost since childhood, if I may say so. I will never forget the moments we spent together in the hallways of that hospital, and how together we had discovered the cancer that consumed her and sealed our friendship. We remained united throughout her ordeal. We stayed together to the end, and today I am here to pay final tribute to my great friend, blah-blah-blah...* In my delirium, as soon as I finished my speech, I would begin to cry copiously, while Brian held me up so I wouldn't faint. Hold up. *Why Brian? Why not Peter?* That's when my connection and I heard: *Planet Earth calling Amanda*, or something like that, deep in the background of my dreams. And, the next moment I was overtaken by the terrifying idea that death was near at hand. Almost at the corner; I could feel it breathing down my neck. But fortunately for me, it was at the corner of Jocelyn's house and not mine. I remember that my eyes

107

welled up with tears. I tried to control them so she and the doctor would not notice my fragility. But it was too late. He held out his hand with a box of tissues. As I pulled one of the tissues, trying not to look directly at Jocelyn (proximity to death had made us intimate), he began his diagnosis. "Jocelyn has a node, but I can't affirm anything just yet. We need to do more exams to reach a conclusion," he said. I stood there, silently. For the first time in my life I could not formulate a simple question in front of a medical professional. Nothing! "Let's begin with the biopsy. It's a procedure..." I watched him speak, but his voice seemed far, far away. And his monologue was endless. Jocelyn, in turn, also seemed distant, almost disconnected from the event, as if it were not her problem. Not that it looked like she didn't care. No one in their right mind would have an "I don't care attitude" for a problem like that! It was different. It seemed like she couldn't believe what was happening. The whole scene was sad. Heart-wrenching. Especially if we consider a heart as fragile as mine, which will need one - or maybe two - bypass grafts in just a few years. I left the room with some papers in one of my hands and the other helping to prop up Jocelyn, who I thought was about to faint at any moment. I felt her legs trembling. She was pale and weak. She certainly hadn't eaten a thing all day. I wasn't sure of what to do with those papers, but a nurse accompanied us and set up an appointment for a biopsy in three days. Jocelyn just agreed by nodding to all the questions that were asked to her. She was dumbfounded, without reaction or emotion. She was probably thinking of the consequences if the diagnosis came back positive. What to do in such a situation?

We exchanged messages for a few days until Peter took the initiative to invite me to dinner again. This time at his place. I thought it would be rushing things to accept such an invitation, because the intentions were clear. Dinner and then... well, only God knows. I decided to accept after Marc convinced me that to solve my lack of sex problem, firm attitude and daring behavior would be needed, like arriving at his place, and after the first glass of wine feign drunkenness and jump into bed with him. It almost sounds like Marc doesn't know me at all. We've been friends for at least three years; ever since I met him while he was completely drunk in a bar downtown shouting horrible things to an ex-boyfriend who was threatening to call the police if Marc didn't shut up immediately. It was terribly embarrassing to see a man that size crying compulsively out of love. Julia and I spent hours trying to console him, and in the end, we became friends.

Fully recovered, he now serves as a thermometer that measures our actions when men are the subject. Only those who have a gay friend know how well they know men and how their advice is normally right on the money. Maybe because emotionally speaking, they live in the middle, between the male and the female. Sentimentally hybrid beings.

This time Peter didn't give me an exact time. He just said to arrive between eight and eight thirty.

I rang his doorbell at precisely 8:10, wearing tight jeans and a sleeveless blouse with strings of beads dangling that created a shiny look whenever I moved. He answered the door with a huge smile of satisfaction. The aroma from the kitchen practically guided my steps into the apartment. I was starving and the pasta he had prepared looked wonderful. He could definitely cook. From the presentation of the plate, the combination of wine and finally the flavor, everything was delicious. We dined and talked excitedly. We spoke about theater, books, music preferences, and even about favorite TV series. He told me of his passion for *Game of thrones* and *Narcos*, and I told him a little about my obstinacy for medical series and my new discovery, *Dr. Oz.* "I'm a big fan!" The evening was moving along just right for the desired finale. Bed, wild sex, and if everything went well, my problem with frigidity was just about over. But when we finished dinner, I felt my plans would not be fulfilled.

I offered to clear the table and help with the dishes. He quickly refused, which I found odd, but decided it was just another gentlemanly deed. He grabbed the dishes and went into the kitchen. I insisted, gathering the glasses and silverware, and I entered the kitchen just a few seconds later. What I saw left me perplexed and ruined my expectation of having found the man of my life.

The kitchen was clean; there was nothing wrong there. It was what Peter was doing that disturbed me. He was putting something in those tiny plastic containers we use to put things away in the refrigerator. So far so good. I also use them to put things in the refrigerator. I'm strange, but not off the wall. What shocked me was not that he was putting away the food left over on my plate.

He was saving the food that had been left his plate as well. "Was I seeing right?" I thought. Yes, I was. My mind was racing in one direction. There had to be some explanation for him to get the rest of the roast (already chopped) and pasta with four-cheese sauce I had left on my plate and put it in a container to be taken to the refrigerator, I mean. I always, save the extra food I cook, but taking food that had touched my mouth and fork. Does he even know how much bacteria are contained in a human's mouth? *He hands out food to the needy, that's it! But it wouldn't be that noble of an act if he took food that had already been touched by others, would it? I think not. There must be another explanation. Did he have the intention of saving my leftovers as some prize or fetish, perhaps? Yeah, I know, that would be a ridiculous idea.* I looked about for a motive, no matter how simple. I watched him for a few moments, with the dirty glasses in my hands, unable to approach. Then, he finally noticed my presence, came up to me and took the glasses from my hands:

"No need to bother. I can do this myself." A moment of silence that seemed like an eternity. I think that was when things began to add up. The air was suddenly very heavy, and I and my big mouth couldn't resist, so I said: "Do you have a dog?" In my thoughts, I was begging for him to say yes. *Yes! He has a dog, and all is explained. He's not some nut case who saves food off plates of people he has invited to dinner. He's just a generous and kind guy who rather than feed his dog with dehydrated and stinky rations, prefers to feed it steak and pasta. I actually began to think, what a lucky dog, and what a cool owner. I never asked God for an affirmative answer with such fervor,* I thought to myself. Up until then I had not noticed, seen or felt any trace of any pet around the apartment. There was no newspaper spread in a corner; no box for a cat to do its necessities. Nor did I see any toys for pets like a plastic bone or a water dish for dogs. No sign of chinchilla fur or fur of any other domestic rodent people have the bad taste to raise at home. "No. In reality, I don't like pets in the home," he replied, visibly embarrassed. I saw his face redden instantly. I didn't need to have a fit or simulate a convulsion to head for the door and get out of there. The air was so thick you could cut it with a kitchen knife. Peter had been able to do something unheard of in my life as a hypochondriac up to then. He was able to add another phobia to my already huge list. Just to recall, I have claustrophobia, agoraphobia, necrophobia, verminophobia, nosophobia and now I have leftover food bacteria phobia, too. Congratulations to me! I think I graduated with honors from the school of magistrates in bad luck! Even the enchanted prince in my story doesn't turn into a frog, which is totally acceptable and understandable. After all, all men have their prince/frog side. But no! Mine turns into a PIG! Ahhh! That's disgusting! Repugnant! Crushed by my suppositions that Peter, the perfect, had a weird food fetish, I dragged my beaten body back to my apartment. I am nosophobic so I got home and ran to the bathroom. I stuck two fingers down my throat and threw up, not just dinner, but all the deception and frustration as well. I was back at the starting point.

9

Of course, I was there when Jocelyn had her biopsy. And so was Robert this time. She was confident and kept repeating non-stop, almost hysterically: "*Come on, come on, I'm ready for them to take this thing out of me. Let's get it over with.*" The doctor had already explained the whole procedure. Everything he was going to do, removal of the entire node for analysis, etc. Although she didn't seem very calm, Jocelyn went through the entire procedure without the slightest twitch. Only her eyes revealed her affliction. No wonder. She didn't sigh once or even grumble about anything. No complaints about pain, nothing of the sort. *Just like I would be*, I thought.

In the waiting room, Robert and Sabrina, friends of Jocelyn's who had also come to offer support, were biting their nails waiting for me to appear to give them the news. I was the only one who wanted to accompany her to the procedure. Do you think I'd miss something like that? Watch a procedure like that as a spectator and not as a patient would be awesome. Jocelyn actually asked Robert to go in with her, but he refused. Just like any cowardly man. Men... honestly, what do we need them for? Oh yeah, I remember. For nights of lasciviousness and wild sex.

In fewer than two hours, she was ready to go home. The doctor said the result would be ready in two days and he would call her to give the report. Apparently calm, but still in shock, Jocelyn went home with Robert, who promised he would spend the next two days with her. Between you and I, that's the least he could do. I couldn't work right for those two days either. I couldn't do anything but imagine what they would find in that piece of tissue they took from Jocelyn's body. Mutant cells? Green slime resembling liquid kryptonite? An orange-colored mass? What would be inside that half centimeter in diameter lump? A saffron colored powder? Maybe.

Forty-eight hours of suffering and imaginary fits. I couldn't get the subject out of my mind. Having breast cancer was something that consumed me. I took a veritable dive into the universe of the dying. I already imagined having all the symptoms, of the disease quickly taking possession of my body, and when I was about to have a breakdown and ask for a biopsy of my own, for God's sake, we got the verdict: it was nothing!

Nothing? What do you mean nothing? She doesn't have anything? It can't be. And the lymph node? And the cancer that was eating away at her body from the inside out? Was this all reduced to nothing? While my reaction was making Sabrina, who had called to give me the good news, outraged, I was having a fit, feeling fooled, deceived and duped. Hoodwinked or worse. Jocelyn has a fibroadenoma, very common in women of her age, but it's benign and just needs to be monitored with periodic exams. Maybe every two years. She'll be fine. I know I could have reacted better. I'll admit that. I could have been happy and all. But you must understand. Jocelyn's disease was supplying all my hypochondriacal needs, and for the first time in years I had put my own health on the back burner. While I worried about her health, I had almost automatically forgotten about my own fragile health, and that was so good for me... Knowing that Jocelyn was not going to die was excellent news, no doubt. But, it was also the reason that I would return to my torment, my own private hell, my own Via Crucis. I hadn't gone to a doctor's office for days. I wasn't concerned about taking medication and I even allowed myself to run out of Neosporin and Advil at home. Going back to my previous life was depressing.

I called Jocelyn immediately. I told her I was happy to hear the result, but I warned she must be cautious about the result. I swear I'm not one of those people who forebode evil or anything, but when it comes to illness, I prefer to believe that two opinions are always better than one. I'm just wary, that's all! I know what I'm talking about. Jocelyn thought about going with me to a big named specialist. Meanwhile, I decided to vent my feelings to the only person who would really understand where I was coming from: my mother. "Mom, the diagnosis could be wrong. I honestly hope it's nothing, but you never know. Please, listen. It's not possible. I mean, it's possible, but... well... I hope it's possible, but it's improbable that it's nothing. That doctor is too young. You should have seen that baby face of his. Practically an adolescent. He couldn't be over 20. How does a 20-year-old have a medical degree? That's why I don't believe doctors. Their careers are based on weak foundations. There are no schools of medicine like there used to be, because if there were, that boy would never have gotten a diploma. He can only be mistaken. I saw the node, mom, I saw it. It was gigantic!" I tried to argue with her and convince her Jocelyn was still at risk. "I need a second opinion. I mean, Jocelyn needs a second opinion."

"Amanda, cut it out. Leave the lady in peace. She's been through a lot the past few days and thank God it was just a big fright. You're not helping her, honey," she begged. But, I wasn't listening to her. I was determined to find an error in the diagnosis that would prove either she was truly not sick, which would be great, or that she indeed did have cancer, caught at the outset and thus in time for treatment.

"I'm going to look for the best specialist in town. I'm going to find the best. That's it. I'm going to find him and ask him to review Jocelyn's case," I decided. "Then I'll talk to Robert and he'll convince her to go with me for the second opinion." "Amanda, this is not some college exam. Review a biopsy? Honey, accept the fact that your friend is fine. Get this out of your head and get back to your life. Just try to move forward like everyone else in the world," my mother was preaching on behalf of happiness. Meanwhile, *my best friend since childhood* was being eaten alive by a gang of assassin cells. And she wants me to forget everything and be happy. "You need to find yourself a boyfriend. Maybe that will be the solution to your health problems," she concluded, her patience running thin. She said she had to get dinner ready because she had a guest coming over.

A guest? Who? Who's the guest? I called again to find out who it was, but she obviously ignored the call as soon as she saw my number on her caller ID.

"Forever" by Drake was playing on my Spotify as I waited for the elevator in a charming building on the corner of Park Avenue and 57th. I was alone in the hall waiting for one of the elevators to open and take me directly to an appointment I had made two weeks earlier. I was to meet Jocelyn at precisely 8:40 in the morning in the waiting room of the greatest specialist in breast surgery in the country.

I confess I was particularly anxious even though neither I nor my health would be receiving the attention of Dr. Nathan Holderick. Famous for his professional competence and for his TV program on medicine, the guy is already a legend. He is also a constant in the Manhattan social columns. He circulates among celebrities and dates TV and movie actresses. Not long ago he even played a leading role in a divorce gone public: he and his ex-wife, the only heir of a millionaire Arab, disputing custody of their children in court. Tabloids, rags and gossip sites had a field day, thrilled by every new declaration she made. She would give details of her husband's cheating and said she could no longer live in the shadows of such an egocentric and egotistical man, who cheats and lies. Hundreds of stories were invented, but nothing was actually confirmed, just suppositions and insinuations about possible central figures to the betrayals. No one was ever able to prove anything. He maintained his reserved attitude and was never seen with another woman. Photos of old flings with married actresses began to resurface from the ashes to become a nightmare in the lives of those involved, which caused great frisson and plenty of gossip. He threatened to sue newspapers and magazines, while the supposedly betrayed husbands kicked the *paparazzi* on the corners of their homes. In short, the media and gossip industry with their brazenly sensational headlines did not miss the chance to rake in a few million dollars with the scandal of the divorced man I was about to meet.

But, I wasn't there for pure and simple voyeurism. I must confess I was extremely curious, but I had noble reasons for visiting that office: Jocelyn's state of health. We needed a second opinion on her case. And we needed an opinion from the best. From what I had been able to determine, he was the best, so...

We waited 45 minutes to be face to face with Dr. Nathan. Although we had arrived on time, the man is a celebrity, a legend, and even paying a fortune for a single visit, his patients had to be patient. His behavior is worse than a pop star on the rise. I know you are going to think I'm a terrible person and have too many defects, but believe me, I'm cool. Just don't make me wait too long, because another of my minor defects is to easily lose my patience. I hate waiting. I went up to the receptionist at least five times demanding to know the reason for Dr. Roderick's delay. That's my job, to complain. Demand people's rights and correct injustice. We had an appointment, so we would like to be seen on time. Very simple. Two plus two. Anyone disagree?

"My dear, what happened to him in there? Did he die? Or better, did the patient die? Only something of that nature would justify such a long wait, with a previously scheduled and confirmed appointment. The rude woman didn't even bother to respond. She just raised her eyebrows and looked at me in a gesture of pure indifference. Then, she lowered her head again and continued entering notes in a brown leather daily planner with the name of Dr. Nathan written in gold.

Controlling my temper so Jocelyn wouldn't get even more nervous, I went out to get some hot chocolate for both of us. The exercise of walking to a coffee shop and back helped dissipate my adrenalin a little and for me to calm down. By then I already hated the guy, even before setting eyes on him. I thought everything he was going through, the messy divorce and airing his dirty laundry in public was all deserved.

When I got back, nothing had changed. Jocelyn and three other women were still sitting in the enormous waiting room with its comfortable sofas (at least that; if we have to wait, it was at least in comfort), tense faces and some who were even teary-eyed. A very sad scene to be honest.

I was happy to see the hot chocolate helped cheer up Jocelyn a bit. She even made a joke about a story she was reading in one of the old magazines from the waiting room. That's right, I thought the same thing: comfortable sofas and old magazines, great combination. They could at least have had the latest editions of *Vogue, Bazaar* and *Cosmopolitan*.

Now face to face with the breast surgery phenom, I opened my little notebook and began to explain Jocelyn's case, the procedures run thus far and my suspicions in relation to the false negative diagnosis. He listened to everything, taking notes and intervening with some questions for Jocelyn, who could barely move, petrified by fear and shaken up because she was going through all this again.

"Jocelyn, do you have the exams with you? I want to take a look at them, but let me first say that your initiative to seek a second opinion is correct. Everyone should do that. Doctors are not special beings. We also make mistakes." No need to say that statement really stroked my ego. It seemed like an approval message for my hypochondriacal behavior; finally, a doctor understood me. I looked at him with a smile and quickly, before she could make any effort, pulled the exams from her handbag and spread them over the desk. Dr. Nathan spent a few minutes in silence, looking like a specialist, pensive, and then he began to speak.

"The other doctor wasn't wrong. The node that was removed for biopsy really is benign and presents no risk to Jocelyn's health. That's the good news." "That's great..." and then he interrupted as I celebrated and Jocelyn smiled from ear to ear.

"But..." I knew there would be a BUT... My intuition is never wrong. Jocelyn had a real problem. "I see something else in these exams and I would like to be sure before I say anything. I can't pinpoint what it is, but I am absolutely convinced you need new exams," he said, looking into Jocelyn's eyes. "I'm really sorry. I know you would like me to just confirm the other diagnosis. But, I must be responsible. I truly feel that an ultrasound and perhaps another biopsy are needed," he added. We left his office bewildered. Jocelyn was back in her nightmare. I felt guilty for putting her in that situation, but deep down inside I knew it was for the best. Just before we left the office, Dr. Celebrity handed me some requests for exams and instructions about her case. One sheet most especially caught my attention. First, because he had spent such time writing it on a prescription sheet; second because he made slow movements with his lips that gave the impression he was having fun as he wrote the prescription; and finally, because the prescription had been made out to me. He folded the sheet in half and carefully wrote: *For Amanda.* As we left his office, I thanked him for the attention he had given her, and after he left us at the door of the elevator, I gave Jocelyn all the forms for the exams, except for the prescription he had made out for me. I was so curious I could barely control myself. I had found a handsome and famous doctor, who besides everything else even used telepathy with his patients. What other explanation would I have for the fact I had never mentioned the pain I felt in my elbows? It's something horrible. A sharp and relentless pain. They hurt when I bend them and even more when I stretch out my arm. Only I know how much it hurts. No one believes anyone can suffer so much from pain in one's elbow. But, I swear it is true. And, then suddenly, Dr. Nathan guessed that and gave me a prescription without even asking. Of course, none of that would be the case! He probably had a few additional instructions for Jocelyn and just wanted me to read them first. Had to be that, I thought. But I couldn't have been more wrong.

10

In reality the note said: *Would you like to have dinner with me? If you are available, give me a call and we can set something up.* What? Could it be that someone up there finally decided to look after me? Did I win the lottery without buying a ticket? A gorgeous, famous and longed for doctor had invited me to dinner. I couldn't believe it. Pinch me, I must be dreaming. Or better yet, don't pinch me, because my delicate skin bruises easily.

The prescription even had his cell phone number for me to call and confirm dinner. Confirm? Could he really have any doubt I would accept? No woman in her right mind in this city would reject such an invitation. Maybe the well-married ones, but me? That was my Prince Charming in a smock! And there was no doubt he knew how to apply the Heimlich maneuver and the tracheostomy using a pen. Too good to be true.

I waited two days to get back to him. I didn't want to seem desperate. It was all part of a well thought out strategy to make his interest in me grow even more. Men love women who don't show much interest, which is what I read in a well written article in *Cosmo Girls* last month. The day I gathered the courage to call, he answered on the second ring. My heart was beating so fast and loud I'm sure he could hear it over the phone. Terrible, I know! But how could I avoid it? My heart was doing flips in my chest.

"Hi. This is Amanda. Jocelyn's friend. You asked me to call. Remember?" My voice began to fade so badly at the end of the sentence I was afraid he'd say no. Yeah, as the years go by you begin to suffer from low self-esteem. A gorgeous man gives you his phone number and asks you to call and you still think he was making fun of you. "Of course, Amanda. I've been waiting for your call. How have you been?"

After a few minutes of futile and redundant conversation, he finally reaffirmed the invitation and we set a dinner date for Tuesday night. The week went by so slowly that I had the opportunity to experience an aneurism, tonsillitis, degeneration of neck skin and mycosis on the back of my thigh because of all the anxiety, for finally having met the man who would make me happy for the rest of my life. So, I thought. I had been cared for so often at the Lenox emergency room that the last time a doctor threatened to prohibit my entrance, for disturbing the peace, if I ever returned there with any disease with a pre-established diagnosis. Or any theory about some supposedly fatal disease. *You are making my patients restless and scaring them with your theories,* he had said. The weekend was even worse. I lost count of how many pills I took; many I suppose. But, what was I supposed to do? I had a sore throat, earache, headache (classic and moderate migraine) and diarrhea. My Lord, how I suffer! I even considered not going on the date. But on Monday, he sent me a message confirming everything and I didn't have the courage to tell him I was on my deathbed or suffering a nervous breakdown and thus could not see him, much less have dinner with him.

On Tuesday, a little more at peace with my real emotional state, I went to Bloomingdale's to buy a new dress. After all, before being a hypochondriac, I am a first and foremost, woman. I bought a beautiful dress. A halter dress, with laser cut ruffles in the fabric, without any finishing. *Haute couture*, awesomely *chic*. Lauren is going to go nuts when she sets eyes on it. I can hardly wait. During my lunch break, I also had my nails done and took advantage to do something with my hair. A necessary investment to be at the side of such a special man.

I left the office at six, swung by my place, showered, put on my new dress, silver shoes, and grabbed a tiny silver and gold pocketbook. I put on some daring make-up, not normal for the basic kind of person I generally am. I allowed myself to use a little more and it looked great. A few accessories and I was ready. I got to the restaurant, one of the hottest in New York, the kind you need to make reservations for a month in advance or to be good friends with the manager to get a table without a reservation. At first glance, no sign of Nathan (I think that from now on it doesn't sound right to call him doctor). Did I get here too early? A very skinny young man with dark circles under his eyes, probably suffering from some sort of liver problem (I almost asked Nathan to check, but contained myself), approached and asked if I was Amanda. As soon as I said yes, he asked me to accompany him. We passed by the main room, which was full, and went to the back, and there he was, standing at the side of the table, ready to welcome me. "I'll take over from here. You can leave us alone," he told the young man, and with a lovely smile on his lips, he greeted me.

"Have you been here before?" he asked, staring into my eyes. "No, but I am loving it. It's all so..." I stopped for a moment, wondering if it wouldn't be too humble to say what I was thinking. The place was truly splendorous, and I had never been in a restaurant like that before. And look, I've been in plenty of high class places in New York. "It's an excellent restaurant, no doubt. Great choice," I added. "I took the liberty of choosing the wine to start. It goes well with salad as well as seafood. I hope you like it." Like it? This wonderful man is actually concerned that I may be upset by the fact that he chose the wine even before I got there? Huh? Not at all. For me, he could choose the wine, the dinner, from the appetizers to dessert, and I would still think everything was excellent, beautiful and very romantic. He is a kind and courteous gentleman. What could ruin my night? Oh yeah, I remembered: maybe if he wanted to split the tab at the end. That would probably ruin my evening.

There was a piano bar a little more to the back. The pianist was playing beautiful songs as Nathan and I talked excitedly. He enjoyed every dish and tasted each glass of wine with the pleasure of a true gourmet. I don't know if I have mentioned this before, but I love men who know how to appreciate a good meal. I was feeling a little intimidated, but he was somehow gradually making me relax. Perhaps because from time to time he would take generous forkfuls of lobster from my plate, with simplicity and gentleness. I even risked trying a little from his plate, too. And the scallops he had ordered were divine. He is a master. Master in the art of making women feel secure and worthy of his attention. He not only enjoyed the dishes, but also every word that came out of my mouth. I had never felt so important on a first date.

Just before dessert was served, he decided to risk a few steps on the dance floor. Even though I swore I would trip over my own two feet, he insisted. And so, we went, waltzing through the room, like characters in some old movie. The people around us watched in admiration at the boldness with which he led me with perfect rhythm, in perfect timing not only to the music, but also the moment.

When we sat back down, he cast curious looks at me and I can bet his curiosity went far beyond finding out my favorite TV program. It was more like "I wonder if she wears G-string panties?" I think that was the moment he began to realize he could really be interested in me. And I think I felt the same. Not that I was imagining what sort of underwear he was wearing. As I daydreamed about a future romance with this wonderful man, one of the restaurant employees approached and said a few words in his ear.

"What happened? Any problem?" "No. Just... Could we leave now?" he said, hesitating a little. "What about dessert? You just ordered it... What's the matter...? Did you change your mind about our evening? Did I say something...?" "No. Of course not, you did nothing wrong."

Of course, you didn't do anything wrong, silly. What could you have done? Mispronounced the name of the dessert? Or stepped on his pinky while you were dancing? "So, is there some medical emergency?" I know I should have stopped asking, but I'm just impossible. I can't stop.

"No. I would just like to go," he said, a little irritated and with a notable alteration in his voice. "Sorry. Of course, we can go," I replied, grabbing my pocketbook. I added, "I'm really sorry. I didn't want to irritate you with questions, it's just that..." I tried to control myself so he wouldn't see the two fat tears ready to roll down my cheeks.

"Sorry. Look, I'm really sorry, okay? Truly sorry. Maybe some other night, who knows, we can try it again. But today I think things could get a little complicated," he finished while signing the receipt for the meal paid with his *diamond* credit card. A bell went off in my head the very second the word "complicated" left his mouth. What could become complicated? What is he talking about? Could he be feeling something? A slight upset feeling in his stomach? Heartburn? NO! Diarrhea? It can't be. Oh my God! He's not feeling any intestinal discomfort now. Is he? Please say no, say no. What am I going to do? Could I just come out and ask? Like: *Nathan... are you feeling something? Like some irresistible urge to go to the bathroom, right now, immediately?* Or should I suggest something more subtle, like: *Ahhh.... Nathan, did you know I have a free sample of an excellent medication for intestinal problems in my pocketbook? You probably know it. I think I'm going to take one. Would you like one too?*

With a stern look on his face and penetrating eyes, he led me to the exit. But when we were almost outside the door, the same restaurant employee who had whispered into Nathan's ear stopped us and suggested we leave through the back. "Through the back? Why..."

Not a word was said. One minute I was glorious in my Prada heels, and the very next I was leaving the classiest restaurant in Manhattan through the service entrance. There's no need to say I had to raise my dress and hop over boxes of vegetables and greens spread about the hallway that connected the kitchen to the back door of the restaurant. Before we left, Nathan pulled out a hundred-dollar bill. Yeah... wow... he gave it to the young man. Why someone would give an employee one hundred dollars to take him to the service entrance I would only find out after going through the door. I must say that not even in my worst nightmares had I ever imagined something like this could happen to me! Why to me? "Oh, no! Damn!"

"What's going on?" I asked, bewildered by the non-stop flashing lights in my face. "Sorry. This is what I was trying to avoid," he said in the same soft and courteous tone he had used at dinner. "Who are these people? Where did they pop out of?" The scene was grotesque. Several *paparazzi*, at least 20, I gathered, were elbowing each other for the best shot; the shot that would bring in enough cash to pay this month's rent. Flashes were exploding in my face, leaving me practically blind. I even thought that if I suffered an eye injury as a result of this episode, I would sue them. "My driver is waiting for us right up ahead. Come on, Amanda. Can you run with those huge heels?" Oh! How kind of him to think of my shoes at a time like that. Of course, if I had known I'd be going through something like this, I would have worn running shoes. Of course. "Don't worry about my shoes. Just get me out of here!" I was practically shouting. I couldn't understand how such a wonderful date could have become such a frightening situation in less than ten minutes. I jumped into the back seat of the black car, whose chauffeur was waiting, doors open. We went three blocks without my saying a word, and then I decided to break the silence, furious. "What was all that? Could you explain to me what all those guys were doing there? Why were they waiting for you? How did they find out we were there? I didn't do anything wrong. Did I do anything wrong? Are you by any chance still married?" I could feel my face on fire. No! It can't be. I checked everything about him on the Internet. He's divorced. It can't be. I wouldn't have been duped like that. He can't... Could he?

"In reality, Amanda, it's quite complicated. More complicated than it seems. *So explain then! I'm waiting!* I was shouting in my head, almost without patience. Or better, without any patience. "You are..." I cleared my throat before continuing, the sentence almost hurting my throat. "I mean... Are you married?" "Amanda, I swear I was going to tell you, but things just aren't that simple. I couldn't just come out and say... that... that's not how we..." "You are married!" I shouted as if awakening from a bad dream. "Amanda, look. I think it best I drop you off at your place and for us to talk another time." "But what about all those stories on the Internet that say you are separated. That there is nothing between you and your wife anymore and that you are fighting a fierce battle in courts to see who keeps the kids. Is that all a lie?" "Sorry. Part is true and the other part made up. You know... Journalists make up a lot of things about our family."

"Like what? Like you're an incurable womanizer? Is that the big lie they make up? If so, I don't think it's a lie!" I said, furious. "How could you involve me in this? I'm a respected attorney. Do you have any idea what this scandal could do to my career? How could you?" "Amanda, I'm sorry, I had no idea they would find me. I just wanted a little fun with a beautiful and intelligent woman." "What? You just wanted some fun?" I could feel my blood boil. My blood pressure was probably already at a record high. I grabbed my pocketbook and in the blink of an eye hit him in the face with it. The next, I was shouting to the driver to stop the car right then and there.

"Stop this car now!" "But, we are almost there, madam," said the driver who sounded quite used to the whole situation. He must have witnessed this scene several times. "Stop! Stop this car now! Are you deaf?" When he looked at his boss through the rearview mirror as if asking for permission, Nathan just shrugged his shoulders, as if saying: *Go ahead and stop. Let this nut walk home.* As soon as the car had stopped near the curb, I got out and slammed the door with all the strength I wanted to take out on his face. I walked eight blocks with my feet on fire and my emotions crushed. I entered the hall of my building blind with anger. With a few mechanical movements I pressed the buttons to the elevator and I didn't even notice Brian's presence. As he was trying to approach me to say good evening, I practically fell apart.

"I don't believe this is happening. He couldn't have done that to me. He just couldn't." "What's the matter? What happened? Are you feeling okay?" Brian asked with genuine concern. "I'm so stupid." I was sobbing. "No. You're not stupid. You just had a bad day. Happens to everyone. Tomorrow you'll be feeling better." Tomorrow? I hadn't even thought about it. But I think tomorrow will be even worse. How am I going to explain to my boss, my family and friends and... Oh my God, how am I going to explain this to Jocelyn? "Oh! I hadn't thought about that! Tomorrow will be even worse! I'm sure everything is going to fall apart. Tomorrow I will let down my family. I'll be fired and my friends will be furious with me," the tears poured down my face, in total despair. While Brian tried to console me, I was wondering why this guy only ran into me in moments of crisis. Could he have planned all this, with all the details and acme of cruelty? Just so he could be nearby to console me? No, I must be delirious. My high blood pressure must be causing some sort of hallucination. High blood pressure must have that sort of symptom. Doesn't it? "Would you like to tell me what happened? Maybe I can help."

"I don't know. Could you kill someone for me? And after getting rid of the body, could you go to the printing sectors of some magazines and sabotage their machines so they can't print anything for at least a month." He smiled and said:

"Killing someone and getting rid of the body is something relatively easy. But to sabotage very high-tech equipment... hmmm... I don't know about that. But, I'll find some way to solve your problem on the Internet right this moment." "No need. No problem. Anyway, they could release the photos on the Internet. Wouldn't make a difference."

"Release the photos? What photos? What are you talking about?" "Nothing. Forget it. I think you'll get it soon enough. He shrugged his shoulders and growled ah-hah! As if saying: If you say so, I believe you. As he was entering his apartment, I turned around and said: "Brian, could you do me a favor?" "Of course. What is it?" "When you understand what is going on, please don't judge me. It wasn't my fault. And in this case, there are three versions of the story." Even without understanding a thing, he nodded, indicating agreement. He wouldn't judge me. At least *he* wouldn't.

11

No need to say I didn't sleep a wink last night. I kept tossing and turning in bed, from one side to the other, going over the disastrous evening I had had with Nathan. I tried to recall every word said to find a single clue that could suggest he was married. He didn't wear a ring, not even during Jocelyn's appointment. How could I have ever guessed? And besides: what about all that false advertising concerning his tumultuous divorce and custody of his children? Could he be paying for those stories so he can flirt with other women, playing the role of a needy, divorced man? A poor guy whose ex-shrew is trying to destroy him in every way possible? My God. If he does that, he's a monster. Poor guy. Yeah, right.

As I tossed about in bed, I tried to work up strategies to get out of this one. First, I thought: *Amanda, take it easy. This may all be just a bad dream; tomorrow, when you wake up, everything will be okay.* That's when I turned on the bedside lamp and to my total despair saw the dress on the armchair, on the right side of my bed, and my pair of Prada sandals next to it. Okay, so it wasn't a dream. So, I thought of something else. The photographers were there on Nathan's account, and not mine. They don't even know who I am. I tried to cover my face so they probably never got a good shot of me, nothing that would show me clearly. That's it! No need to worry. Early tomorrow, I'll go to the Salvation Army and leave my dress (not my Prada sandals; no way... after all, they are exclusive) and thus get rid of all evidence that could incriminate me. If anyone asks if that's me in the photo, I'll smile happily and say: *Of course not. Imagine that, me. But thanks anyway, she is pretty.* And then I'll leave quickly without anyone noticing I'm nervous and all. Amanda Loeb, you are a genius! Perfect. But, what if someone insists? My mother, for example. My mother always says she can tell her daughters from miles away. That she would never confuse us with someone else. Well, if she really has any inkling, I'll feign an asthma attack. I'll begin to gasp so hard for air, with such despair, she'll have no other option. She'll call an ambulance and take me to the hospital. Worried about my health, she'll have already forgotten about the photo in the paper. But what if none of that works?

The fact is I'm in a pickle. I really am. Definitely in a pickle. I can't even imagine Edward's reaction. He'll fire me on the spot and I'll never get another decent job at a large law firm. With a little luck, maybe I'll get a job at some NGO that handles child prostitution. Which is also praiseworthy work. But I don't want to spend the rest of my days chasing horny and sexually sick jerks who like little kids. I don't have the energy, the stomach, nor am I strong like Olivia Benson on *Law and Order*. Besides, everyone knows my health is fragile.

My mother is going to put me on a plane with a one-way ticket to India. There's no way I could last a month in India. With all that milk-based food, the filth, all those diseases and leprosy. Lord, do not allow my mother to send me to one of the few countries on earth that still has leprosy! And she'll discreetly say: *Oh, one more thing: no need to write or send news. We'll look you up! Have a great trip, honey!* And I wouldn't even be able to blame her. In a single night I was able to destroy my reputation and shame my entire family. If the gods help me and have pity on me, perhaps Julia will be the only person who will have fun with all this and support me. After all, isn't that what friends are for?

I went to work bright and early. I didn't have any doctor appointment, which was a relief, because I don't know if I could face a doctor's office after last night. I walked by the newsstand and took a peek. Wearing a hat with a huge brim and equally large sunglasses so no one could recognize me, I stopped in front of the newsstand, and after a quick check I noticed my secret had not been revealed. It's hard enough finding out I had been duped and fallen for the line of a charming, scum bag of a married man. But, knowing this could be revealed to the entire country, and maybe the world, is just too much humiliation.

When I got to work, I tried to control myself and look normal. I think I gave myself away when Sarah entered my room and casually commented: *Did you see what's going on with that doctor...* And I quickly interrupted her, saying: *That's not me. I know it looks like me, but it's not.* Sarah's eyebrows quickly narrowed in a confused look.

And she continued: *Of course, it's not you, Amanda. Did you hear me? I'm saying they are going to charge that doctor who took care of Michael's health over the past few months. They suspect he died because of excess medication.* She smiled and left my office.

Three days went by and nothing. Not a single photo was published. Not one celebrity gossip site had released even the smallest note on the matter. For a moment, I was actually offended. Didn't it even deserve a footnote on the home page of TMZ or OMG? Those websites are full of D-list celebrities. But, nothing was mentioned. So, I emerged from the world of the anguished, relieved, and decided to go through with my weekend plans.

Monday arrived in a flash. I couldn't even believe it when the alarm went off at seven. I grabbed my clothes that I had, as usual, already separated the night before, and went to the bathroom. Relaxing bath, morning check-up. No anomaly, yet another day of peace in my hypochondriacal saga. I put on a brown *tailleur* with big, gold buttons and an impeccable cut. It was worth every penny I had paid that snobby clerk at Versace. My pair of Jimmy Choo's and my Gucci handbag made of ostrich leather. Yes, I also think I got too caught up in brand names after going on that date with a celebrity. It's a shame my salary doesn't keep up with the investment needed for a woman to show the world how *chic* and elegant she is. I put on SPF 40 sunblock and light make-up, as I do every day. I drank my coffee and went to work. Just a minor accident as I walked the blocks that separated my place from the office. A dog that was doing his necessities on a tiny plot of grass decided to joyfully jump and get himself entangled in my legs. Fortunately, no runs in my stockings. I would have exploded. I was staring at the dog's owner, eyes ablaze, ready to begin an argument about the impropriety of the situation, when my cell phone rang.

"Hi, mom, good morning. Something happen? Why are you calling me so early?" "Amanda, just tell me what really happened and I'll believe you. But tell the truth. That was just a professional meeting, right?"

I could feel my blood boil. She could only be talking about what I imagined she was talking about. My face turned beet red in seconds, and I didn't know what to say. If I confirmed everything, she would be immensely disappointed. If I said it was a business meeting and she found out the truth, she would never trust me again. *I don't know what to do.* I thought in agony. I wonder if I should feign that asthma attack.

"What are you talking about?" I cleared my throat, trying to gain time.
"Amanda, I know you. I know you're intelligent and you know exactly what we are talking about. About your picture with Dr. Nathan Holderick on the cover of *Famous!*"

"Mom, I can explain, look, just..." I stammered unable to explain a thing.

"I hope you have an excellent explanation, Amanda. What were you doing in a high-class restaurant with a MARRIED man?" she almost shouted.

"Well, I didn't know. I didn't know he was married. I only accepted to go to dinner with him because

I didn't know," the tears welled up and I had to control myself to not have a crying fit right there on the street.

"Now, I'm furious with you. I think we had better have a talk after I calm down a little. Honestly, I'm disappointed in you. I always said you could have any man you wanted, so long as they weren't married. You may have destroyed a family. Have you thought about that? Your sister tells me he has four kids. Four!"

"I know. Sorry. I didn't want to be a home-wrecker. I swear," I defended myself, thinking that Lauren had thrown more wood on the fire, and I was the one getting burned.

After talking to my mother, I just wanted to go back home, crawl under the blankets and stay there until the people and media had completely forgotten about me. But, I had scheduled two important meetings at the office and I had to be there. I gathered every last bit of strength left in me and went.

I exited the elevator cautiously, trying to make myself invisible. *I know not everyone reads* Famous, *and to think they will recognize me because of an out-of-focus photo is being a little paranoid on my part,* I thought. I suddenly felt an ice-cold feeling creeping up and down my spine. Sarah reads *Famous*! Oh, my God... she does read *Famous*, and she always comes around to comment about something she finds interesting or extremely bizarre! I wonder in which category she'll include me! Interesting or bizarre? I walked along the hallways and by the workstations as fast as I could. But it didn't take long to hear the first knocks at my door.

"Hi, Sarah. What's up?"

"Hmm... Amanda. Edward wants to talk to you. He told me to give you the message as soon as you set foot in the office."

"Okay, thanks. Tell him I'm on my way."

Not knowing where it came from, a copy of *Famous* suddenly appeared in front of me, in Sarah's hands.

"That's you, isn't it? Could you give me an autograph? I told my fiancé it was you, but he didn't believe me. Could you…"

Without even thinking properly about what I was doing, I scribbled something on the magazine cover, right above the photo, where my face clearly appeared as I ran to the car with Nathan right behind me, holding on to my arm. It was an amazingly incriminating scene. The couple in that picture had an intimacy that never really existed. Nathan seemed to protect me from the photographers, while I looked comfortable, even happy. Concerned only about walking quickly, as if late for an appointment. But, that's not exactly what happened. Now that I see the picture, I understand perfectly well why my mother was so furious. I'm truly guilty. At least, that's what the picture says. How do they do that?

I knocked on Edward's door, and he opened it for me. To my complete chagrin, he was not alone. I saw Robert, Paul and Carl also waiting in the room. That's it. Besides getting fired, there will be public humiliation. The lions are just waiting to devour the prey without pity.

"Amanda, sit here," ordered Paul, my boss' boss. The most powerful guy at the institution.

Paul is one of the Company's founders. He became famous for having shocking scenes published like the polar bears on top of the tiny floating glaciers. Or of the deforestation in the Amazon, or those shots of the Japanese ships murdering whales in the Pacific Ocean. He is the master of the advertising behind our organization. He's able to raise millions and millions of dollars every year for our causes using images like those plus plenty of shrewdness.

As I pulled back the chair to sit down, my eyes caught sight of two copies of *Famous* on the table. It became absolutely clear that the meeting was about me.

"Amanda, I'm going to ask you a few questions and I need you to be sincere with me. You know our organization is very important and respected around the world. We cannot under any circumstance allow negative publicity ruin our reputation."

My heart pounded harder with each word that tiny man with disheveled hair and an uneven beard pronounced in his deep and penetrating voice. I was almost ready to simulate my asthma attack, or even a heart attack, because my heart was pounding in my throat and everyone could certainly hear it.

"I know that, but I didn't want..."

"Well Amanda, what were you doing in that restaurant with a married man?"

"Well I... I didn't know..."

"You were negotiating a donation for the campaign on the importance of recycling cell phone batteries, isn't that right?"

Huh? How's that? What recycling campaign is that? What's this man talking about? I don't know anything about that. And since when do I get involved in collecting money or donations for campaigns?

"Hmm... Yeah. I guess that's it." I had no idea what the man was talking about. But, since I don't want to prosecute pedophiles the rest of my professional life, I decided I would agree with anything he said and that seemed better than confessing to the fact I had been fooled by a married scumbag.

"Very well, gentlemen. All solved. I have spoken personally with Dr. Holderick's attorney and he has ensured me the sum is quite generous," he said, smiling at me. "We just need Ms. Amanda to confirm she was at the restaurant for him to sign the agreement.

Now I got it. The Godfather had sold my dirty little secret and arranged a scenario with Nathan's attorney that would make him a hero and not a villain. Why is it I hate men so much? I feel like everything is a set up. They save the scumbag's marriage, raise money for an organization project at my expense, and what do I get out of it? NOTHING! Just being spared public sacrifice. But I must admit that despite the rotten odor surrounding the whole story, it was pretty ingenious. I wonder who had the idea, Nathan or Paul?

I was obliged to give another press conference to explain things. In reality, to lie about the real motives that led me to go out with Dr. Hero Holderick. The good guy benefactor who sponsored the cell phone recycling campaign. Actually, I was obliged to read the entire campaign and really lay it on thick about the harm caused to the environment by the improper disposal of the batteries. So far, so good. The hard part was getting my mother to swallow the whole story. She's still not convinced even while I'm being called the "model employee at the service of ecology" by the media. The magazines reported it was all a big mistake and they filled their pages (internal, not on the cover, like in the previous editions!) with new pictures of Dr. Holderick handing me the hefty check for the campaign. Among the dead and wounded, everyone was saved.

12

One month had gone by since the sorry (for me) episode with Dr. Nathan, and my life was finally back to normal. On one of those calm mornings, I was opening my emails, sitting deeply in my swivel office arm chair. Actually, I must say that if there is something I simply love at the office, it's my chair. It's a high-back, dark brown, sheep's leather chair. The foam has been softened to perfection by years of use. I feel protected, embraced by it. Pure comfort.

I had just arrived and was sitting comfortably, I was analyzing a lawsuit that had come to me together with a note from Edward, my boss, just saying: *Utmost urgency!* That's when Sarah, my assistant of more than two years, knocked on my door, just before opening it.

"Good morning, Amanda. Here's your copy of the *New York Post*." putting the paper among the pile of other papers on my desk. "Do you need anything else? Coffee maybe?"

Sarah's a good assistant. She never seems to get upset by my hysterics or any unusual request I may make, especially when dealing with my delicate health. She's always available and very cooperative. I think she has only one defect: she talks too much! She loves to talk. Nevertheless, I admit she's funny and at times I have great fun with her stories at the end of a tension packed day. She loves to talk to me about her latest boyfriend. Some six-foot ten guy, long hair, plenty of piercings and tattoos, but that she describes as a really sweet person. As I listen to her endless monologues, I just nod my head, trying to hide my total lack of interest in the subject.

"A *cappuccino* would be great, Sarah. You can get…" As I was finishing the sentence and turning towards her, my eyes caught the morning headline: SWINE FLU SPREADS IN MEXICO! "Sarah, close the door, please," I said in a concerned voice.

Sarah closed the door and turned towards me with a surprised look on her face as she waited to understand what was going on. I picked up the newspaper and began to read the story. My increasingly tense and concerned expression was a sign something very bad was about to happen.

Sarah's face was a mix of confusion and affliction.

"Amanda, are you okay? What's going on? Is there bad news in the *Post*?" She asked non-stop, her deep green eyes wide open.

"Sarah, tell me. Where did Selena spend her honeymoon? Cancun? Did she get back from Cancun last week? Is that right? Am I right?" My expression was now of outright terror.

"Yes. She went to Cancun with her husband. She's so happy… She said it was awesome and that…"

"Thanks, Sarah. I need to be alone. You can go now," I said rather rudely.

"But what about your *cappuccino*?" she was trying to ask as I whisked her out of the room and closed the door.

I couldn't believe what my eyes were reading. Or what my ears had just confirmed. The story said a strong wave of flu had hit Mexico. A tragedy without proportions. In reality, it was the return of a virus that had already made thousands of people victims in the past. Called the swine flu, this disease is, in reality, a cocktail of several flu viruses, containing genetic material from sick humans, birds and pigs. It emerged because of contact with pigs, but today the virus is transmitted from people to people, even without any contact with the animals. More than a hundred people have already died from this new epidemic, which could reach global proportions. *Oh my God!* There are already confirmed cases in the United States, and the population must be aware of the symptoms. The story continued by reporting everything known about the cases – the first person to get the disease was a five-year old boy, who passed away. Then it described the phases of the disease, in all its detail, and concluded with the symptoms.

No! No! No! Will I never have peace in this life! Must I always be vigilant? I thought to myself as I grabbed the phone to call the only person who could calm me down: my mother.

"Mom, it's me. Have you read the cover of the *Post* today?" My voice was shaky.

"No, but I gather you did and didn't like it. Right?" I could feel her smile at the other end of the line.

"Mom, this is serious. Very serious. You cannot go out of the house today. Actually, you cannot go out for the next few months! And Lauren must do the same," I ordered, hesitant.

"Of course, Amanda. My food and medication supply is at maximum level. Don't worry. I'm ready for a nuclear war or another terrorist attack. Thanks to you, I must admit." I have to say I have no idea how my mother finds such things funny. I don't think she takes me very seriously. "But tell me: why are we in a state of alert this time?" Now she was making fun of me.

"A swine flu epidemic has spread throughout Mexico and it is reaching Manhattan. It seems there are already 22 confirmed cases in Queens!" I shouted. "Mom, this is very serious. TWENTY-TWO cases in Queens!!!" I said, desperate, while mentally counting how many subway stations separated Manhattan from Queens. "Only two. Only two, mom!!!"

"Two what Amanda? Two people with the flu? What are you talking about? You just now said twenty-two," she grumbled without the slightest patience.

"Just two subway stations separate me from Queens! Only two! I'm easy prey. A target without any chance of resistance, that's what I am. A potential victim for this cruel and lethal disease, "I screamed completely out of control".

"Amanda, stop! Stop this instant! Enough already! Are you feeling something?" Her tone of voice was sweet now. That's part of her strategy: first, she's authoritarian, and yells, and then she becomes gentle and understanding concerning my problem.

"Yes, now that you mention it, I think I do. I feel a slight pain in my throat and a headache. My body feels weak and feverish," I stopped for a minute. "My legs feel kind of wobbly, too, and…" She interrupted me abruptly.

"Amanda, stop it now! How many times did you read the part on symptoms? Tell me. How many?" She took a deep breath. "You must have been in contact with a sick person to catch the flu. And you haven't had contact with anyone from Queens or Mexico! As far as I know, you don't use any public transportation and you stay away from crowds. So, you're safe."

"Mom, you don't get it. It's an epidemic. No one is safe. No one!" Now, it was my turn to take a deep breath before going on. "And, there's more. This is the worst part. Do you remember Selena? The environmentalist who works with me in the office?"

"The one that just got married?"

"That's the one. The thing is she just got back from her honeymoon. She was traveling with her husband," I said slowly to create suspense.

"And…?" She grumbled.

"And do you know where she spent her honeymoon, Miss Know-It-All?"

"No. But I'm sure it wasn't Queens."

"Cancun. And from what I know, if my geography classes were of any worth, Cancun is in Mexico. Or isn't it?"

"Amanda, that doesn't mean she's sick. Please, honey! You're smart and know that."

I was going nuts. I got up from my chair and walked around my desk. I opened and closed the door to my office six million times to see if Selena was seated at her desk. I rested my head against the half-open crack to watch her every movement. I needed a sign. Any sign, regardless of how small, that could serve as proof and sustain my theory that Selena had brought the swine flu as a souvenir. I was overcome by the certainty that together with the sombrero she had brought Edward, the handmade ceramic vase for Sharon, the poncho for Robert and the hand-painted jars for me, she had also brought that fatal virus into our midst.

"Amanda? Amanda, can you hear me? I'm talking to you. Is the young lady sick or not?" Now, she seemed concerned, finally.

"Mom, she still doesn't have all the symptoms. But this morning, when she was drinking from the water fountain, *I* noticed this strange noise coming from her throat. A sort of light hoarseness, like a casual smoker. You know? Like... hrrr-hmm! But she doesn't smoke! And there's more: yesterday she was asking whether Sarah knew of any medication for nausea. And nausea is one of the symptoms that differentiate swine flu from normal flu. Mom, she's infected, and I know it! She's going to kill us all, I'm sure. I have to get out of here. I have to get out of this office now," I was turning my body every which way as I spoke, searching for the closest way out (without passing by Selena, of course).

My head began to spin. I thought of a thousand things at the same time. I had to act and fast. I had to come up with a plan that got me out of the office that very moment. And for some reason, I couldn't remember which direction the emergency exit was. (Another lesson learned. We never pay attention to the emergency exit until we need it. And when we need it, we don't have any idea where it is located.) I needed a reason to work from home. Something that could justify my not going to the office for about two weeks. An emergency trip to visit a sick aunt. No, that wouldn't work. Edward knows my entire family lives around Manhattan, and no farther away than Connecticut. My mother's sick! No, horrible idea. Edward would want to visit her just to eat the butter cookies she makes and he adores. Sophia? No way. I can't involve that innocent creature in my fits of despair. Lauren? Eric? No, no, no.

"Amanda! I heard a voice calling from the door. When it opened, even before I could invite the person in, I saw Selena walking through. Needless to say, I almost passed out.

"Mom, I have to go. Selena's here in my office!" I said, almost whispering, "and she wants to talk to me." I hung up without hearing her reply. And then I turned towards my sentence. Death was finally knocking at my door.

No problem, I thought. *Amanda, you are strong. A warrior. What could a virus that causes severe headaches, nausea, vomiting and diarrhea ever do against someone as strong as you?* I tried to convince myself. I decided to relax. There was nothing else I could do unless I jumped out the 16th floor window or pushed Selena out of it.

"Hi, Selena. How are you? How are you feeling?" I asked, trying to keep a smile on my trembling lips.

"Wow, Amanda. You are so observant! I'm better today, but some days I feel just horrible. Thanks for asking." She smiled.

Oh my God! She IS infected. She just confessed. I have to get out of here! I have to get out of the office immediately!

"Have you been to the doctor? Are you taking care of yourself?" I asked, with utmost concern, but trying to feign sympathy.

"Of course. She said everything's okay. I'm really well, no need to worry," she smiled again.

She has no need to worry. She really doesn't have any need to worry. She's going to kill everyone in the office, building, district and city, but she really has no need to worry. Of course not! There won't be anyone left to tell the story, not even her. Why didn't she stay in Mexico? How does someone pick up a disease like that and then catch a plane to infect an entire city? That's just too much irresponsibility! Way too much!!!

"Good for you! But... Do you need anything? Something I can help you with?" I asked, hoping to get her out of my office as fast as possible before she touched anything, or worse, touched me.

"Nothing much. I just wanted to give you the invitation to my baby shower," and she stretched out her arm to hand me the invitation. I obviously refused to take it.

Oops... I think I missed something. Baby shower? What baby shower? Who's pregnant? Selena's pregnant? How's that? She caught the swine flu in Mexico, still doesn't know it, and to make matters worse, now she's pregnant? How insane!

"Baby shower? Are you pregnant?"

"Yes, Amanda. Isn't that what we have been talking about? My doctor said I'm three months. And I'm doing just fine. I know what you're thinking... everyone asks me the same thing. I got married three weeks ago and I'm already pregnant. I swear I didn't know. I found out on our honeymoon, and it made us so happy. My husband is bursting with joy."

"But, Selena, are you really feeling well? I mean, you're not feeling anything unusual? Fever, cough, sore throat, nausea, diarrhea, for example?"

"No. The doctor said nausea would be normal. But, I don't feel anything you mentioned. Well, I'll just leave your invitation here," she said, setting it on a pile of papers. "I'll let you work in peace. I just wanted to give you the invitation. You'll come, won't you?" she said, without abandoning the smile that lit up her face.

"Yes, of course. Of course, I will. Thanks," I smiled back, trying to be pleasant and demonstrate how happy I was for her.

As soon as she left and closed the door, I called my mom again.

"Mom. I don't think she's sick. At least not with the swine flu." I said, embarrassed.

"Oh! Good to know. Now you can get back to work without any problems. And, you can give me a few hours of peace before flying off on a tangent again. I hope."

"You're right. I really have a lot of work to do. Sorry for my panic attack. Talk to you tonight," I hung up so fast, I don't think she caught the last word.

I went to the door again. I looked at Sarah, who turned towards me immediately.

"Sarah, could you bring me that *cappuccino* now, please? I need a little caffeine. Thank you." I finished the sentence and turned again towards the pile of lawsuits waiting for analysis, and I thought: too bad I don't have any illness that would justify missing work. I would love to get away from all these lawsuits.

That's when my cell phone vibrated. Out of the corner of my eye, I noticed I had just received a text message.

13

"Amanda, let's change the subject? I just don't think I have to discuss my sex life with you."

What? Sex life? What sex life? Just what I needed. Now my mother has a sex life. Okay, so even snails in Mongolia have a sex life. Actually, the other day, I watched a documentary that showed the beginning of Sigmund Feud's career and he was trying to unveil the sex life of snails WITHOUT any success. I was pleased to know that not even Freud could explain everything and I earned another argument to avoid those therapy sessions even the doorman at my building insists on subtly suggesting to me.

But wait a sec... *I DON'T* have a sex life. How could my mother? She must be joking. Or she finally realized she hates me and wants to drive me insane. Doesn't she know I could have anaphylactic shock caused by a surprise like that? I know it sounds absurd, but follow my train of thought. Anaphylaxis is caused by hypersensitivity to medications, foods, insect bites or physical exercise. My mother is sick and tired of knowing I am hypersensitive to all this and to surprises as well. I end up getting anxious, and when I get anxious I dive head first into tranquilizers. Consequently, I could have anaphylactic shock as a result of the combination of many medications associated with the news. There! Just like that. News like that could kill me.

And, if I truly am the victim of anaphylactic shock it will be of no use for that good-looking neighbor of mine (did I say that?) to try and save me (oh, my God, I did say *good-looking*), because in New York, there is still no law that obliges building owners to have a defibrillator on every floor, not even in every building, that could save the life of a citizen in the middle of cardiac arrest or something like that.

"Mom! So, it's true! I thought it was just another Alice in Wonderland story, you know, some joke by pinhead Lauren. You know how she gets when her hormones are kicking in. Unbearably cruel! And with a very nasty sense of humor. So, is it true or not? You actually have a boyfriend?"

My mother with a boyfriend! That's the worst news I have received since the scandal with that famous anti-inflammatory drug accused of causing the death of more than 25 thousand people due to heart problems. I stayed in bed for two days after I found out, and I didn't even use that medication. Imagine now! *My mother has a boyfriend!* How could that happen to me? It's going to take at least a decade and a half to get over this trauma.

"Who is he, mom? Spit it out. I know. He's one of those distinguished gentlemen from the poker club, right? I remember the one who couldn't take his eyes off of you at the end of last year's tournament."

Silence dominated the other end of the line and I continued babbling my monologue, of questions without getting any answers.

"Where did you meet him? What's his name? Does he work or is he retired? Are you sure he really likes you? You must be careful: men today just want to take advantage. Does he know you have a daughter with fragile health and in need of constant assistance? You did tell him, didn't you? Could you kindly stop ignoring me and start answering some of my questions?"

She continued to ignore me, changing the subject several times. By playing this back and forth game, she was able to change the focus of the conversation using something that tormented me even more than her supposedly new boyfriend: my soon to be birthday.

"Have you decided whether you are going to forget this early aging silliness and have a party to celebrate your thirtieth birthday?"

Sometimes, I hate my mother. I know everyone says that, but believe me, I'm serious. I hate the manipulating woman she becomes when she wants to confuse me.

I'm still not sure, but I think I will need to move out of my apartment, building, city, country, perhaps even planet. I'm going to check Google to see if they are already selling lots on Mars, what the price is and if I can get on the waiting list All because I can no longer take this persecution. This dog, my neighbor's pit bull is addicted to me, or better, my smell. Ever since it attacked me and thoroughly thrashed my clothes, I think my smell has become impregnated in the animal's nostrils, and every time I walk through the door of 4C it begins to bark desperately. Pure agony for both of us.

As if it were not enough for me to have this horrid feeling that the monster doesn't want to just smell me, I also have to put up with its owner circling me and trying to smell out something to justify going on the offensive. I can't handle it. There isn't enough Lexotan in the world to calm down my nerves!

I must confess I loved the cactus Brian sent me. It was truly a sweet and kind gesture, but I cannot understand why he just can't stop apologizing. After all, despite the huge scar (ok, it's just 1 inch long, but it's the emotional wound that counts, the trauma, and there's no cure for that), which I am treating with a powerful cream from the Amazon, the tragedy has already been overcome. When I say "almost", it is precisely because of that horrendous dog that will not let me completely forget everything.

I think I will also need to increase my stock of Valium, because, since, as everyone already knows, my birthday is just around the corner. And, my anxiety is at an unbearable level. I think I could have a heart attack at any moment. My immunity is very low and I have had a sore throat all week. I cannot stop thinking of ways to avoid having people greet me with kisses and hugs on this not so exciting date. All the stress was good for something though: I kept the radar on and noticed that stressful moments like the one I am experiencing now worsen my clinical history tremendously. The trigger to my paranoia is no doubt anxiety. The more anxious I am, the sicker I get, or I think I get.

There are still 60 days left before decreeing what I call the race to death. Although I think I am going to die at least twice a week, believe me, the intuition is even stronger now. Contrary to what everyone believes, I know the finish line (or starting line to the other side) is very near. Don't ask me how I know; I just do. I've already begun to suffer. I can't stop thinking about it. Not that I'm someone without anything better to do, quite the contrary. My work has been exhausting; my family needs me; my friends want my attention; my frigidity is already irreversible (at least in my head); I haven't had a romantic date since Obama left office, and the last man who came close enough with sufficient intimacy for me to feel his breathing was my dentist last week as he tenderly held (sign of my need for affection) my chin to examine my molar. And, that doesn't include my health, which is in need of constant assistance.

Nonetheless, there's just no way. The thought I cannot get out of my disturbed mind is trying to find strategies to get around my friends and co-workers alike and pretend that judgment day is in reality just like any other. How can I do that? Don't people realize that including a geriatrician to my list of specialists is more painful than pulling a wisdom tooth? And, in my case, without any anesthesia, since I have serious side effects from local anesthesia. And, there's more: the simple idea of having a disease related to old age, like Alzheimer, Parkinson or rheumatoid arthritis could make me lose sleep for months.

The other day I found out one of those little secrets my mother insists on hiding. She says for my own good. Tell me another one! I call it hiding precious information that can ensure the survival of your own daughter! Won't she ever get it? Well. I found out my great-grandmother on my mother's side, God rest her soul, died of a heart attack at 34! Thirty-four. Can you imagine how that news shook me up emotionally? No? Then, let me spell it out for you.

My great-grandmother Angela had a hard life. She came from Italy while still a child, in her mother's arms. She learned to speak English; worked as a labor in a clothing factory where she met my great -grandfather, a self-defeated, alcoholic Irishman. They had EIGHT children; and this must be made very clear, before she was even thirty. Her weak heart could not handle it and she died at the age of 34. After a life like that, it's no wonder!

I can even accept that this happened in another time; that the woman had eight children and that when she was alive there was not sufficient technology for a preventive diagnosis. But, for the love of God! Those genes are in me now! A woman from my family, just three generations before mine, died at the age of 34. That is completely scary! She was just four and a half years older than I am right now!

The information itself was enough to bring on one of my attacks. I created thousands of theories about women with weak hearts in my family. I called my aunt asking to tell me the truth and not leave out any valuable information. My grandmother did die of old age at 89. My mother is already 55 and her heart is quite strong as all evidence points out. My aunt also never complained about her heart ever giving any trouble nor did any other organ in her body.

On my part, I can ensure I will not relax. I'll have a complete check-up next month. I'm going to ask the doctor for complementary heart exams. My great-grandmother's case has only confirmed my suspicions that my heart is a time bomb ready to explode, which only worsens upon examining my medical history. But, that's okay. Now, I know everything and have a plan. Do the check-up and if the exams point to some anomaly, I'll immediately put my name on the list for transplants, with the recommendation to only accept a heart under 20 years of age. *Could I do that?* Otherwise, let me die in peace. And, if the exams prove my heart is as strong as an ox, I'll look for other hereditary diseases to occupy my free time while I'm still alive and don't have a boyfriend.

14

Where could I find a book about that? - I thought to myself during my pilgrimage in search of the perfect gift for my brother-in-law. *Think fast, Amanda. Bearings? Engineering? Forklifting? Think fast!* I frantically ran through the millions of square meters of bookcases and shelves, with books on almost every topic that one could ever imagine (with the exception of bearings for forklifts, of course), of the new Barnes and Noble on the Upper East side. I had been there for more than half an hour, without being able to come to any conclusions. Actually, I had come to one conclusion: I would like to find a book for him. An amazing book. I was determined, but completely lost, when finally, it occurred to me that I needed help to complete my mission: buy a book about bearings for forklift trucks, to make a good impression at the dinner in honor of Eric.

I was exhausted; I had worked all morning on a case that I could already tell was going to exhaust my neurons beyond repair. For those who don't know, a neuron that is lost, is a neuron less in the brain, point blank. There is no return. They do not have the ability to reproduce, or anything like that. We are born with a limited number of neurons, some of us with a very limited quantity, and we die with less than half of them; there is no remedy for this. With that being said, not even a great and peaceful night's sleep would be able to replenish the loss. Sleep? I wish! I have had horrible insomnia for days now. The kind that will deceive you, and let you sleep peacefully for two or three hours, and then wake you up at about four in the morning, and you only fall back asleep at six, knowing that your alarm clock will go off at seven. I have tried everything. Warm milk before bed, herbal medicine foot massage, reading and tea, but I haven't had any luck. I am looking for a specialist in the field.

It wasn't even two in the afternoon, way too early to think of going home and having some well-deserved peace and quiet. I had to go back to the office and face the rest of my day, and that was only part of my lunch break. Buy Eric the book, and then, pick up a salad at any convenience store was the plan. But, the salad and the store would have to wait.

As I passed by the medical section, I couldn't resist. I had to stop. I stopped long enough to completely forget what I was doing there in the first place. I lost precious time looking for new developments in the health field. I took a good look at the new releases and ended up buying a copy of the new edition of the Merck manual, last updated. This was so typical of me.

There was no need for a book to plummet on top of my head for me to go back to what I was really there for: to buy a book for Eric. *I am here to buy an amazing book to give to Eric.* I tried to stay focused. Lauren had called me two days before to invite me to a dinner at her house with very few guests. Just a few single friends (she made it a point to stress that), who work with him, two couples that were very close friends, my mom, and I. The dinner was to celebrate Eric's long-awaited promotion to director. Lauren had dreamt of this day for a long time. She couldn't wait to have a corporate credit card, those that only directors and the wives of directors had the privilege of using. As the manager's wife, she didn't have that luxury. That's right! In command of the company that Eric works for is a woman, the granddaughter of the founder. As soon as she took office, one of her first measures was to authorize corporate credit cards to all the wives of the directors. I know saying it like this might make it seem a bit frivolous, but I think it was a very smart idea indeed. According to her, it was to avoid the constant fights about the wives' excessive spending habits. The card had a limit to essential expenses, which was not much, just enough to cover expenses ranging from a manicure to a small treat, such as a Balenciaga purse, Fendi cloths, jewelry from Cartier, Harry Winston or Tiffany & Co. This would make the wives happy and the husbands at peace, they worked more and made more money, with less stress. "Happy wife, happy life," as they say. Lauren couldn't way to lay her hands on her credit card.

Either way, this is a very special moment in the career of my brother-in-law. He has worked for the company for 15 years. He works hard, loves what he does, and even has fun with it. He can talk for hours about the automation systems for the production of bearings for forklift. Fascinating! I would like to somehow participate in their joy with a symbolic present. But, need I say that the possibilities for a symbolic gift at this point were slim to none.

I had almost given up and bought him a Mont Blanc pen, (exactly what I thought, so uncreative!) when I decided to ask a sales associate for some assistance. The worst part is, that I don't even know where to start. Engineering? Automation? Robotics? Industrial production? Production line? What kind of book would be useful for the director of a rolling bearing industry?

Eric loves to read books. He received his Master's degree from a prestigious university, and it was there, in the middle of the books in the library, that he met Lauren. She was majoring in Modern Art, and he was getting his Master's degree in Computer Science. It was love at first sight. He was the cute *nerd* with a promising future, and she, a girl full of charm who was studying arts to become an excellent housewife who has smart things to say at business cocktails. You could definitely say they are the ideal couple. Pardon my sarcasm! It's pure envy.

A nice young man has just informed me that perhaps a book called the Engineering of Automation and Systematic Production Applied to the Development of Products and Industrial Raw Materials on a Large Scale can be a good one. I don't know. I called Lauren in hopes that she would give me a good idea, but, as always, she didn't answer the phone.

"Ok, I'll take it. Do you guys gift wrap?"

I finished the odyssey in search of the perfect gift for my brother-in-law and I went back to the office, where a lot of work awaited me. Getting to my office I realized that my cell phone had no service, which always happens. Cell phone reception in New York wasn't as great as one would assume. My answering machine was full of voicemails. As I hung up my light, summer jacket on the back of my chair, I pressed the button to start listening to all of them.

Message 1: Hi Amanda. Why don't you answer your cell phone? Is there a problem? I have been looking for you all morning. Call me. I need to speak with you.

The person didn't identify himself or herself, but I knew exactly who it was. Julia.

Message 2: Amanda, for the love of God! Could you please return my calls? I really need to talk to you. What is going on? Are you preparing yourself for a biological warfare? Or do you think that a new virus is contaminating us via telephone? Answer the phone! I need to talk to you, and its urgent!

The second voice, troubled, anxious and rude didn't identify themselves again, but it was Julia. What? A Virus transmitted via telephone? SEARCH ON THE INTERNET – PHONE VIRUS. I wrote on a post it before listening to my next voice mail.

Message 3: Amanda, honey, its mommy. (I hate when she starts off like that, brings me gut wrenching feelings.) I would like to know if you RSVP'D to Lauren's dinner. Can you call me later? Call as soon as you can. I will be out shopping, but my cell will be on. Kisses honey. Mommy loves you.

No comment: I still have a gut wrenching feeling.

Message 4: Hi Amanda, it's Lauren. I am returning your call. I couldn't pick up before because Sophia was choking on a piece of that doll's arm that Dalton gave her for her birthday, and that I've always hated. Remember? I think it was because I had already foreseen something unpleasant. I felt like something bad could happen the second I looked at her. Well yeah, her fore arm detached and Sophia swallowed it. I think I read her too many stories about ostriches! It's my fault. I had to help her. But she is fine, no worries! Do you need something? Don't tell me that you're sick, and not coming to Eric's dinner. Amanda, stop right now. You know that I don't tolerate your attacks! Save them for mom. By the way, she confirmed that she is coming to the dinner. She is even buying a new dress and is bringing... (the signal of the end of the recording interrupted her speech).

Does Lauren think that an answering machine was created to catch up on gossip? What was mom bringing to the dinner? Dessert? Or a book about *Systematic Production Applied and Development of Products, or Whatever?* Oh, no! I hope she didn't have the same idea as me.

Message 5: Amanda, the law project for the territorial demarcation of the park Lake Village is amazing. The engineers have done a great job preserving part of the lake and the animals, and with reforesting that stretch hit by the fire. It is wonderful. We need to speed up the submission to the congress. Please, give me a call. I will be out of the office until four o'clock, but I want an update today. Thank you, Edward.

While listening to Edward's message my eyes scanned through the e-mails I had received on the same topic. Amongst them, three were from Edward. He certainly is dedicated to this project.

Message 6: A-M-A-N-D-A!!! I have triple pneumonia and the doctors say I only have five more minutes of life. My last wish is to talk to MY BEST FRIEND!

Wow! I think I should listen to the other messages later and call Julia right now, I thought as my fingers dialed her number.

Before I could even put in a word, she groaned like an animal in despair.

"He is going to ask me, I know he is. I saw it!"

"Hi, Julia, do you need to talk to me? Or do I have to sit here and listen to you scream and groan?" – I asked as I held the telephone away from my ear.

"I saw it! I know I shouldn't have snooped through his things, he trusted me with the keys. But, I can't contain myself. I saw it!"

"Saw what?" –My God. What did she see?

"The ring! It's beautiful. The most perfect engagement ring I have ever seen in my entire life."

"Hold on! You're telling me you were looking through your boyfriend's belongings and you found an engagement ring? And, you assume that it's for you. But, he hasn't said anything yet. So, you're not really sure, are you?"

"Of course, I am sure! The ring is huge, with a humongous diamond in the middle and four smaller ones on the sides. Beautiful! He's given me all the signs lately.

He is perfect, loves spending time with me and doing everything together! Last week he went to the nail salon with me! Isn't that the cutest thing you've ever heard a guy do?"

"I don't know. Is it? I go to the nail salon with Marc all the time and I don't think it's that cute. Especially when he wants the same nail polish color as I do – I hate when he does that!"

"Amanda, stop fooling around."

"Ok. But has he said anything about marriage? Asked anything?"

"Of course not. He must be waiting for the perfect moment to ask me."

"Julia, be careful. You always assume…"

"Amanda, please. Will you ever be happy with anything? He loves me. It's that simple. He loves me and he bought an engagement ring for me."

"You always make assumptions and then…ok. Maybe you are right. Let's celebrate! How about some cocktails at Café Noir tonight? It's been so long since we've visited our friend, Carlo. It will be fun."

"I would love to see Carlo. But, today I can't. I am going to meet up with my love for a couple of beers at Sweet Vicious. Maybe tomorrow?"

"Tomorrow I have Eric's dinner. Lauren will kill me if I don't go."

"Ok, we'll talk later then. You'll be the first person to know after he asks. I am so nervous…and so happy! I can't believe that I'm finally going to be the fiancé of a cool guy, who has the money to buy me a beautiful engagement ring."

It took me more than fifteen minutes to finally be able to hang up. Julia was exuberating happiness with the possibility, even if it was imaginary, of being asked to marry someone. *She had practically planned the wedding and bought her dress already.* For a second, I felt anguished. My heart was tight, as if it had shrunk. No, it wasn't a symptom of any disease. It was just sadness. Things were moving way too fast. Everyone's lives seemed full of surprises and changes. Lauren was enthusiastic with her corporate credit card; Eric, with the challenges of his new position as director of bearings. Marc got a job in the studio of a renowned artist. Mom had a mysterious boyfriend, and Julia was most likely getting married. What about me? What about my life? I've been at the same job for almost five years. I know that saving the planet from the unscrupulous capitalists who only seek profit by destroying the environment is not a bad job, at all. Sometimes, I even feel like a superhero. Super-Eco-Girl! But, I can't even hope for a promotion, because in this business you don't exactly have a career plan. I could dream about having a political career, but I do not believe that I have the strength for it. And, my health problems wouldn't help because they are getting worse by the second. I continue to have nightmares, when I actually do sleep, about the idea of seeking psychological treatment. And, the endless search for my soul mate is exhausting. Not to mention the fact that my birthday is so close that I feel the breath of old age only a few feet away. Stupid life! Stupid. I sunk into my chair, and wanted to cry. I withdrew the crying, took a deep breath and ordered a coffee from Sarah. I had a lot of work to get done.

15

"Hi mom. It's me, Amanda." As if she didn't already know.

"Amanda, honey, I'm getting my hair done. Can we talk later?"

"Sure, mom. But…"

"Amanda, you promised your sister you'd go to this dinner party. Don't come up with any last-minute illnesses now. I promised her you would not miss it. She's excited to introduce you to some of Eric's friends."

Why is it that nobody ever lets me speak? And what's the deal with her trying to find me a boyfriend? It's so embarrassing to realize my mom and sister feel they need to conspire to find me a boyfriend… as if I wasn't capable of doing that on my own.

"Mom, that's not it. Listen! What did you buy for Eric? Please, don't tell me it was a book about production and automation."

"No, honey. I bought him a Prada wallet. I considered giving him a Mont Blanc pen, but then I figured you or your sister could have thought of that. So I decided on the wallet. Why?"

What a relief. How could I possibly think of another gift now, right before the party? The truth is, since Lauren and Eric got married, I have never gotten him a gift he actually liked.

To make matters worse, he always gets me wonderful gifts *that Lauren buys for him to give to me.* I am clearly at a disadvantage! Last Christmas I learned that Eric hates green. Too bad I found that out just as he was opening the hunter-green Polo Ralph Lauren sweater I'd paid a fortune just to impress him. The face of dissatisfaction he made is forever captured in a picture we took together.

"No reason, I'll see you at dinner, then." I hung up and continued to pick out an outfit and gather my makeup.

I stepped out of the cab in front of Lauren's lobby on time, just two minutes early. I said good evening to Charlie, the doorman, and walked towards the elevator. Standing next to me was a very handsome man. Young, no more than 30 years old, and very elegant in his Ermenegildo Zegna blazer. His hair was ashy-blonde with an impeccable haircut, and he wore a distinctive cologne. Simply marvelous. The cologne and the guy. As soon as the elevator arrived, he smiled at me and nodded for me to go in first with his head. I walked in and he stood right in front of me. The gift in his hand immediately caught my attention, because it looked exactly like mine. I did not allow myself to panic, because purchasing a book at Barnes & Nobles and asking the clerk to gift wrap it was not uncommon, after all. It certainly wasn't exclusively for me, right?

The elevator door opened and he took just a few steps to Eric and Lauren's front door, followed by me. When Eric opened the door, he looked absolutely thrilled. Not for the arrival of his guests, I suppose, but because of his promotion.

"Greg, buddy, you came!" It sounded kind of fake. Eric looked surprised that Greg had actually shown up. They didn't seem very close.

Greg stretched out his arm and handed Eric the gift. From that moment on, everything seemed to happen in slow motion. I can't even explain how it happened, but it was a disaster! A complete disaster, worthy of Amanda, the lunatic of the family. I swear I spent the whole evening trying not to embarrass my family with the events that ensued.

Eric started unwrapping his gift right in front of me, as we all walked into the living room together. I remember seeing Lauren walking towards us, but I have no idea where Sophia came from. By the time I noticed her, there was nothing I could do.

I already knew the gift from the stranger in the elevator had been bought at the same store as mine. I figured it was a book. I just couldn't imagine the stud from the elevator, who was only a few steps in front of me, would give Eric the book *Automation and Systematic Production Engineering Applied to the Development of Products and Industrial Raw Materials on a Large Scale* and, even worse, that Eric would love it!

"Wow, I can't believe it! I was so excited to read this book, Greg. How did you know?"

"Truth is, I didn't know. I asked your secretary and she told me you'd asked her to buy it… so…"

"Wow, thanks. Thanks a lot!"

Great! Just great! I'm furious. I finally found the perfect gift for Eric and along comes a snob, with the help of Eric's cocky secretary, and ruins my night. Why didn't I just buy a simple, sophisticated Mont Blanc pen? I didn't know what would be worse: not giving him a gift or giving him the same gift as someone else? I thought about it hastily and decided that not giving him anything was the best option. I could say I bought him something but left it at the office. I could say I didn't have time to buy anything and would send him a gift later. Or I could simply shut up and say nothing.

Quietly, I dropped the present onto the floor, near a tall ceramic vase right next to the door and sighed in relief. Just then, Eric came and hugged me. "I'm happy you're here. Will you entertain us with your funny stories about diseases?" I looked at Lauren as if looks could kill. I had already asked her a million times to please explain to her husband that my health issues are serious, even though everybody thinks hypochondriasis is a joke. But, in return, she gave me a warm look and shrugged her shoulders as if to say: I'm not to blame for my husband's rudeness. Well, then.

As soon as the long hug was over, Eric and I felt something tugging at the bottom of our pants, begging for attention. I looked down and there she was, beautiful and smiling, with her huge cheeks. It was Sophia, my niece, holding my present.

"Daddy, open Aunt Amanda's gift!" She said, with the biggest smile on her face.

I tried taking the gift away and mumbled "this is not for you." But it was too late. He had already opened it. "Oh... You called my secretary as well, Amanda?" He said smiling.

The worst part is that I didn't. I spent my whole lunch break thinking and searching for the perfect gift. And all my hard work turned out to be for nothing. Damn it!

"You can exchange it for something else. Maybe Automation and Systematic Production Engineering Applied to the Development of Products and Industrial Raw Materials on a Large Scale - Part 2?"

"They've published part 2?"

"I don't think so, but this book will most likely be a hit! So, we should expect one." *Amanda, shut up,* I thought.

At this point, Lauren was tired of watching me humiliate myself and the whole family's image.

"What do you guys want to drink? Greg, would you like a Martini? And you, Amanda, the usual?"

All I could bring myself to do was nod my head, as everyone stared and pitied me.

Who would've guessed that this dinner party Lauren had planned for Eric would be a box of surprises? Starting with the single guests. Lauren really outdid herself trying to find me a date this time. There were five of Eric's single friends, three of whom were interesting. The other two were bald. And, off the bat, I had to eliminate Greg, because of the whole gift issue. I couldn't possibly start a relationship with someone based on bitterness and resentment. And what had just happened by Lauren's front door will be etched in my memory for a very long time. So, there were two contenders left: Patrick and Alex. I then moved on to a preliminary investigation. I had to know if they were also interested in me and if they were in some sort of relationship. Even if it wasn't anything serious, I needed to find out.

The truth is I didn't even need to dig very deep. Alex soon started babbling about some girl he met a few weeks before. Lucky girl. The sparkle in his eyes said it all. He was in love. *Okay, fine,* I thought. *Patrick is very handsome, smart, and has a great sense of humor.* I tried to get closer to him, and we talked a lot for a good portion of the party. The chemistry was great, and he was lovely. Even during the most stressful moment of the party, he stood by my side and offered me support, helping me catch my breath when the big surprise of the night came.

Let me make this clear, the big surprise was solely for me, because – as far as I know – the whole family was already aware of the facts, except for me.

A few moments before Lauren started serving dinner, the intercom rang for the last time. I took the liberty of getting up and answering it. Lauren had a lot on her plate, and Eric was busy entertaining his guests. Besides, the last guest was my mom; she was the only one who hadn't arrived yet. I told Charlie to send her up, and he said they were already on their way up. *They? So, it isn't mom, it must be other guests.* I waited by the door for three minutes, which was the time it took for the doorbell to ring. I then opened the door and the first person I saw was Dr. White.

Yes, Dr. White, the monstrous doctor who never believes me and always questions my diagnoses. The one who's constantly trying to admit me into a psychiatric clinic, suggesting therapy treatments. Now I understand why my mom insists on it so much. Suddenly I saw her, right behind him, holding his hand! I immediately understood why. She had been abducted. He's brainwashed her and now she's part of the New York doctors' conspiracy against me. So, he is the mysterious boyfriend. I can't believe it! I just cannot believe it! Why didn't anybody tell me? Did Lauren already know? Of course, she did. Sophia came running to the door and threw herself into his arms. Children do not lie! I should've asked her who mom's boyfriend was. She probably would've told me the truth while Lauren and Eric were mom's accomplices in this plot against me. But, why? Does she really think I'm so insensitive I couldn't be happy for her? Does she really hate me? My own mother kept this kind of secret from me; she doesn't consider me her friend. She trusts Lauren, but not me. I'm disappointed, devastated and agitated. I cannot believe my own family would keep something like this from me.

"How long now?" I asked before even saying hello. "Tell me mom, how long has it been?"

"Amanda, we'll talk about this after dinner, okay?"

Lauren came over and quickly took them both to the table before Amanda, the lunatic, made a scene.

Amanda, the lunatic, can't control herself and has no manners. Is that what they think of me?

"We were just waiting for you to start. Come! You too, Amanda. Patrick wants to show you something online. Then, please, bring him and Eric to the table."

Wonderful food, indigestible dinner and unpleasant surprises; apart from Patrick's presence, the party was a bizarre experience. Seeing my mom all touchy-feely with my doctor was the end of the world for me. Since my dad passed away, I hadn't seen her with anyone. I must say it wasn't easy. Not that I'm bitter and think she doesn't have the right to be happy again. She does, but... she could've waited for me to get married or at least find a boyfriend first, right? Rationally, I know things don't happen when we want them to, or how we want them to. Love just happens! I also know this isn't a treasure hunt, but I'll be turning 30 years old soon! Thirty years without ever being in a serious relationship. Always dreaming up the perfect guy – preferably a doctor, of course – and now my mom, who had been happily married for many years and all, has a cute, charming boyfriend, and he's a doctor! It's so unfair.

Dinner was almost over, so I announced I was leaving just as Eric offered some liquor and Lauren served coffee with mint chocolate.

"I need to wake up very early tomorrow."

"Stay a little longer, Amanda. We can share a cab home and talk a little" said mom, the traitor.

Oh, now she wants to talk! Now? Oh, she won't have it that easy. She'll have to explain everything in detail to me, but not now. I'm too tired, too shocked, and too upset to have this conversation right now. I need to think. To understand a few things and formulate thousands of questions she'll need to answer if she wants my approval.

"I really am tired. We'll talk later."

I said bye to everyone except Patrick, who insisted on bringing me home. He seemed worried. How adorable! Before I got out of the cab, we exchanged numbers and he promised to take me out to dinner. A date! Finally, it looks like I've found a nice guy. He affectionately kissed me on the forehead. So cute! I think I'll try to forget tonight's disappointments and dream about him. It's the best I can do.

I came in through the glass doors, leaving behind the image of Patrick going away in the cab, praying he'd call me. I pressed the button to call the elevator. I was daydreaming, totally absorbed in my thoughts when I heard loud laughter.

"Good night, Amanda."

It was Brian. He looked gorgeous, in a blue and white striped shirt. His remarkable haircut and cologne added the final touch that amounted to what I'd classify as a just-right man. But he wasn't alone. For someone who was always insisting I go out with him, he didn't waste any time. Got tired of being rejected and just found someone else. Pretty fast, right? Men! They're all the same. It took only about three "nos" in a row for him to give up. How about her, you ask? Beautiful. Long, shiny hair, perfect face, immaculate skin, beautiful smile and a Barbie-sized waist. He really is very smart. Behind that innocent look, I knew there was a womanizer. I knew it! He didn't fool me.

"Good night, Brian."

"This is Sally."

"Nice to meet you, Sally. I'm Amanda, Brian's neighbor."

By the way, be very careful. His dog almost killed me one day. He's a canine killer. But, other than that, Brian is actually a good guy. Have fun! – I felt like saying, but I bit my tongue.

We went all the way to the fourth floor without exchanging a single word. I noticed them glancing at each other, as if were sharing some inside secret. They both had wide smiles, communicating only through their eyes. Just one look and they could understand each other's thoughts. It was obvious they were pretty intimate already. I could tell it was a long-term relationship.

The elevator reached my floor, which coincidentally was also his. We got off the elevator and said our goodbyes in front of Brian's door, which came before mine. I finally got home and all my thoughts were again focused on mom and Dr. White. I tried to stop thinking about it, but I just couldn't. While taking off my makeup, I thought: why didn't she tell me? Why did she trust Lauren and not me? I thought we were friends, I always confided in her. My problems at school, work, my health, my fights with Julia, everything! And now, just like that, she stabs me in the back. What a disappointment!

16

I woke up humming "Toxic" by Britney Spears, and was so energized I just went on dancing (mimicking the choreography from her music video) in the shower. It's amazing how some pop culture artists can help brighten people's lives. Sometimes Britney can lift me up as if she were my best friend. But, the reason behind such a wonderful mood was not Britney's songs, of course.

To whom it may concern, good news: Patrick called! *Yes! Yes! Yes!* He called last night and we spent more than two hours chatting. I think I have a date! Actually, I don't think so, I'm quite sure. He invited me to dinner at Le Cirque tomorrow night!

The guy is a lord! You know, like those with a title of nobility and all? I have a theory. I believe when someone is born an aristocrat, the title of nobility follows that person into the next life, and this has absolutely nothing to do with how much money the person has. Patrick was that kind of guy; or so it seemed.

I arrived ten minutes late because traffic on 58th Street and 5th Avenue was chaotic. While still in the cab, I sent him a text: "I'll be 10 minutes late, sorry. See you soon." I was expecting a cold and feisty response, typical of New York men. He replied: "Don't worry; I'm waiting for you at the bar, with a good wine." And a smiley face. He's so sweet, isn't he? He is.

As soon as I arrived at the restaurant, I saw him sitting at the end of the bar, gorgeous. Carefully styled hair, flawless shave and radiant skin, like that of a woman addicted to cosmetics. He was wearing a pair of jeans that, I could tell by the wash, had to be Diesel, an Armani t-shirt and Prada shoes. Perfect. The final touch was the cologne, *Incanto* (Salvatore Ferragamo), which I knew well. It was the same one Eric wore.

Patrick was so different from my inconvenient neighbor... The one who's always asking me out to dinner. Who keeps cornering me in the elevator, in the supermarket, in the building's hallways and on the street. The one who wears faded jeans that are way too snug, skintight t-shirts, so hot... um... I mean, too tight, sneakers and that leather jacket he never seems to take off. No, really, you can't even compare the two. Patrick is a man. He's wonderful! The man of my dreams, perfect.

We both ordered the same appetizer, green salad with shrimp. As for the entrée, I ordered a salmon fillet with fine herbs reduction and he ordered the lobster risotto. The food was divine; so delicious I could barely wait to try the dessert. For me, *crème brûlée*; and for him, a delicious *bombolone* with coffee ice cream – I tasted it as he kindly fed me a spoonful.

Great dinner, great chat, great company, what else could I want from a man, I thought, as he ordered me a cup of coffee (the last treat of the evening) and the check. I was still sipping my coffee when the check arrived. I recall thinking: I don't even want to see it. Well, too late. He opened the fancy leather check presenter and announced, loud and clear: "It's $190 for each, including tip."

Huh? Wait a minute. I think I missed something. Who invited me? Who picked the restaurant? Who made me think this was a romantic date? Who's misled me with a perfect gentleman's façade? And now I have to pay the bill? Where has chivalry gone? Oh my, this is a first date. Or isn't it? Oh, I don't know, I'm confused. I thought, as I rummaged through my bag, looking for my credit card.

Another scene that unintentionally came to my prodigious mind was me explaining to a police officer how my stiletto heel ended up smack in the middle of Patrick's brain, having entered through the fool's left temple and gotten stuck there. I'd present my defense arguments right there, while everyone stared in disbelief at my shoe, still lodged in Patrick's head as he leaned over a pool of blood on the table at Le Cirque, staining the immaculately white tablecloth and the fancy china that only the most refined and expensive restaurants, such as this, use.

It's very simple, officer; this scoundrel invited me to dinner, made promises of love, let me to believe this was a romantic date and I was the woman of his dreams. After all of this, he asked me to split the bill for dinner! Our first dinner, mind you. I'm not the type of woman who'd exploit a man. But it's there, written between the lines of the relationship etiquette manual, haven't you read it, sir? Believe me, it's there: a gentleman pays the bill on a first date to demonstrate interest in the lady. Be honest. Don't you think he deserved a lesson, sir? I agree I underestimated the power and speed of my blow. But, you know what? Physics was never my favorite subject in school. Still, I don't think I deserve to go to jail, wouldn't you agree, sir? I played this out in my mind, while I looked for the credit card. Can I call my mom and my lawyer, or will you let me go right now? Then, I woke up from this wonderful dream.

I paid the bill, savored my espresso to the last drop and got up from the table without another smile. I took away his title of nobility, got into the cab, alone, and headed home.

He even had the audacity to ask if he could come over. *Excuse me? Wake up, buddy. Am I the only one with a brain here?* And to think I was so naïve as to think he had blue blood running through his veins. Quite the opposite, he has red anemic blood. Thin and inconsistent! I was so frustrated I couldn't even talk about it with Julia or Lauren. I decided to simply erase the night from my memory, rather than to think about it. Phone calls were received (by me) from a number (his) whose name no longer showed up on my cell phone's screen, because it had been deleted. Such calls have not been answered (by me) until the caller/sender of the messages understood (finally!) that his calls would not be answered, under any circumstances, and gave up.

Latest news on my health: frigidity has become a chronic condition. I'm afraid I no longer have hopes for a cure. But life goes on.

Whenever I have unpleasant surprises, such as what happened between me and my traitor mom, and there are aggravating factors like the disastrous date with Patrick, for example, I fall into a deep and involuntary depression. I fight it as hard as I can to avoid being carried away, but on days like today, in which I'm spending my time organizing my medical schedule, adding in names of new specialists, cataloging symptoms of new diseases, archiving my medical exams in alphabetical order, and making a thorough list of medications to update my inventory, I realize the damned depression has grabbed hold of me.

At this point, I analyze the possibilities and, if my chances of coming out of this crisis are minimal, I surrender. I dive in headfirst, with an open heart. I'd rather face the one thing I'm sure I know well – my condition, hypochondriasis – than to confront emotional troubles and innermost issues that I'm not familiar with. Since I'll have to find a physical reason to head to the hospital and solve my problems with a prescription for some happy pills, then, let it be soon. This way, everything can be resolved painlessly, especially considering that my heart is already beating so hard it hurts my chest.

I remember the last time I got depressed as if it were yesterday. I spent two days locked in the house, feeling sorry for myself. I had messy hair, a dirty house (I was really unwell), bitten nails, and horrendous breath. It was a nightmare. I spent both afternoons eating junk food loaded with trans-fat and drinking Diet Coke, in addition to the old cliché tub of ice cream, of course. I watched all of the most useless shows TV had to offer. Shows about trips I'd never go on, cooking shows teaching you how to make the best hamburger anyone could ever ask for, gossip shows that kept talking about that guy who is famous because he has eight kids. You know the one? Yeah. Then, I stop and think: my grandmother, my dad's mom, had five kids and raised them until they were all hard-working adults. And, the poor lady never even received a religious medal for this. Why was this guy famous again? Then I remembered, his sperm is similar to that of Superman's and he had six kids all at once, aside from the two he already had. It certainly is a great accomplishment.

Back to my depression, after that bizarre weekend, amongst tears, horrible food and useless culture, Monday came and I had to work. Depressed or not, work to me is sacred. I only miss it in case of a serious health problem. I woke up on time, took a shower and went through my checklist to see if there was anything abnormal in my body. You know I do this on a regular basis, so nothing new there.

I had breakfast and headed to the office. The day went by slowly and painfully. I couldn't focus on anything and pretended, very well, to work hard. That is until, late in the afternoon, an intruder began to battle with my tongue.

I moved my tongue from one side to another, feeling inch by inch of my palate, and noticed it had installed itself right in the middle of it, at the very top. A tiny blister, which would torment me for over six months.

Exactly 48 hours elapsed from the moment I first noticed the blister until I actually did something about it, and some really odd things happened in this short period of time.

Oddity #1: I didn't panic immediately. At first, I didn't pay any attention to the fact that this blister was taking up a space dedicated exclusively to my tongue. Which, for a hypochondriac, is terrifying.

Oddity #2: I waited for the blister to spontaneously disappear, just as it had appeared. At the time, this seemed very logical.

Oddity #3: The blister had the extraordinary power of changing size. At some points during the day, it was so small I honestly thought it was going away. At other times, it was so huge I thought it would take over my whole mouth, which was scary.

I checked the size of the blister with one of those round mirrors that dentists use every 20 minutes, and with my tongue every two minutes.

All night long, I did not lose control. I admit, I did do some online research, but I couldn't find anything specific on the topic. Likewise, there was nothing in my medical encyclopedia that closely resembled my mutant blister. It was only when I woke up the next morning and realized the intruder was still there that I decided it was definitely time to start panicking.

First, I called my mom, then two dentists and one orthodontist. Only one of them had time on his schedule to fit in an emergency appointment. If this wasn't an emergency, then what was?

I called the office and let them know I wouldn't be going to work that morning. I grabbed my bag, made sure my insurance card was in there, and went to the dentist's office. It was a tiny office downtown. There was a very small counter in the left corner of the waiting room, behind which I could see the secretary's head, and a three-seat sofa where another patient was already waiting to be called in. I was probably going to be next, right after him.

I tried to control my anxiety by drinking gallons of water from the water fountain and going to the bathroom as many times as needed. The receptionist finally announced that I could go in.

I walked into the small, cramped office, behind a door with a sign that read *Orthodontist Surgeon and Maxillofacial Traumatology*, followed closely by the receptionist. She led me to the chair and reclined it so that I'd be in the ideal position for the examination. Then, a tall man appeared. He seemed to be about 50 years old, I'm not so sure, with a mask on his face and ready to start. He placed my file, containing my name and other information, on a small table next to his chair and began asking questions and taking notes.

"So Amanda, what's going on in your mouth?"

What a stupid question. I already knew I didn't like him. Can I go home? I don't need to find out what's going on in my mouth. The answer I was dying to give him was: *If I knew it, I wouldn't be here.* Here's what I really answered:

"This blister has suddenly appeared on the roof of my mouth and it's constantly changing size. It's irritating."

"Okay, let me see."

I opened my mouth as wide as I could, as if saying: welcome in.

"Yup, there it is."

Oh! I thought it had gone shopping. Of course, it's there, I can feel it! I didn't come here to be told it's there, I came here to have it removed. Do you get it? Or is it too hard to understand?

I'm sorry, but I have an issue with inaccurate statements. Before you talk to me, please formulate a sentence correctly and consistently. Let's give it another try.

"It appeared two days ago and ever since then I've noticed a variation in size. What is it? Will it go away on its own? Is there any medication to get rid of it? Do I need to undergo surgery for immediate removal? Or is this a tumor and I might as well request my extreme unction now?" I said this clearly and objectively, as he looked at me in dismay.

"Well, we'll need to run some tests to confirm, but I believe this is a case of mucocele."

"Huh?" – while my mouth was still open.

"Mucocele is a swelling of the mucous membrane. 75% of the cases happen in the roof of the mouth and are floating; they vary in size and sometimes even change place."

"Can we get to the important stuff? Am I going to die?"

He laughed and continued to explain: "We still need confirmation, but if that's what it is, we'll remove it. The prognoses in most cases are good. But we need to do a biopsy of the material collected."

"Biopsy? I'm going to die. I knew it. This small talk doesn't fool me. If a biopsy is needed, the diagnosis is a tumor; if the tumor is malignant, then I have cancer and if I have cancer, I'm as good as dead."

"Amanda, please calm down. Nobody said anything about cancer. I'm just explaining the procedure. You don't need to be frightened. It's all very simple."

Simple for whom? Not for me. The guy will take out a huge chunk of my mouth –I hope I don't need it someday – then he'll send it to a lab and I'll be anxious all week, waiting for the results; a whole week of distress and agony. Yet, he tries to convince me everything is fine. I ask again: fine for whom?

"One more question. How did this happen? The blister wasn't there three days ago. How did it just pop up out of nowhere, like magic?"

"It could be bruxism."

"Bruxism? I told you it appeared like magic. I knew it, black magic, someone is trying to harm me." *Oh my God, help!*

"Amanda, I'm a dentist. I don't believe in magic."

"So, it's a tumor. It's cancer. You believe in cancer, don't you?"

"Not in your case. You're too young and you don't have a family history of it. But we'll run some tests. I've also never seen someone your age who was such a hypochondriac, so maybe it is cancer."

That actually sounded strange, somewhat satisfying. *I know, I'm crazy. Actually, not crazy, I'm sick.* I let him finish his explanation about bruxism before bombarding him with more questions.

"Bruxism is the habit of clenching and grinding your teeth. It's very common for patients to report that they wake up with headaches and experience excessive wear of the teeth or jaw joint disorder. Bruxism is 100% associated with stress and emotional tension in your living environment. It is more common in patients between the ages of 15 and 35 and it affects women more than men."

Nosophobic patients have the ability to predict the future. If the future is dark and scary, then it becomes even easier for them. I call this a cognitive-intuitive skill. Julia calls it plain old pessimism. Well, since positive thinking isn't something hypochondriacs tend to do, I got this notion in my head, full of hair and sick thoughts, that this would turn out to be a big deal. And, it did.

One week after my appointment, I went through surgery to remove the blister. I questioned Dr. Walton's competence (or lack thereof) from the beginning, but did he have to prove me right?

On the day the damn blister was to be removed, to my disappointment, it was almost imperceptible. As a result, Dr. Walton removed only part of it and three months later I had to undergo surgery again because the blister, my companion on this journey, had come back with a vengeance!

There was also the anesthesia issue. When I got to the dentist's office, they immediately started preparing me. I went into the same cramped, small room and sat down on the reclined chair, exactly like I had on my first appointment. But, this time an assistant came to prepare me for surgery. She first applied an analgesic ointment all over the roof of my mouth, then she injected the local anesthetic. The first injection was very painful, but bearable. Then, she applied a little more and asked, "Are you okay?" Given the circumstances… "Yes."

"I've applied it twice. Now, let's wait a little while. I'll be back in a couple of minutes to see if you're numb, okay?" Given the circumstances… "Okay."

After five minutes, she came back. "Is everything okay?" I don't think the circumstances have changed in the last five minutes, so… "Yup."

"I'm going to pinch your mouth with tweezers. If you feel any pain, just let me know and I'll apply more of the anesthetic, alright?"

Given the circumstances… "Alright."

"Do you feel it?" (Pinched.)

"Yes."

"How about now?" (Pinched again.)

"I still feel it."

More anesthetics.

"How about now?" (Pinched again.)

"Yup, I still feel it." But, at this point I confess I wasn't really sure anymore.

"Listen, I've given you enough anesthetics to knock down a horse. Are you sure you can still feel it?"

"Yes."

"Well, either you're a hypochondriac, or you're a drug addict."

"I am."

"What? An addict?"

"No. A hypochondriac."

"And you waited this long to tell me that?"

"You didn't ask." I answered, knowing this would irritate her.

I went through my entire stock of natural tranquilizers while waiting for the biopsy results. No amount of chamomile tea could possibly soothe that kind of anxiety. So, with good reasoning (or good arguments), I went to the doctor's office and demanded a prescription for a sedative. From there, I went straight to the pharmacy. The pharmacist, who obviously already knows me, was shocked when I took out the prescription from my bag; an actual, authentic prescription, duly stamped and dated. "Do you carry this medicine, please?" I asked, full of confidence and strangely proud, I must confess. He handed me the box of Diazepam and asked if I wanted some water to take it right away. I said yes, of course. My hands were trembling from the anxiety, how could I refuse? I went home from the pharmacy, with my nerves still shaken, but feeling that the medicine was starting to kick in already. In the end, I tested negative for lymphoma. My first reaction: um… okay! I wonder if these results are correct. My second reaction: Thank God! That was a close one. After all the fuss, everything turned out just fine.

Then I asked myself: where's my depression again? I'll call my mom right away so we can plan to meet up and talk. She'll have to explain how come she's dating MY doctor, the meanest one of them all. Oh yes, she will. I'm not going to risk being a victim of bruxism, black magic or whatever it is ever again. No way.

17

No way, not again! No! No! No! Last week was a total disaster already. First, Lauren's dinner party; then meeting Brian and his little girlfriend in the elevator; and finally, the dreadful insomnia that had been tormenting me for several nights. When I would finally fall asleep, it was always past five in the morning and my alarm clock religiously went off at seven-thirty every single day. At work, most days I was yawning in everyone's faces. How pathetic! I even took a nap during my break one day and was awakened by none other than my boss, knocking on my door and walking in as I tried to regain composure. Terrible! And, now that I'm finally home, trying to go to sleep early and get some much-needed rest so I can recharge my old damaged batteries, my noisy neighbor decides to throw another mid-week party. Really? Please, who do these party animals think they are? Don't they work? Or wake up early? I don't think so! Well, he better be ready for this, because tonight I've had it. I'll put an end to this guy party. I need to sleep and tonight, I will!

I got up from bed, where I was snug in my pink flannel pajamas with green hearts, possessed by fury and anger. A mixture of boiling hormones (Yes, I am PMSing.

Why? Is there a problem?), combined with frustration, plus feelings of helplessness, fatigue, stress and every other emotion that could bring out a person's animal instincts. In other words, I was a wild beast about to whack someone with my claws and sharp teeth. I didn't even consider my total lack or arguments to end a party at nine o'clock. By law, it was too early to call the cops. He paid rent just like I did, and could throw as many parties as he wanted, as long as there were no drugs and it was over by eleven. The noise wasn't a strong enough argument, because I could only hear it from my apartment. I didn't notice this until I walked through the door with my soft red slippers, which had a huge Minnie Mouse face on the front, and headed towards his door. In the hallway, my ears were invaded by peaceful silence. Wonderful. I could put my bed right there and would certainly sleep like an angel. But, in my apartment, this had become a difficult mission in the last few weeks.

Ever since Thomas moved into the building, two months ago, his weekly parties were driving me crazy. At least two days a week my apartment was taken over by unbearable electronic music – I don't know how anyone can possibly listen to this without getting a headache. The noise of high heels on the wooden floor next door, the laughter and the smell of marijuana made my existence increasingly painful. I even considered moving out. But, the thought of finding a new apartment near a good hospital and redoing my catalog of pharmacies and doctor's offices in my neighborhood discouraged me.

I rang the doorbell to his apartment, which is opposite mine. Between my door and his was the elevator; our apartments are conjoined. Our wall is as thin as an eggshell. I can even hear a sneeze from the other side.

I noticed that someone was looking through the peephole, but I didn't back down. I clenched my jaw, pulled off an angry look and rang the doorbell again. When the door opened, a tall man, around 40 years old and extremely cheerful, showed up with a glass of wine in his hand.

Everything happened so fast I can't even remember the details. I was thrown into the living room of a high-tech apartment. Plasma monitors all over the walls, colored lights and a huge bar. It looked more like a club. People were happily engaged in conversation all around me and I stood there, in pajamas and slippers, holding the glass of wine that was previously in the tall man's hand. How did this happen? I don't know. I think it went sort of like this:

"Hi, you must be Amanda. Nice to meet you, my name is Thomas. I'm your new neighbor. I love living here... the building is amazing and the neighbors are incredible. I feel so good here..." he was talking nonstop. "You know, the other day I almost rang your doorbell. I've been having excruciating pain these last few years. Some doctors say it's rheumatism, others disagree. I can't stand this pain anymore, it's unbearable. God! Where are my manners? Come in!" He pulled me inside. "Have a glass of wine with us. We can talk about my problem and maybe you can help me. I heard that you know all the best doctors in town and that, if my problem has a cure, you're the right person to help me."

I don't really remember the rest of the conversation. But, now that I've had a chance to breathe and understand what is going on, I realize I'm not the only one in pajamas here. I think other people were bothered by the noise and tried to put an end to this as well. Needless to say, they had all failed.

"So, you were also disarmed by our seductive neighbor?"

The voice that came from behind my left shoulder, almost whispering, was Brian's. He wore gray pajama pants and a white V-neck t-shirt, tight but not too tight, just enough to show off the muscles on his chest and biceps. So hot, and I couldn't help but notice. He wore rubber flip-flops on his feet; his impeccable nails immediately caught my attention. His fresh breath and the strong scent of toothpaste gave away that he hadn't taken a single sip from the glass of whiskey in his hands. It probably ended up there the same way my glass of wine had come to me.

"I think so. How did he do it to you?"

"He started babbling about his last trip to Europe and his gastronomic discoveries. Said we needed to talk, because he had amazing tips for me to spice up the menu at the restaurant. I think the rest you already know... he pulled me into the room and put this glass in my hand. And, I don't even like whiskey."

I couldn't help but laugh, for the first time in days. He smiled and asked, "And with you? What was his manipulation strategy?"

I felt my smile fade and my face harden. I looked away, trying to ignore the question. I was uncomfortable.

For a second, I felt too embarrassed to answer. I was ashamed of myself. How could I allow myself to be manipulated by a stranger like that? Someone who doesn't even know me had just used my reputation of being obsessed with diseases to make me back off from my initial intentions. How? How could I be such a fool? How could I allow this to happen? How could I allow others to toy with my condition? How?

"So, what did he say to change your mind?"

"He asked me for, um… advice. Advice about… about a case he's involved in." – I lied. I lied because the thought of admitting that hypochondriasis was imprisoning me once again was unbearable. I lied because the mere idea of mentioning it without looking like a fool was ludicrous. I didn't want him to think I was crazy or something. Although I know that's exactly what some people think.

"What kind of case? Don't tell me it involves the last building he lived in. I wouldn't be surprised if his former neighbors were suing him." Brian smiled mischievously.

We started talking about the absurdity of the situation and came up with numerous strategies to get away from there, like accomplices, two kids trying to escape their punishment. But every time we got up and walked towards the door, staging a goodbye or going for an Irish exit, there came Thomas with another drink in his hand and his pointless conversations, convincing us to stay. We gave up on the third attempt and decided to stay and enjoy the party, in which every 20 minutes another guest in pajamas showed up.

At around eleven, the get together finally ended and we could all go back to our own apartments and get a good night's sleep. I can't deny that I enjoyed myself. Brian is very charming. I think mom was right, after all. He really does seem like a good guy.

Before going to sleep, I replayed the conversation with Brian numerous times in my mind, hoping to see him again soon. When we said our goodbyes in front of my apartment, he invited me out for dinner again. He really is very persistent. He made it a point of reminding me this was probably the tenth time he had asked me to dinner. But, this time it was different; I said yes.

Finally, the weekend has arrived. I had such a stressful and busy week I didn't even realize until now, the end of the workday on Friday, that Julia hadn't called me in over 48 hours. She's having problems. I know she is. She's been my best friend for years, and I know her very well by now. Julia is a very sweet and laid back girl, but she can't handle real-life dramas very well. Whenever she's all bubbly, she never stops bragging about the reasons for her happiness. But, if she has problems, things change completely. She disappears. She doesn't return any phone calls from her parents or friends and isolates herself until the initial impact has been completely absorbed by a depression or until she falls into a coma due to alcohol poisoning in the small studio where she lives, in Chelsea.

Last time she disappeared like this was when she didn't pass her Master's degree exam and heard it from her most repulsive professor. He apparently felt a special pleasure in announcing she'd have to attend one more semester and then try taking the test again. She was devastated for weeks. Her boyfriend at the time was the one who found her naked, completely drunk, humming an unspeakable tune inside the elevator in her building. He told me she hadn't showered for at least five days and her breath could knock out even an experienced drunk. "An alcoholic! That's what she's become!" he would scream, in total despair. A few months later he'd use that same statement as an excuse to break up with her.

So, now I have more than enough reason to believe she's hibernating with some sort of problem this very moment. The situation demands urgency. I need to go to her place right away.

I left the office, went home for a quick shower, jumped in a cab that was leaving a passenger at the corner, and hurried to her building. I was there in less than 15 minutes, with my finger against the intercom button, pressing it frantically. I knew she was home, but would refuse to answer. And that's exactly what happened. When my finger was about to get numb, she appeared in the lobby, panting. Her eyes were puffy from too much crying, which indicated I was right as to what she'd been doing these last few days. The reason behind it was still unknown, though, and that's exactly what I was there to find out.

"What happened?"

"Nothing" she said, opening the door.

"Nothing? Who spends two days crying over nothing?"

"I don't feel like talking to anyone. What are you doing here?"

"What am I doing here? Is that a question you ask a friend who's trying to save you?" A trailer immediately started playing in my head. In this gruesome movie I see Julia in emotional distress, laying in a pool of disgust and wine. I burst in the door and throw her in the shower lovingly cleaning her as her knight in shining armor.

"Are you trying to save me? My life *isn't* in danger. I don't want to hurt myself! I want to *hurt* him! It is Luca's life you should be protecting."

I knew it! I knew he had something to do with this. Our Lady Patroness of Hypochondriacs and Feeble People (in this case, Julia), please help me! This seems to be more serious than I had initially thought. Julia never talks like that. She's always so positive, yet today she seems possessed. Her eyes are bulging with hatred and she's fuming. And I'm still standing here in the lobby, clueless as to what happened.

"Julia, what happened? Last time we spoke, everything was great. You were about to get engaged to…"

"Ugh!" she hissed, when I said the word *ENGAGED*. "Hush, Amanda, don't say that word ever again! And don't you ever say that guy's name in front of me again.

"But what happened?"

"He wasn't for me…" she said, before breaking out in tears.

"Honey, don't be like this." I hugged her. I was actually a little terrified. I'm not exactly the type of person who knows how to comfort someone, else let alone myself.

Julia was crying uncontrollably, taking small breaks to regain her breath just to start up again. In between these crying spells, she was able to briefly explain to me what had happened. Apparently, she'd been hasty, thinking the ring she'd found was for her. She was plotting antics and dropping hints to find out when Luca would propose. Until, finally, she couldn't take it anymore and asked him flat out. From what she told me, Luca went crazy. He said it was preposterous that she was going through his things, that he had placed his trust in her when he gave her the keys to his apartment and that he felt invaded and betrayed. After lecturing her, he decided to explain where the ring came from. David, his best friend, had bought the ring for his girlfriend, but since they lived together, he asked Luca to keep it for a week until the day he planned to propose to her. Once everything was explained, she couldn't even argue with him. Luca asked for his keys back and said he needed some time. He wasn't sure Julia was the cool girl he thought she was anymore. I must say I can't blame him and, deep down (even though I could never say that to Julia), I think he has reasons to be suspicious of someone who snoops around his apartment to find something that was supposedly hidden.

"Julia, calm down. Taking a break doesn't mean breaking up. At least, I don't think so."

"Don't you see, Amanda? He took the keys back and said he wasn't going to propose to me. That it was all in my need. He doesn't love me. If he really loved me, he'd forgive me and forget about this petty, pointless fight. He led me on. He made me think we were heading towards the altar. And now, he abandons me?"

"Julia, this is not so pointless. Some people value privacy, you know? And, you can't say he led you on. He never mentioned anything about it. You saw the ring and assumed he would propose. As a lawyer, I can tell you one thing: everyone has the right to defend his version of the facts. But, that doesn't mean there are two truths. There is only one truth. This was a big misunderstanding. Don't blame Luca for it. You need to accept it."

As soon as I shut down, she started crying again and asked, as if I were an expert (I wish), how she could fix this.

As if it wasn't hard enough for me to face the fact that I'll be getting older in a few weeks, thousands of unexpected events have fallen on me like a ton of bricks in the last few days. Someone, please, have mercy on me! My skin is flaccid, my hair is thinning and my face is pale. My teeth are getting yellower each day. My bones are losing calcium, my nails are weak, my feet are callous, and my cuticles look like huge mushrooms. I'm so frazzled I can't even deal with simple emotional issues, like my mother having the boyfriend of my dreams. A doctor! My mom has a boyfriend who's a doctor. As for me? I don't even have a boyfriend. This stress is killing me. It's adversely affecting both my mental and physical health. The other day I forgot an important appointment – a sign that my memory is failing me. It's all wrong. Everything is out of whack. And why? What for? Is there anyone who can tell me one positive thing about getting older? And don't give me that wisdom crap, I really don't buy it. If someone had given me the option to exchange wisdom for the perky breasts I had when I was twenty years old, I would have gone for option number two in the blink of an eye. At twenty years old, all the girls are happy, even though they lack wisdom.

I believe my monster-doctor, part of my alter ego is manifesting. Maybe, it's time to lie down on a therapist's couch. A comfortable, soft, warm, and cozy couch. Well, this is truly worrisome. I'm considering going to a therapist. I'm either going nuts or severely depressed.

18

I need to get myself admitted into some sort of medical facility. No, I'm serious. I've never been more serious in my entire life. The world is crumbling all around me and I need to do something to protect myself and not be swallowed by the mushroom of smoke that occurs following an atomic bomb explosion. Do you know this feeling? No? Lucky you, because it's horrible. My feet are skidding in fast movements on the slippery floor. I can't think of a safer place to be until this storm passes than checked into a luxurious clinic, claiming extreme fatigue. That's it. I've made up my mind: I'm going to admit myself into a clinic and my excuse will be that I'm mentally worn out. Now, I just need a good excuse to be incommunicado as well.

I can't handle so many problems any more. Julia and Luca broke up, my mom is dating Dr. White (I don't even like to remember that), I've been having problems at work, my health is increasingly frail and, to make matters worse, I can't even find a man to kiss every now and then. What's going on with me? Does anyone up there have any idea? An explanation, maybe? It could even be that whole karma theory, anything. I asked and looked up at the sky.

As if God had nothing to worry about, other than my inactive sex life.

I was going to bed and imagining myself in a room at the clinic. Everything white, a high bed, clean disinfected sheets. Interesting machines all around me, with flashing lights monitoring everything possible to keep a person alive. The nurses' attention 24 hours a day and the doctors, divided into six-hour shifts, visiting me and asking if I am feeling well. And, the best part, listening to all my complaints. What a dream! Not to mention the medication. Aaaaah, the medication. All those medicines at the reach of a button. I feel a tiny pain, press a button and there comes a nurse, offering me the latest painkillers in the market. I'm going to call my health insurance tomorrow to see if they cover a nervous breakdown.

I began to feel relaxed, like a baby that counts sheep to fall sleep. But an inconvenient neighbor decided to ring my doorbell just as my favorite doctor was starting his shift.

The shrill noise of the doorbell sounded three times. On the first ring I woke up from my dream into the cruel reality of my lonely bed. On the second ring, I jumped to see who the idiot was outside my door at this time of the night. And, by the third ring, I was so mad that I ran to the door and tried to see through the peephole who I'd have to smack if it rang a fourth time. But, I didn't see anyone.

I opened the door slowly, assuming the night attacker could be shorter than average or some other child. But there really was nobody there anymore. At first,

I thought it had probably been a mistake, or that the person had given up. Only after carefully scanning the hallway I noticed a post-it note placed just below my peephole. And there was only a single sentence on it: "Dinner at eight on Sunday. Stay tuned for more details."

I remember thinking: this is a mistake. For sure. I crumbled the post-it note, threw it in the trash can in the kitchen and went back to bed – the one in the clinic.

I know everyone thinks I'm crazy, but considering we're all a little bit crazy and a little bit of a doctor deep inside (that's what my mom says), I feel it's completely sound for me to declare that this morning I woke up with such a severe headache I even considered changing my will again. This time, to add in that Lauren can have my new Prada bag and that Julia shall have my Miu-Miu dress, my Fendi Baguette bag and my GG belt – she never takes it off anyway; it would be a mere formality.

I talked to Julia early in the morning and she seemed to be recovering. Luca has apparently called her and they were going to meet up and talk. She may be able to salvage their relationship, after all.

I decided to take a stroll around the neighborhood. After all, it's Friday and I have absolutely nothing to do, because I don't have a boyfriend and my best friend is depressed. Walking around the city can sometimes be a good option; it certainly beats staying home and watching *Sex and the City* reruns.

I had Taylor Swift's "Love Story" playing on my Spotify and was wearing a tank top with gorgeous embroidery on the back and lose, tailored white pants. I kept watching the people around me, trying to find something in their behavior that would justify my own. All I saw were outlandish people and electronic schizophrenics. It's incredible how technology has turned us into lonely virtual creatures. People walk around like they're zombies, isolating themselves from the world with their headphones. Others are happily talking, apparently to themselves, on their tiny cell phones. Or they're engaged in group chats through their handheld devices. The world really is full of disoriented people. I am certainly not the only one; but, then, how come I feel so alone with my problems?

I walked a few blocks thinking about life and feeling sorry for myself. I hate it when I do that. Sometimes, I hate my life so much I wish I could disappear. Then again, since I'll necessarily take myself wherever I go, I end up coming to the conclusion that it's better to just stay where I am. But something needs to change. I feel an overwhelming urge for changes in my life. I can no longer live with this disease; this is a nightmare. A bad joke that someone upstairs decided to play on me. But it never ends. Never.

After aimlessly walking through the streets of Manhattan, and even crying a little, I stopped by the pharmacy and bought some colorful antacids – my inventory was low – then I went back home.

When I got there, I found another post-it note on my door. This time, it said: "Don't forget, Sunday at eight. Dinner and dancing."

I smiled, not knowing who the note was from, but thinking this was all very fun. Suddenly, I paused and thought – could this be from the party enthusiastic neighbor? Oh, no! The idea of it made me nauseous. I chewed a Tums tablet, picked up a pen and wrote on the post-it note: "No, thank you!" I went towards Thomas' apartment and stuck the post-it note on his door. I then came back to my apartment, took a shower and went to bed thinking: *Can you believe his audacity? First, he makes me attend a party I didn't want to be at. Now, he wants to drag me to a romantic dinner. Is he crazy? I think some people in this building need a therapist more than I do. In fact, if a psychologist lived in this building, he'd be rich. This place is full of crazy people!*

I woke up feeling good on Saturday, which is a miracle after a night of insomnia and crying. I felt energized and ready to run errands, so I went on with my list. After checking off errand by errand with a feeling of accomplishment, I decided to go grab some coffee and then came back home. I was anxious, anticipating the latest films that would come out on Netflix. Everything was going on as planned: an afternoon of housework and errands, movies, and ice cream. I turned off my landline and put my cell phone on silent. Today, all I want is my own company. I don't want to see anyone, talk to anyone, or listen to anyone. Just my own thoughts, my laziness and me.

At around five o'clock, the intercom rang. I thought it was probably the guy from the dry cleaners, bringing back my sweater. I'd asked them to wash and deliver it to my house as soon as possible. But, I'd been told it would only be ready on Monday morning... I thought it was a bit strange, but this wouldn't be the first time they sent back my clothes ahead of schedule. I answered the intercom and asked whomever it was to come up. I waited by the door and, when the elevator door opened, it wasn't the guy from the dry cleaners, it was a guy from the flower shop. With a huge bouquet of flowers in his hand and a small box.

Oh my God! Why can't people just let me live in peace? Somebody else is trying to assassinate me now? I'll make Thomas swallow this, petal by petal.

"Amanda Loeb?"

"You can take these flowers back and tell the person who sent them that next time I'd rather have some arsenic-stuffed chocolate."

He looked at me in dismay, like a small frightened bird.

"The flowers aren't for you, only the box and the post-it note."

"Oh, thank you! Sorry, it's just that I hate... you know, I'm allergic... I'm allergic to flowers. Sorry."

"Okay, just sign here please."

I signed the slip and returned it with a five-dollar bill. Usually, I'd give him a two-dollar tip, but the fear reflected on his face was so great I felt obligated to compensate him for the stress I'd caused.

I went inside and opened up the small, delicately wrapped box. Before looking inside, I decided to read the note: Hi, small cactus! I believe this will be a very interesting evening. Casual attire. You'll receive the last set of instructions tomorrow at 7:45 p.m. Be ready.

I opened the box and inside was the most beautiful cactus I'd ever seen in my life. So beautiful, so delicate and yet so strong and sturdy.

19

It was past seven when my cell phone buzzed. I'd fallen asleep in the bathtub and lost track of time. It was a message from an unknown number: AT 7:45, FOLLOW THE FOOTSTEPS, OPEN THE DOOR AND MAKE YOURSELF AT HOME.

It was him. He sent me the last clue from his cellphone.

"Damn it! I'm late! I don't even know what I'm going to wear."

I hopped out of the bathtub, wrapped a towel around myself and ran to my closet. Panic took over. I hadn't thought of that. What am I going to wear? I don't even know what awaits me. Dinner with several people, or just the two of us? Is this a romantic date, or does he just want to talk some more, like we did at Thomas' place?

"Oh my God!" – it suddenly occurred to me – How about that vicious dog, Ali? That dog can't see me, or he'll want to chew my leg off. I think I'll need a bite-proof outfit this time.

I had only twenty minutes to get ready. How can a girl get ready in twenty minutes? I know. I'll wear what I was wearing on Friday. He didn't see me and will probably never know I wore this outfit for a walk in the park. Everything is fine. It is cool and casual. Everything will be alright. I tried to calm myself down by saying: "Yes, everything will be alright."

No, it won't work! I cried, looking at my feet. The outfit I had planned on wearing called for sandals and my feet, well, my feet were hideous, callous, with chipped nail polish, and my cuticles looked like mushrooms. What am I going to do now? I don't have time to fix this.

I picked up my nail kit and ran to the bathroom. I took off the polish, cut and filed my nails, then tried to trim the cuticles, but soon gave up. I sanded the soles of my feet, put on a moisturizing cream and went back to plan A, which was to wear the blouse with the embroidery on the back, the tailored white pants, and the brown open-toed sandal.

I sloppily blow-dried my hair. It looked nothing like it does when I get it done at the salon, but it wasn't bad. I brushed my teeth, flossed, rinsed with some mouthwash, and applied the final touch, a little dab of perfume. I grabbed a clutch, just to put my keys and credit card inside (I don't know why I'd possibly need a credit card, but I was nervous – cut me some slack, okay?) and two condoms (yeah, I surely had bad intentions – or good ones, it depends on the point of view. I could not ignore the fact that this could be the perfect opportunity to solve my frigidity problem and I did not want to miss it). I took one last look in the mirror and left. I went to the door thinking he might be by his door, looking and waiting for me to leave. Just to make sure he wasn't, I looked through the peephole and saw no one.

I started giggling as soon as I stepped out and saw the footprints – orange paper feet stuck onto the floor, coming from my apartment and leading me to Brian's. He's really creative, I thought. I walked up to his door and paused to read the message. It didn't say anything about ringing the doorbell or knocking on the door. Just *Open, come in and make yourself at home.* So that's what I did.

I opened the door and was stunned. I came upon an incredible living room, decorated with the most minute details like a Bedouin tent. Colorful fabrics and bright pillows, lots of pillows, lit candles, hookahs, vases and other oriental artifacts altogether composed the perfect ambiance, which transported me to a desert night. There were no flowers, but many small vases containing cacti of different colors and species. In the middle of the tent, on a small table, there were several plates with Mediterranean dishes and two wine glasses, which were empty for now. The twilight was slowly giving way to a medium light and along with it came a handsome, tall man. It took me a while to understand what was going on and to articulate a response. At first, I felt like a pray, a little mouse going right towards the trap, where a delicious piece of Swiss cheese sat; one wrong move and it could literally lose its head. Then I thought: *Who is this man? Who spends so much time and effort trying to impress a woman just for one night of sex? Who would do that?* He interrupted the silence and my thoughts with his low, soft voice.

"Hi Amanda. I hope you like Lebanese cuisine."
"I... I... I... I loo-oo-ve it."

He smiled, realizing I was nervous. Meanwhile, I was hoping I'd remembered to bring my Prozac. I bashfully opened up my clutch, so that he wouldn't notice it, and began to one-handedly look for the pill I thought would be in there, but wasn't.

"Take your shoes off and sit here" – he said, pointing to one side of the coffee table, where there were cozy pillows waiting for me.

I quietly sat down. I couldn't feign a mature and coherent reaction, so I opted for a straight face and a coy smile. I was totally overwhelmed and felt pathetic. He was literally in control of the situation. He did it, he caught me and completely disarmed me. Brian opened a bottle of wine and started talking about the benefits of a Middle Eastern diet, about why he had picked those wines and about the weather, the full moon and I don't know what else. It took me a second glass of wine to start to loosen up and join in the game.

"The food is wonderful. Did you make it?"

He laughed at my question, making his lack of skills in the kitchen obvious.

"No, it's from my restaurant. I have invited you so many times to go and try it, but you never went… so I decided to bring it to you."

"And the decoration?"

He chuckled, as if to say: Oh! I always do this when I have a new victim.

"It's from one of the party rooms at the restaurant. Do you like it?"

"It's beautiful. I feel like I'm in one of the *Scheherazade and the 1001 Nights* stories. You went through a lot of trouble. All of this for me?"

"Don't you think you're worth this and so much more?"

"I don't know. Do you?"

He smiled and offered me more wine. I didn't know if that was a yes, a no or a maybe. But at that moment, I promised myself I'd show him I am worth that and so much more.

"Where's Ali?" I asked, realizing I hadn't seen the beast around.

"Don't worry, he's with the pet sitter tonight. He's not home."

He could tell I was relieved and added: "I know you had a bad impression of him. But, believe me, he's a good boy. I'm sorry he bit you that day, but I have to say, if he hadn't, we might not be here right now."

Huh? What was that supposed to mean? Seriously, his dog had to bite me so we could have a date? Wouldn't it have been easier for us to have simply bumped into each other in the elevator? Like, both of us trying to press the fourth-floor button at the same time? You know how it is, glancing at each other and stuff. I had to go to the hospital? I totally disagree.

"That's in the past. Let's try to forget about it, okay? Why did you name your dog Ali? Was it in honor of Muhammad Ali?"

"In fact, it was. I'm a boxing fanatic and Ali was the greatest of all time, in my opinion."

"Makes sense. If I had a beautiful, charming and sensual Persian cat, I'd certainly name her Madonna."

We toasted and continued talking. He would ask questions about me with a curious childish look on his face and I'd go on with my stories.

"Tell me more about you, Amanda. I know you're a lawyer, have a thing for medications, you hate flowers and dogs and your mother is very nice. What else?"

I spent at least an hour talking about myself, in a never-ending monologue. He didn't seem bored at all. On the contrary, he'd sometimes pitch in, craving to know more and more. Every time I paused, trying not to bore him with my soliloquy, he'd react by asking for one more story. Since I have unlimited stories about hospitals, diseases, and drugs, he had a wonderful time. Laughter, wine and more wine.

I was always a lightweight when it came to alcoholic beverages. I could say this is one of my weaknesses. I gave myself entirely, body and soul, to that wine, without any concern. After all, I was only a few steps away from my house. What could happen to me? Have a night of wild sex with a hot guy? I don't think that would be so bad. Actually, I believe if someone was at risk here, considering my current situation, that someone was not me.

When I was just about to pass out, and having noticed that Brian was one of those good guys who wouldn't have sex with a drunken woman, I told him it was time for me to go. I tried to get up on my own, but I couldn't. My legs didn't follow my commands. So, he lifted me up and gently held me in his arms. He picked up my clutch, carried me to my apartment, and asked me where my keys were. Since he got no reaction from me, he probably (from this moment on I blacked out, so these are just assumptions) opened up my clutch, took the key, opened the door and put me in bed.

I woke up the next morning with the alarm ringing at the exact time I always wake up to go to work. I was still fully dressed and had my makeup on. My clutch was on the sideboard by the door, open in such a way that you could see the credit card and the two condoms inside.

"Oh, no! How embarrassing." – My face began to burn. But, I was so late I decided to cure my hangover and my shame (or lack thereof) on the way to work. – I need a shower, some medicine for my liver and an aspirin!

20

I wasn't hit by a car on the street (thank God!), I didn't fall down the stairs, I didn't jump into the elevator shaft (what a stupid thought), I didn't trip and fall on the street, no crazy delivery boy ran me over with a bike, nothing. Nothing happened to me. At least I don't recall anything that could justify this pain. The fact of the matter is I woke up super happy and bouncing off the walls with excitement. And, that was exactly the problem. As I was jumping for joy, I felt the little toe on my left foot throb in pain as soon as it touched the ground. I swear the pain was so intense I felt the throbbing deep in my soul. It started as a small sting, then it turned into a marching band of drums spreading throughout my foot. And, I believe my toenail, I mean, the tiny piece of cartilage that coats the tip of my pinky (can't even call that a toenail, can you?), is about to fall off. I have no idea how this happened.

I'm trying to retrace all my steps, literally speaking, since the time I met Brian last night, when I was in perfect physical condition, until the moment I woke up in my bed this morning, with this wretched pain in my foot.

In case you didn't notice, I said I woke up IN MY BED this morning, with severe pain in my pinky toe. Making a huge effort to remember all the details from last night, I started to piece together what I could recall. I worked my memory like a puzzle and I was then able to fill in the parts that were hazy due to the enormous amounts of alcohol that was still in my bloodstream. In a nutshell, I'm still slightly drunk, my toenail is black and blue and falling off and my pinky toe is shattered into pieces. On the other hand, my frigidity problem, I can assure you, is a thing of the past.

I met up with Brian at Nobu for dinner. Edamame, sushi with sake, sake with sashimi, tempura with sake, sake with sake and so on – and sake forth – my memory was gradually turning vague. After the fourth shot of sake, it would be frivolous of me to affirm the following account is accurate, but I promise I'll at least try to maintain some sense of reality and a (sore) foot on the ground.

As far as I can remember, Brian and I got into a cab on Hudson Street after dinner and headed home. On the way here, Brian asked the cabdriver to stop by a deli so he could grab some M&Ms and a bottle of water. I know M&Ms don't go with a night of sex and lust, but we were both craving something sweet. It was a late summer evening and the weather was beautiful, warm enough for me to wear a satin dress, but not so hot as to leave the dress wet and pasted onto my body with sweat.

In front of our building, while Brian paid the cab driver, I noticed two beautiful transvestites. Both were tall and wore blonde wigs, miniskirts, sequin tops and stiletto heels. They talked excitedly to each other, across the street from us.

"Hot guy!" – one of them yelled as soon as the cab drove away. "You're a lucky girl!" – the other one screamed. "Take advantage of that delightful body, honey!" – this comment threw me off. "Enjoy your night, kids!" – shouted the second one.

Brian laughed a charming laugh. "Thank you, ladies, I'm sure that's exactly what we're going to do!" – and he gave me a naughty look. I felt my face burn. In a moment of spontaneity, I squealed euphorically and said bye to the transvestites, making my intentions very clear to Brian. *Yeah, I'm looking forward to an incredible night with you too.*

We opened the door to the building and things started to get steamy right away. Brian didn't even care that the doorman was there, napping. When the elevator arrived, we were glued to one another as if we were holding on to a sinking ship. Instead of feeling nervous and panicking, my body was taken over by a strong urge to have sex with him. In the hallway, the first dilemma. "Your apartment or mine?" – He asked. Without taking my lips off his, I answered: "Yours; it's closer." *It's closer? How desperate, he must've thought. But if he did, he pretended he didn't and just kept at it.*

He fumbled through his jacket pocket looking for his keys, opened the door and a second later we were on the couch. Then, some other concerns (my concerns) went quickly through my head. *I wonder if my waxing is decent. Am I wearing the hottest lingerie I own? Will he notice I didn't get a pedicure this week? Do I smell good? Bad breath? After all the sake and raw fish…*

He panted while slowly taking my clothes off, as if unwrapping a much-desired gift. He looked at my body and made me promise I wouldn't be uncomfortable with anything that could possibly happen. I promised.

Biting my neck, licking it in soft, up and down motions, his hand slowly caressing my inner thighs… this was only part of his repertoire to provoke me! Everything was done at the right time, the right way. If he wanted to drive me crazy with all the foreplay, I have to say, it worked. I was about to shout out for him to go straight to the main course, but I held back and allowed him to serve me the entire feast as he desired – and it was totally worth the wait. After some unusual maneuvers, it finally happened.

I will not share intimate details with anyone. All I have to say is Brian is a little perverted (love it!), but some things are best left to the imagination. For those with prude minds, perverted may mean he likes to lick my toes. For those with dirty and disturbing minds, well… the sky is the limit.

I exploded in orgasm while staring into his eyes, in a magical symphony of the senses. Perfectly aligned with my pleasure, connected to my soul, he came too. We cuddled all night. And no insomnia. To be honest, I slept like a baby. There was no second round. Brian did not strive to display an athletic performance, just a top-notch one.

He woke up early the next morning and went to work. He left a cute note by the bed, kissed me on the forehead and left. Saturday is his busiest day at the restaurant. While Brian worked, I would spend my day getting x-rays of whatever was left of my toe. Actually, I just remembered, in one of Brian's maneuvers last night I felt my foot crack. That's it!

When I got to the ER at Manhattan Hospital, my little toe looked like a huge thumb. Swollen and painful. I went into the reception room hopping on one foot. I filled out the form with all my personal data and insurance information and sat down to wait.

In the triage, a super-skinny nurse bombarded me with questions before sending me to get x-rays.

"Are you on birth control? Do you have an IUD? Any type of contraceptive?"

"No, nothing." – But this reminds me that I need to see my gynecologist to decide which would be the best contraceptive for me, since my sex life is finally active again.

"When was your last period?"

I wonder if nobody has informed this woman I came here simply for an x-ray of my toe. I know I need to control my paranoia, but I'm starting to think this woman suspects I had a night of orgies and wild sex. Only after telling her all about my sexual history, which she heard in disbelief, but intently, including details about my frigidity and how Brian was so considerate and managed to cure me in a single night, that's when I began to suspect she simply wanted to know if I was pregnant.

After the triage, I went straight to the x-ray room, which was surprisingly empty. The technician handed me a heavy vest and helped me get it on correctly, then positioned my foot in the machine, left and shut the door behind him. Like a giant Polaroid, the machine began to photograph my foot in different positions. It took no more than five minutes and I was then led to the waiting room.

I limped all the way to a tiny room with only a few chairs at the end of a large hall and was soon informed that the orthopedist had gone out for coffee and would take about 30 minutes. Only then I realized I hadn't had breakfast either. Skipping and limping, I went to the cafeteria and ordered a ham and cheese sandwich and a cappuccino. On TV was a rerun of the Dr. Oz show about food that can prevent illnesses. Needless to say, 30 minutes went by and I didn't even realize I'd waited that long. I finished eating and went back to the small room down the hall.

It didn't take long for the doctor to call me, with my charts in his hands.

"Amanda Loeb." And there I went, happily skipping, still thanks to Brian. After all, what's a broken toe compared to the end of my frigidity issue?

"So, doctor, is my toe broken into a million pieces?"

"No, actually I need to take a look at it because the x-ray doesn't show anything wrong with your toe."

What do you mean it doesn't show anything wrong with it? I feel excruciating pain, I can barely put my foot down on the floor, and the x-ray doesn't show anything? That machine must be broken. I want another x-ray.

"Doctor, I would like to re-do the exam. The machine must be broken."

"This isn't a Biology test. The machine is working perfectly fine and we don't need to re-do anything. Just let me look at your toe, okay?"

"Okay." – What else could I say? These doctors are so bossy... so conceited. The doctor moved my toe from one side to the other. At each crack I would scream in pain. Don't assume that he minded, though; he couldn't care less and continued to torture me. The more I moaned and screamed, the more he messed with it. *Thank you very much for making me feel worse, you soulless person!* – I thought. He would say, "Does it hurt here? What about now? Is it still hurting?" – I would answer: "No, not at all! The pain is just as bad as pulling out a tooth without anesthesia, but that's okay, I'll make it." And I'd convince myself I was strong enough to survive that.

"Listen, Amanda" – he sighed - "you shouldn't be feeling as much pain as you're describing, because the x-ray shows nothing wrong with your toe. Are you sure you're in that much pain?" – he looked at me with a look I knew all too well. The one that says: *you're nuts, addicted to codeine and you're here in my office trying to make a fool out of me just to get a prescription.* I can't stand that look. I lost my temper and almost told him to go to hell. But I really needed to uncover the mystery surrounding my tiny and beloved toe.

"With all due respect, doctor, I woke up with intolerable pain in my pinky toe, which, as you can see, is twice the size of the pinky toe on my right foot. So, I must say I am, yes, a hypochondriac, but my pain is real. The x-ray machine is not working properly and I need something for the pain, right now!

I don't know if my enraged outburst convinced him or not. But, I walked out of there with a prescription for a mild pain reliever, a bandaged foot and a text from Brian: *Your scent is with me, I'll call you at night. Have a nice day, little cactus.*

21

As I lazily opened my eyes this morning, I realized my appointment with Dr. Herman Dean was scheduled for today. Two long weeks of waiting had gone by since my initial consultation with him. I think it goes without saying that I had been consumed by anxiety these past two weeks. I've had nothing short of an aneurysm and a perforation in my intestines (I swear my stools were going somewhere else instead of being expelled from my body), in addition to a suspected pancreatitis and confirmed (by me) appendicitis. Don't ask me why, but I've been obsessed with my digestive system lately. The funny thing is none of these diseases were ever on my top list of concerns. On the official list are: brain cancer, breast cancer, lung cancer (I know I don't smoke, but so what?), aneurysm, cirrhosis, hepatitis, meningitis and vitiligo (the disease Michael Jackson swore he had; well, I'm terrified of that too).

But it was my suspected appendicitis that made Brian wake up at 4:30 in the morning and take me to the emergency room at Cornell. He simply couldn't understand when, two days ago, I woke up with a terrible pain in my abdomen and the right side of my womb. I couldn't even touch it; the pain was unbearable. I ran to the bathroom and felt burning while urinating. Then, I realized the previous week I'd had several warning signs that my intestines were punctured. That was it; I woke Brian up right away, totally freaked out.

"Wake up! I need help. You need to take me to the hospital. It's an emergency."

"What happened? What are you feeling?"

"I have an infection in my appendix and I need emergency surgery."

He laughed. A loud and contagious laugh. Unbelievable, given the urgency of the situation and the fact he had just been awakened in the middle of the night – I would have been in a terrible mood.

"You need what?" – he asked, smiling.

"I need to go to the hospital right away. I need a urinalysis, an x-ray of my abdomen, and if my diagnosis is confirmed, which I'm sure it will be, I'll need to go through an emergency surgery." I said as I organized some personal belongings, pajamas and flip-flops, in a small suitcase – things I'd need while I was hospitalized.

Brian watched in disbelief, but didn't contradict. He called a car service company and asked them to have a driver wait in front of the building for us. Ten minutes later, I was filling out the forms in the emergency room.

In the triage, I explained all my symptoms. I mentioned my previous suspicions and last week's perforation of my intestines. I explained I had not seen a doctor then because I thought I needed additional evidence. I said this as if I were justifying myself, apologizing to the nurse for not going to them sooner.

When a real doctor finally saw me, he did the obvious: touched my stomach around my belly button. While I moaned in pain, he continued the preliminary tests so he could then request an x-ray, which is essential to this type on diagnosis.

"Amanda, you have no signs of appendicitis." He said calmly, while still touching my abdomen and staring at a fixed spot on the wall, clearly focused.

"NO? What do you mean? You have barely started examining me. That was so fast, how could you be so sure? Aren't you going to request an x-ray or a urinalysis to be sure?" – I panicked at the thought of becoming the victim of a medical error.

"Amanda, your ovaries are swollen and so is your abdomen. When was your last period? Are you on birth control?"

Oh, no! He must be kidding me. As if I, an almost 30-year-old woman who's been getting her period since age 12, could possibly not know when I am PMS-ing. This is ridiculous!

"You mean to tell me this pain is nothing but PMS? Or that the pill, which yes, I 'm taking, is causing all this pain?"

"I'm saying your ovaries are swollen and this could mean one of two things. Your period is either very close, or you need to go to your gynecologist and ask to switch to a different birth control."

Totally crushed and with Brian watching me, I had to confess.

"Yeah, I switched brands about 20 days ago. My doctor recommended this one because the previous brand was making me very irritable."

"So, the appendicitis case is solved. Now you can go back home and try to sleep. I'll just prescribe something for the discomfort, but I think you should call your doctor and make an appointment ASAP. Okay?"

Do I really have to answer this? The man is a tyrant and so very rude. But, at least he solved the mystery of my appendix and assured me that, for now, I'll be able to keep it intact.

The day of my appointment had arrived. I was still at the office, trying to go through some cases, but the fact is I couldn't take my eyes off the clock on the wall. Not the hand that tells hours, but the one that counts seconds – that was the one I was focused on.

I was too anxious to work. God knows how long I've been avoiding this appointment. I didn't want this person in my life. This was the one medical specialty I did not want in my schedule. I didn't think I needed someone to tell me what to do. Point out my problems and criticize my condition. What for? I was happy. I had a life, a solid career, a boss who loved me, friends (not too many, but enough), a family, a social life (not so much) and an amazing, caring and dedicated boyfriend. *What more could I possibly want?* – I asked myself. However, despite my daydreaming and reluctance, I knew the answer. I needed to be normal, to act like a normal person. Someone who didn't wake her boyfriend up every morning suspecting a new disease. Better yet, someone who didn't panic every time her temperature was one degree above or below the expected range. Someone who can use public transportation without having heart palpitations, or who doesn't check her own pulse 34 times a day. Thirty-four is my lucky number. I was tired of all of that, too.

I got to his office on time. Standing by the door, I felt my body stiffen. My arm couldn't bring itself to press the buzzer for suite 8C, where I was supposed to meet Dr. Herman Dean. I was breathing heavily and erratically. I realized if I didn't calm down, I'd have a heart attack right there – which wouldn't be all that bad, because then I'd have an excuse not to walk through that door.

After a few breathing exercises and a piece of candy to elevate my blood sugar level, I managed to press the button. A stern voice answered and, without many questions, told me to go up. The door then automatically opened and I went in.

The lobby was huge; nothing too impressive or expensive, just huge. There was abstract art on the wall and a couch in front of the two elevators. Since I wasn't apt to make any choices, I pressed both call buttons. The first one to come was the one on the right. A happy, blissful couple came out of it. I couldn't help but feel envy and commiseration. Even though I was with Brian and things were going well, my not-so-optimistic and compulsive thoughts led me to believe our relationship wouldn't go very far.

I felt worse with each floor the elevator reached. My hands were sweaty, my legs were shaking and my stomach felt empty, although I had eaten just two hours before. By the eighth floor, I felt so bad I turned around and tried to hold the elevator door with my hands, in case I decided to get away from there. I stayed in this exact position for an impressive 30 seconds. When I was almost about to give up and leave, one foot back in the elevator already, I heard the office door opening and someone calling my name.

There's no turning back now, I thought. I have to face my fears and my doom. The only thing that comforted me was the idea that, in an unusual way, I was in charge of the situation. *In charge? Yes, you're in charge, Amanda. Think about it, you're here because you were forced to come. But you know you need it, so accept it. He's now your analyst; you're paying him so you can do it your way* (I erroneously thought!). *The secrets are yours. If you want to open the doors to your dirty little world for him to enter, you can, if not, don't do it! You ask the questions. Show him who's boss. Take control. Do with him as you do to all your other doctors. Show off your confidence, your knowledge; tell him you're not interested in trite advice. That's it. You're in charge.*

It worked. Full of confidence, I took a deep breath and walked towards the open door, where I saw a really tall man, at least six feet tall, I suppose. He was about sixty years old, hair almost completely gray, face riddled with deep wrinkles, signs that a person has suffered a lot or doesn't have the slightest idea what anti-aging lotion is. In his case, maybe both. His smile was friendly and his expression made him seem trustworthy, which probably came from his professional experience. It didn't seem spontaneous, but it didn't bother me.

"Amanda?"

"Yes. Dr. Dean?"

"Yes. But you can call me Dr. Herman."

I walked through the office door, still fearful, like a child entering the principal's office at school for the first time. I scanned the room for a few seconds. There were huge bookcases all around, like a mini library, with many books on various topics. In the center of the room there were two sofas. One was a big, comfortable black-leather sofa, rugged but still charming. The other one was smaller, an armchair basically, also in black leather and the same style; they matched perfectly. He directed me to the large sofa, waited for me to sit down, and sat in the armchair across from me. Next to me was a small table with an empty glass and a small bottle of spring water. There was also a huge box of Kleenex. I wondered why that was there, but my question was answered soon enough.

We were both sitting, waiting for the other to take some kind of initiative and start talking. But nothing happened. Neither of us seemed willing to break the silence and the ice.

Is this his technique? To make me feel uncomfortable for two hours, take my money and call it a day? Is this therapy?

I kept staring at the walls and the ceiling, while my fingers held on tight to the arm of the sofa. I analyzed every inch of that room, evidently trying to ignore his presence. On the other hand, he stared at me, with his hand on his chin, as if he was already analyzing me, and he would clear his throat every now and then, as if to remind me he was still in the room.

"So… what is your line of work? I mean… are you Freudian? Or do you follow some other theory? I don't know… Melanie Klein? Lacan? Reich, maybe?"

"Freud. But I don't follow it to a T."

"Oh, okay. Got it."

After five more minutes observing me, tired of my silence, he decided to start from somewhere.

"Amanda, is there anything you might like to tell me?" – with his hand still on his chin.

"Something? I don't know, like something wrong I've done? Like horrible things, sinful or obsessive thoughts, or things that people usually confess to the priest before mass?" – I said, still not paying attention to him. I kept pretending to be interested in the books on the bookshelf.

"No, nothing like that. Your day-to-day things that bother you. People whom you don't like but need to coexist with… something you saw or heard in recent times that left you insecure, anxious, stressed or nervous… perhaps?" – when he pronounced the word PERHAPS, he raised his voice a little, clearly asking for my attention.

Terrible idea. I forced myself to look him in the eyes, and I didn't like what I saw. My eyes quickly scanned his face, but they were fixated on a specific detail. His ears. He had humongous ears, with large tufts of hair sticking out of them. HUGE TUFTS! I thought I'd have a panic attack and want to run away, never to come back again. Quite the opposite, the tufts ended up having a positive effect. While staring at them, I answered all of Dr. Herman's questions and, after a while, the conversation flowed so naturally I can't even recall what exactly I had told him. I went into a temporary trance, as if the tufts had hypnotized me and I couldn't look away. A mixture of horror and humor took over my thoughts. While speaking about my life, I thought: *Why doesn't he trim those tufts? I need to find out when his birthday is so I can give it him as a gift.*

Exactly 50 minutes went by, the length of a session, when I woke up from the trance and realized I'd used up almost all the tissues from the tissue box. On my way out, while heading to the elevator, I passed by a mirror and couldn't help but notice my eyes were puffy from crying so much. From the looks of my makeup, red eyes and nose, I had probably cried a lot.

Feeling a lightness in my soul, I went outside with a smile on my face. I was in a state of relaxation I'd never experienced before. And, all I could remember from the whole session was Dr. Herman's tufts of hair. I wonder if this is a new form of therapy? I called Sarah at the office and asked her to clear up my schedule every week during this time. I didn't specify why; I just told her that every Wednesday at this time I would be unavailable.

22

The second session was even easier than the first, and by the fifth one Dr. Herman was actually amused by my many diseases, stories and attacks, and by the way I dramatize everything, making it all sound so funny.

"This is your armor, Amanda, you know that." – he said. Of course, I knew it; it didn't take a genius to see that. It was so obvious… making fun of my own misfortune instead of feeling self-pity made my life a little more bearable. I'm a hypochondriac, but at least I still have a sense of humor. The day I told him about how I met Brian, I could see that, behind that serious and reliable façade, there was a curious child, who was enthralled by the story.

As our intimacy grew, along with my trust in him, I slowly started to knock down the wall I'd put up, until one day all of my fears and truths were exposed. I told him how pathetic I felt for thinking I'd die every ten minutes. But, that I had no control over it, or over the fact that I supposedly had an aneurysm and two heart attacks per week, a suspected cancer and a dozen colds each month. Welcome to my world, Dr. Herman.

"How are you feeling this week, Amanda?"

"I had another stroke last week. I was leaving the office after an exceptionally stressful day. I was supposed to attend a cocktail party after work, a happy hour with environmentalists, lawyers and my office mates, but I couldn't."

"Why not?"

"I was walking home, planning to take a bath and change into comfortable clothes, then go to the cocktail party, when I felt a sharp twinge in the back of my head. I stopped to catch my breath and tried to think positively. I swear I tried, just as you always tell me to. I tried to control myself and not imagine the worst. But, it was too late. I felt the left side of my face turn numb, and then all the other symptoms. Pain in my arm, blurred vision, nausea, dizziness, tachycardia and finally panic."

"What did you do?"

"Usually, I'd have asked my mom to get in a cab and come help me, because I was dying. But this time it was different; I was aware it was just a panic attack. So, I spared my mom. I called Brian and he answered on the first ring. I must confess that simply knowing he was available to me whenever I needed him made me feel slightly better right away. I then explained what was going on and how I was feeling," – I took a quick break as my eyes filled up with tears.

"And then what happened?"

"He calmed me down. No medications, no running to the nearest hospital. Nothing. He just talked to me, asked me not to get aggravated because of the happy hour, and said I didn't need to go if I didn't want to. In the end, he even joked and said everything would be okay. He always says that. Every time I need to get a hold of myself, he says: *everything will be okay.*"

"And it is."

"It's as if someone whispered magic words into my ears. But, that also ends up being a problem."

"Why do you think that?"

"Because I'm sick. Hypochondriasis is a serious disorder. I'm addicted to this. Whenever I'm in trouble, or when I feel anxious and cornered, I need an excuse to get away from it all. Then, I get sick. That's terrible. I don't want to find another addiction to replace this, you know what I mean?"

"Explain it to me further, please."

"I think I'm replacing hypochondriasis with dependency. I'm becoming dependent on Brian to make me feel better, which, in my opinion, is also bad and it scares me a lot. Because one day he might not be around when I need him. Or he might break up with me, or disappear without a trace, or die like my father did and…"

"I think we've reached an interesting point. You've never told me anything about your father."

"It's because I don't like talking about it. That's it."

"We can talk about this now or later, but one day you'll have to talk about it. How about you tell me things from your childhood that involve your father?"

"You know, today I woke up with the worst sore throat. My voice was almost gone and I called my mom to ask her if I could possibly have contracted the swine flu. As always, she said "Amanda, stop it right now." I hung up and went online to get help. I got into my favorite medical site to search by symptoms and within five minutes I had concluded it wasn't the flu, because my voice was getting raspy way too fast. Then, I suspected my tonsils were inflamed and that I'd be missing them for sure this time. They'd be removed and my body, already so frail, would be missing yet another piece. I won't allow this to happen. I won't let any doctor remove my tonsils. No one can convince me they aren't necessary. If we didn't need them, why would we be born with them?" – as you can see, I've completely changed the subject.

Did he really think it would be that easy to make me reveal my most intimate agonies? No way! I know he's an excellent therapist and that's his job. But I can't ignore the fact that he's a doctor, so he may very well be part of that doctors' conspiracy that spreads from New York to Connecticut (yes, it has already crossed the state barrier), to drive me crazy.

Ever since I was a kid, I've always been obsessive. When I was five, I swore I'd be kidnapped. While my friends were worried about being adopted (I never had any doubts about that, absolute certainty reigned in my soul), I thought I'd get out of the house one day, go to school and never come back. I convinced myself the attacker was my dentist. I was so adamant about it that my mom even confronted him once.

But, I realized I was different (meaning: obsessive, compulsive and hypochondriac) around the age of ten, when my father was diagnosed with brain cancer. This was not the first time I'd been faced with a terminal illness. Before this, there was my grandfather's illness, which originated my initial attacks. Childish stuff, just for the attention, my mom used to say. It was only after my father's first surgery for removal of the tumor that I really acknowledged the problem.

At the age of ten, I didn't cry. I was determined to fix the problem. I spent countless hours at the hospital, talking to nurses and doctors, always interested in every detail. I'd go to the school library and research the disease in depth so that I could drill the doctors with questions and save my dad's life. I was tireless. I became familiar not only with the diagnosis, symptoms, and lab results, but also with new treatment options and medications. I clung to each possibility, anything that could give me some hope that I'd bring my dad home, cured. But, when things didn't go well and his health started to deteriorate, I'd begin to feel dizzy and have severe headaches. For a long time, this was my way out; making up my own illness helped me forget about my dad's. My mom, as usual, split her time between taking care of me and my father, neglecting Lauren. I still ask myself today how come she doesn't have any traumas. It must have been difficult for her too. There's another thing that consumes me: guilt.

After he was defeated by the disease and passed away, I was convinced that a terminal disease could strike anyone, regardless of age or financial situation. I embraced this idea and started to display another strange behavior. I started to manipulate the facts to get special treatment. I loved seeing my teachers' and my classmates' mothers' eyes fill with tears as I told them how hard it had been for my family and I to cope with my dad's illness and his tragic end. Suddenly, magically, I began to be excused from tasks and assignments in school and in the community. My life became easier and I'd use my fragile health and my family history to get out of any task I did not wish to do. That's right. I'm a manipulator. I don't think I'm a bad person because of this. I didn't do it on purpose. I wasn't an evil little girl using my own dad's illness and other people's weaknesses for my own benefit. At least not in a conscious way. I was also suffering. I couldn't concentrate on the things I had to do. It was the most painful moment of my life and I had no emotional support. I wasn't able to digest the impact of the news, the treatment and the loss. I wasn't able to accept my dad's death and move on.

I know when I put it like this, it sounds like I had a disturbed and dysfunctional childhood. However, don't forget I have specialized in the art of manipulating, playing with people's emotions and making myself the victim. I'm sick, don't forget that.

Even though the doctors would state I was in perfect health, my attacks became commonplace. I could name over a hundred diseases I managed to contract before turning 20 years old. I don't know. I honestly don't have answers to questions like: why do I refuse to believe I'm perfectly healthy? Manipulation tactic? Today, I no longer believe that; I am a responsible adult and I don't run away from my duties. I have no reason to use this as a tool to make life easier. Because, believe me, it doesn't work anymore. Escaping? Maybe. Escaping the boredom and problems of my adult life is a possible answer. Or maybe I'm bringing attention to a fundamental fact: I am not happy.

I am tired, tired of living this way. But, I have hopes that I'll be able to achieve not the cure, but some sort of control over my illness. Next week, I'll start attending the Hypochondriacs Anonymous meetings. Dr. Herman found out about this group and suggested I go, as a supporting treatment, and I agreed. Will it work? I don't know. We'll see.

23

Manhattan is chaotic. Traffic, as usual, is unbearable. A huge lineup of cabs took over Fifth Avenue, forming a huge yellow river. People are wild and Halloween night will likely shake the city's foundations, as it does every year. The weather so far has been good; we are in the middle of a cold, New York autumn, but we've had two warm nights that reminded me of mid-summer weather. I even had to sleep with the windows open.

Of course, with my luck, I forgot to close the screen panel and a swarm of mosquitoes savored my sensual body, slender and provocative (for the insects!). I was all itchy, covered with red bumps. I've used up tubes of antihistamine cream, but it didn't help one bit. I went to work with a short-sleeve shirt and a knee-high skirt. Despite the mosquito bites, it looked good. I took a light jacket with me just in case, but I didn't need to use it at all. That guy from TV with the blonde and shiny hair, I'm a big fan, the one who tells us every night what the weather will be like the next day, promised that today, October 31st, would be wonderful. According to him, the temperature will go up and we might get a few drops of rain, but that's it. Then, it should be all good. We'll see.

Halloween is the only popular celebration I actually love. The fact that you need to go out in the middle of a crowd or spend the night in packed bars and clubs doesn't bother me at all. I think it's because this is the one day I can exorcise my hypochondriasis and even wear a war mask and no one will notice.

I remember when I was a child I'd wear my princess costumes (always! Now, can you blame me for still dreaming of Prince Charming?) with wigs of various sizes, and go through the neighborhood trick-or-treating, filling up my pumpkin-shaped bucket with sweets, candies and chocolates. The only thing that could ruin my fun would be to eat something rotten and end up in the emergency room, throwing up colorful, sugary snot. But, thank goodness, it's never happened – even though each year I swore it would.

Since Halloween isn't a real holiday (as it should be), I worked the whole day. This week at the office has been the busiest in over six months. Many cases were being expedited so they can be tried before Thanksgiving and Christmas, so I couldn't leave the office before nine any day this week. As a result, I haven't had time to buy my costume, yet. But, I have a plan: I'm going to leave work at around five today and run to Ricky's. There'll probably be lots of people at the door, already waiting to get in. Lauren told me she waited more than 40 minutes to get to the door yesterday. And, all of this hassle just to buy a fancy ladybug costume for Sophia to wear to her school party. Seriously, 40 minutes! Oh God, please give me some patience, because I have none. Well, if He didn't give me the virtue of patience, no problem, I'll go to the nearest pharmacy and buy an anxiolytic. At moments like these, anything will do: Lexotan, Nervium, Valium, Clonazepam or Diazepam. The important thing is to balance my mental sanity with the stress this long line will definitely cause me.

That's just what I did. Finally, at 4:50 p.m., I dismissed Sarah, wrote my last e-mail of the week and went running to Ricky's. Just as Lauren had said, the line was there waiting for me, full of freaks. There were teenagers and young adults, all desperate for a sexy costume and a blonde Lady Gaga wig, many gay men, children, women, and me, all on a single file line that seemed endless. However, to my surprise, the wait was only 25 minutes. I was lucky.

As soon as I walked into the store, I realized one thing: most of the people there, just like me, had no idea what they wanted to buy. Everyone was walking around aimlessly, disoriented by shelves overflowing with costumes, their eyes carefully scanning the shelves so they didn't miss what could be the ideal look, the right costume. As for me? I did the same. I went through all the shelves on the first floor three times. Amongst superheroes, monsters, ultra-sexy or scary witches (there was no in-between), hideous silicone masks and a huge array of sexy mini dresses, from pirates and vampires to Tinker Bell and Barbie, I couldn't find anything suitable. So, I took the clerk's advice and decided to check out the basement. As I walked down the stairs, I found a feather boa hanging on the corner of a wall that interested me. I didn't know exactly what I wanted to wear, but I knew I wanted something cheerful, fun and not too revealing this year. After all, my frigidity issue had been put to rest and, since I have a boyfriend, I'm okay with that.

Last year, I dressed up as a nurse. Obviously, this had nothing to do with my traumas and health problems. Of course not! By the end of the evening, I was tired of hearing all the corny pick-up lines: "don't you want to come over to my house to take care of me?" or "I need mouth-to-mouth." Ugh! My holy-spirit-of-Halloween-night, please help me! And more – I now remember quite clearly – I almost ended up in the hospital for eating a spicy candy. And, I still have no idea how it got into my mouth in the first place. You know how it is… after the third shot of tequila and a few cocktails, I begin to suffer from alcohol-induced amnesia. That candy gave me indigestion, and I spent the whole weekend like a queen, sitting on the throne! Actually, that's not accurate. The truth is I went from my bed to the toilet, from the toilet to my bed, in a never-ending ritual, until that poison was completely eliminated from my body. There was no medicine that could make me feel better.

I picked up the feather boa and continued down the stairs. In a small room right before the costumes area there were a few pairs of huge, rounded toecap shoes. I loved them! I bent down to pick up a pair. They were huge, blue with pink flowers, very cheerful. When I got up, I could see that, right above the shoes, there were a few accessories that could turn me into a colorful clown. As soon as I laid my eyes on a red hat that came with a built-in green wig, a huge sunflower and blinking lights, I knew I'd found what I was looking for.

In addition to the feather boa, I bought the hat, the pair of shoes, a huge yellow tie with polka dots, a pair of yellow disproportionate glasses, a large colorful jumpsuit, and a set of six red, round noses. I think it goes without saying that my nosophobia spoke louder than reason at this point. Of course, I have only one nose – and many times I thought I had problems in my nasal passages; they never worked as they should and, therefore, I've never been able to breathe properly. But this was my reasoning – I think it makes sense, at least for me: *It's Halloween!* People drink, swap costumes, use each other's masks, and so on. And I'm sure some people will think it's cute to rip off my nose and put it on, but I can't take the risk of being contaminated by some plague that might come from a drunken person's sweaty nose. We can't ignore the fact that we're living amongst the remains of the swine flu, can we? Well, I can't. In fact, in a world where you open the newspaper on a sunny Sunday, hoping for good news on the global economy, and the headline reads: *WHO estimates that the H1N1 virus will affect 2 BILLION people worldwide!* I believe the only rational way out of this is hypochondriasis.

I left the store in less than an hour, an all-time record, but still a torture for me. Completely satisfied with my purchases, I skipped home to get ready for the big night. Marc, Julia and I had already made plans. Julia would stop by my house with Luca (yes, they've finally made up), both dressed up as members of the Enterprise crew from Star Trek. He would be Dr. Spock, with the wig and pointy ears, and she would be Uhura. I couldn't wait to see this. We'd meet up with Marc at around 9:30 p.m. somewhere along the Chelsea Parade. Then, we'd go to a local bar and end the night at TownHouse, a gay club that Marc simply loves. I know it seems odd for a straight girl to be at a gay party but, believe me, it's guaranteed fun! And, since I'm not searching for love or sex, it'll be great fun with friends. Brian can't go: Halloween is one of the busiest nights at the restaurant.

The first shot of the night happened at Molly's, where we met up. To my surprise, Marc was dressed up as Britney Spears. Britney Spears! I think dressing up as Madonna, Britney or Priscilla, queen of the desert, at least once in their lifetimes is recorded in the chip of every homosexual in the world and, therefore, it was also recorded in Marc's RAM memory. There he was, standing 6 feet 2 inches tall, flashing his muscles in his tiny red dress with fringes at the neckline, sky-high heels, a blonde wig and, astonishingly, breasts so large that Pamela Anderson's seemed small in comparison.

My weatherman friend made a mistake, a huge mistake. The parade went on under torrential rain. It took less than an hour for me to look like a sad clown, with my makeup completely droopy and the brim of my hat flopping down. The same happened with Marc and his makeup – it had taken him over an hour to hide the signs of a beard. Tired of so many Lady Gagas, Michael Jacksons, vampires and sexy costumes, we left the parade and went to a bar in Greenwich.

Two shots of tequila and the first cocktail of the night. The bar had a small dance floor and a DJ. Marc couldn't help it; he went up to him and asked for a Britney song. In response to requests from the crowd, inflamed by Marc, the DJ played a sequence of her songs. While the audience danced, screamed and cheered, Marc put on an impeccable performance appearing as practically Britney herself. We all laughed and had so much fun. But, Brian's absence made me a little down. I looked to one side and there was Marc, shaking his blonde wig; I looked to the other side and saw Julia and Luca engaged in so many public displays of affection that I was getting nauseous. I'd never wished to have someone by my side as badly as I had tonight. Someone who would be there and who could have fun with my friends, make me laugh, and genuinely enjoy being there, just like me. A companion in the moments of joy, a partner for all times, a best friend in times of confidence or struggles. In other words, a true love. I know my relationship with Brian is still at the early stages and I need to have patience for him to become that person. But I must confess: I'm an anxious person, and waiting is not something I can do without sacrificing my health.

It was a little past one in the morning and I was visibly tired as we arrived at TownHouse. In fact, by the time we got there, Britney was the only one who was still super excited. We bumped into some of Marc's friends as soon as we arrived and he was taken away by the people at the bar. Julia and Luca disappeared ten minutes later, hugging and kissing – that is the good part of making up. Just a few weeks ago, they were still at each other's throats over the ring incident. And now, even though they hadn't fully gotten over the fight, they were as happy as two infatuated teenagers. Love really is beautiful.

All by myself, I looked for a place to sit near the bar, and tried really hard to get the bartender's attention. Picture that... a crowded gay bar, on Halloween night, and I'm a woman, to top it all off. Getting a drink under these circumstances was almost an impossible mission. Luckily, the priest next to me offered to help. I ended up getting a drink and a nice chat. Three more shots of tequila and two mojitos later, there I was, confessing.

"You know, I started therapy a little while ago and I'm having issues with my therapist. I can't seem to tell him the source of my problems. I-can't-open-my-heart-up-to-him, you know?" (Completely drunk and talking slowly, I tried to explain myself.)

"Don't worry so much. The issue there is more financial than emotional." He smiled.

"Financial?" I didn't understand – I asked, completely confused and thinking he was way too drunk to have a rational conversation.

"I went to therapy for many years and I've realized the more you delay spilling out the beans, revealing your true torment, the more expensive the treatment becomes."

"Oh! I hadn't thought about it like that."

"I was in therapy for six years. One day I went there and simply said: I'm tired of this shit. I've been coming here every week for six years; I've paid my car's worth for regular appointments throughout the years and what for? Just to find myself?"

"But did you find yourself?"

"Listen, Lilly Pop (he had nicknamed my costume unhappy clown, because of the dripping makeup. I have no idea how many shots of tequila he's had, but I can assure you he's had plenty), to tell you the truth, I finally realized I'd paid a fortune and spent a whole lot of time of my life in the pursuit of the wrong goal."

"What do you mean?"

"My problems started when I was a child. At the age of six, I realized I was different from other children, especially boys. I never liked to play aggressive games and, every opportunity I had, I was playing with the girls and I was happy like that. Until one day, I was around eight, my father realized this. As you can imagine, he was not very happy about it. You see, I was raised in a very religious family. My dad was the pastor of the parish in our community…"

"Now I understand why you're dressed as a priest."

"While my father worked, I stayed home with my mother and five sisters. My mother could never fathom what was going on with me. She didn't understand. But, one day my parents discussed the matter and decided to send me off to a seminary, thinking it would resolve the issue."

"Wow; what did you do?" – I was totally interested in the conversation.

"I was only twelve years old. I stayed at the seminary for three years and when I felt confident enough to face my family, I went back home and said: "There's no point in denying the facts; I'm gay." His tone of voice rose and his face hardened as he said these words.

"What happened then? Did your dad try to kill you? Did he kick you out?"

"All together at the same time, honey. It was a mess. It took a long time for me to recover. When I decided to do therapy, I thought it would help me find myself. Or heal these wounds from the past. But, one day I woke up and realized what I wanted was not to find myself; I wanted to accept myself and to lose myself!" – he said, laughing.

"I understand."

"So, honey, don't worry so much. The answers will come at the right time. Just relax and tell him whatever you want to tell him. Changing the subject, have you noticed that Joker over there won't take his eyes off me?" (He pointed to a young guy, with an amazing body. His face was a mystery, because it was completely plastered with his perfectly done Joker makeup, from the Batman movie).

"I think you're totally right. He looks interested."

"So, if you'll excuse me honey, I think I'll go lose myself, or find myself in his arms right away!" – and he left, leaving me with a half empty mojito in my hand and an empty soul. This could only mean one thing: I miss Brian.

I left Julia and Luca making out in some corner of TownHouse and Britney happily dancing with Madonna. I headed to Brian's restaurant; I wanted to surprise him by getting there with my clown costume… a little drunk, but willing to help him close the restaurant. So, I went to the bathroom, removed the makeup, put on some lipstick and hopped onto the first cab I could find. When I got there, he was by the door, talking to a couple from the Addams Family, Morticia and Gomez, who were finishing up their dinner. As soon as he saw me, he smiled and came up to the door. He kissed me affectionately. We closed the restaurant and hooked up right there. On the kitchen countertop, we ate cheese, drank some wine and made love. Oops! That last part was supposed to be a secret.

24

I've repeated my loving boyfriend's favorite statement (Amanda, everything will be fine!) about 272 times to try and calm myself down, but I must say: it's not working.

Brian boarded a plane to Paris 72 hours ago, leaving me here alone with Ali. As you all know, my relationship with this dog has never been great but, for Brian's sake, both Ali and I have tried to coexist cordially. But, without Brian around I can't even imagine what that dog can do to me.

When I asked for the fifth time if he really thought this would be a good idea, he lost his temper – which hardly ever happens – picked up the phone and called the dog hotel, asking someone to come pick Ali up for a seven-day stay.

Consumed by guilt, and not wanting to disappoint him, I erroneously gave in and said he didn't need to. I can do it. After all, it's only for a week. An adult woman, intelligent and informed as I am, can certainly care for a dog, even if he has once attacked her. "We'll be fine!" – I told him, trying to sound excited. It's about time

I get over the past and try to get along with my boyfriend's best friend.

"If he gives you a hard time, call the hotel and ask for someone to come pick him up, okay?" – he seemed worried. "Talk to Kathy; she knows us and knows exactly what to do."

"No need to worry, I mean it. We'll be fine." – I tried to convince him, and myself, that the idea was not completely nuts.

I'd have to spend an entire week without Brian, which was pretty hard to accept in and of itself. Since we started dating, I've become somewhat dependent on him. Gentle, affectionate and extremely caring, he always manages to calm me down in the middle of a crisis. This has also made my mom and my sister's lives easier. Now, just like that, I'll have no emotional support for a whole week and, what's worse, I'll be spending time with a dog that hates me.

Brian was called to Paris urgently. He got a group of investors to open up a branch of his restaurant over there. The work should begin next week, but apparently the architect is late with the project, in addition to several other documentation issues that may also delay the work. So Brian, tired of excuses from their lawyers, contractors and others, decided to take the next flight out and solve these problems on his own.

One week! I'll be fine, I'm positive. Seven days, what are seven days? I said out loud, trying to convince myself I could really pet sit this pit bull for a whole week. When Brian comes back at the end of this week, Ali will be alive, well and healthy. And, I hope the same will be true for me. Not counting on well and healthy, though. That would be too much to ask. If all of my limbs are intact, that's good enough.

Everything was fine the first couple of days. I went to work normally. I left enough food and water for Ali for the whole day, and then gave him the special dog food for dinner. At night, we went out for a walk. He'd do his business outside, I'd pick it up and we'd head back home, both exhausted, but feeling lighter, due to the caloric expenditure of hiking through the park, and he was relieved and happy.

Before bed, I'd give him an extra helping of dog food. Brian left me strict instructions not to do that, because the vet said Ali is overweight for his size and age. But I had to disobey. I can't take the chance of sleeping with this huge and hungry dog right next to my bed. What if he wakes up delirious and hungry, and mistakes my arm for a piece of beef jerky? The vet will have to forgive me, but Ali will be overfed every night this week. What's the big deal if a dog becomes obese? Is he looking for a wife, by any chance? Is he taking a crack at a modeling career? Besides, if he needs help losing weight later on, I can always give him some sibutramine (I think!).

By the third day, his presence started to annoy me. My obsessive side wanted a little order in the house, which was always immaculately clean. But, now there was dog food lying around everywhere and Ali spilled water everywhere, leaving huge, wet stains in the carpet, which obviously didn't make me happy. Each day that went by, the animal's anxiety grew, and so did my concern regarding what he might do to my neck while I was sleeping. I thought it would be wise to take the initiative and do something for him to feel better and less agitated. That's when a brilliant idea came to mind: *let's go to a dog spa.*

I spent hours doing an online research, looking for places that offered things like dog massages, manicure and pedicure (Ali's nails were horrendous), dentist (his breath was funky!) and, in addition to these services, had some cute fashionable clothes. Marc told me about a great, upscale place. It looks like that's where New York's celebrities take their pets to be pampered.

"Hi. I'd like to make an appointment for a soothing bath, a massage, dentist, manicure and pedicure."

"What's the name?"

"Amanda Loeb."

"Is Amanda a cat or a dog? What breed?"

"No, I'm Amanda."

"What's the pet's name please?"

"Oh, ummm… sorry. His name is Ali. He's a dog, a pitbull."

"Bath and haircut?"

"No, just a soothing bath. I think he's stressed, you know? I read on your website the soothing bath is great for…"

"How old is Ali?"

"He's 4, I think. Is this relevant?"

"Do you need someone to go pick him up?"

"No, I can take him myself."

"I have time tomorrow at nine, Monday at two and Wednesday at five. He'll be here for approximately five hours."

"Tomorrow at nine is perfect."

I quickly glanced at my schedule and mentally planned out my day. I'd wake up early, feed Ali, have breakfast and leave to take him to the spa. I'd work all morning and leave my lunch break for later, eat something quickly, go pick up Ali and bring him home. That would give me enough time to go back to the office and work another three hours before calling it a day. This would only work out if traffic was not too bad, of course. Even though my office is right next to my house, I'd have to cross town to get to the spa.

The alarm went off and my busy day began. Ali was very cooperative and acted like an excited and anxious child. It's as if he knew he'd be pampered like a prince all day. Brian probably wouldn't approve this, so I kept it a secret. Sharing secrets creates some complicity between two people. Therefore, I can say Ali and I are pretty close now. I wouldn't tell Brian about the spa and neither would Ali; we had a pact of silence that we'd keep till the end, at all costs.

My plan went on as expected. I left Ali at the spa and went to work, convinced that one of these days I'd have to spend $250 on myself for a spa treatment as well.

Two days later Brian was back and, to his total surprise and joy, he found Ali and me living together as good old friends, in perfect harmony. It's amazing what a day at the spa can do, right? Even for a pitbull!

25

I've been thinking a lot about death lately. The deaths of Michael Jackson, Brittany Murphy and more recently, Mac Miller, all very young, and especially my own death. As Madonna's said once, there were many coincidences between Michael and me and a little bit of envy as well – from my part, not from Madonna, of course. Not because he was the king of pop, a brilliant singer and an exceptional dancer and I'm nothing but a hypochondriac lawyer trying to save the world and striving to have my work recognized by my mother, proud of her offspring, or by my boss, satisfied with my performance. But, for the mere fact that he wore his anti-germ masks for the world to see and no one thought he was ridiculous because of it. It was a matter of style. I'm so jealous! It's a shame it didn't become a trend. I wish I could get on the subway and have no one notice I was wearing a mask, a black long-sleeve shirt and gloves in the middle of summer. But, my troubles don't stop there. If even he, the King, the ONE, had a tragic and premature death, then oh my God, what shall happen to me, a commoner, with no title of nobility?

Speaking of nobility, the disease that's currently afflicting me, frankly, is deplorable, nasty and not a bit charming. It's difficult to even say what I'm going through out loud. I wish I could be dignified and modest enough to keep this a secret but, as always, panic and distress took over me. And here I go telling Brian what's going on, after he interrupts my death ravings with at least 82 knocks on the bathroom door, from what I've counted so far.

"Brian, please leave me alone for a minute. I have gastrointestinal problems and would not like to share this with you. Even when a couple is really close and gets along well, people still need some privacy and alone time." – I huffed.

"Amanda, I'm just worried. You've been in that bathroom for 40 minutes. What's going on? Is there something wrong? Open the door, please."

"I can't."

"Why not? What's going on, Amanda? I'll knock this door down, I swear." I heard a muffled giggle after that last sentence.

How could I ever explain to my boyfriend that I'm having problems with my… Ugh, shit! I can't even say it out loud to myself. How could I possibly say it to him?

It all started about a week ago. For a week, I've been alternating between mild diarrhea and constipation. I'd not given much importance to the matter at first. After all, I'm a woman. And what woman has never had a week like this? But today, I must say, bowel cancer is haunting my fertile imagination. I woke up happy in the morning; I'd had a great night of wild sex with the most gorgeous and loving man on the face of the Earth. I know this sounds like something an infatuated person would say, but so what? I am in love. This is so good. Julia is always saying that, when I talk about Brian, my excitement is such that the triangle formed by my mouth and my cheeks looks like a heart. Imagine that!

I went to the bathroom to brush my teeth and eliminate my toxins. As soon as I sat down on the toilet, it was clear: I'm constipated again. I'm not the type of person who tends to push things along, you know? I prefer more efficient and less painful ways to deal with this sort of issues. A full day's diet of fresh fruit and yogurt, for example. But, honestly, this morning I was all out of patience and decided the good old moan, along with abdominal contortions and a little bit of pushing would do the job. I pushed so hard I felt the elasticity of my anus (there, I said it!) being tested to the limits. After unbearable pain, came relief. Hard blocks of an indescribable thing (out of respect for you) fell into the bowl. All it took was a quick glance at the material and I was terrified. Blood. This alone was cause for alarm. A lot of blood in my stool. I cannot explain the trauma involved here. I was in shock, paralyzed and felt like crying. I've spent almost 30 years in this world and I'd never been through something like this. Now what? How will I be able to live with this? Cancer was something I've always expected to have one day. I've had nightmares about this ever since I was a child. But, a decent cancer, one that would preserve my dignity to some extent. Now this was ridiculous. Bowel cancer was not something I could cope with. How would I tell my friends? They'd all stare, holding back laughter, I'm sure. Instead of getting some compassion out of people, I'd be the victim of a cruel joke.

After much insistence, I opened the door for Brian to come in.

"What's wrong?" he seemed genuinely worried.

"Severe abdominal pain, constipation, and blood in my stool." – my goodness, I cannot believe I've just said that to my sweet and hot boyfriend. – "I don't know what to do. I'm scared to death. I think I have bowel cancer."

He looked at me calmly, with a grin on his face, and said: "Don't you ever consider a disease that's simple and less fatal? Hemorrhoid, for example?"

Hemorrhoid? My boyfriend is a genius. I don't know why he didn't go to med school; he's a natural. Just like a magical sparkle, Brian's idea enlightened my mind. I ran to the computer and went to my favorite online diagnostics website. Among the many sites I know, I love *the ABC's of health*. I searched for hemorrhoids, and there it was; everything I needed to know.

Hemorrhoid is a condition in which the veins that normally surround the edge of the anus, at the end of the rectum and in the anal canal, become engorged or inflamed. It can be internal or external and there are four different stages.

I printed out the page that listed all the symptoms and ran back to the bathroom with the list and a small mirror. I quickly locked the door, before Brian could even think of following me, and started self-diagnosing. Holding the mirror in one hand and the sheet with the symptoms in the other, I started examining every inch of my private parts.

I'd never really looked into that area before. Very interesting, I must say. I became quite familiar with my anus within a few minutes of observation, and I found it to be lovely. Step by step, I went on analyzing my symptoms, looking for something that would explain what was going on down there. The appearance was normal. The color was normal. Only one small detail worried me; part of the edge seemed inflamed. There! I've found the sign of anomaly I was looking for. I focused my attention on the list of explanations and found something terrifying.

Stage one: The hemorrhoid size increases, but does not pop out of the anus.

Stage two: The hemorrhoid pops out of the anus during evacuation and voluntarily goes back in afterwards.

Note: mine didn't voluntarily go back in. Should I be worried? I don't know. But, just in case, I'm panicking.

Stage three: The hemorrhoid pops out of the anus during evacuation, but goes back in afterwards (as I have already mentioned, mine hasn't gone back in). In case it doesn't, you can push it in with your finger, and it should stay in.

How disgusting! What a degrading situation. I've just had a bowel movement and now I'll have to take a shower and put my finger in my (…) to push my rebellious hemorrhoid back in simply because it refuses to cooperate and go back in on its own. What did I do to deserve this? I must have been a horrible person in my previous life. That has to be it.

Stage four: If the hemorrhoid is always out and, even when pushed back in, comes right back out, call a doctor. You may have a real problem and may require surgery.

Call a doctor? To talk about an embarrassing problem such as this? Whoever wrote this article has to be kidding. I wouldn't dare go to a doctor with a complaint like this. The last thing I want is to go through a colonoscopy, anoscopy and proctosigmoidoscopy again. Yes, I know, the names sound horrible, don't they? So, just pray you'll never have to find out what it's like to go through this. Seriously. For now, doctors are not an option for me. I'll try to use my finger as a tool and, who knows, maybe with a little bit of luck I can fix this right at home.

After I went through the whole checklist for hemorrhoids, I was feeling like the Hunchback of Notre Dame. My back hurt and I had a headache and indescribable muscle pain in my arm. I took a nice shower and carefully washed the area that was the source of my health issues. Right there, in the shower, I made my first attempt at trying to push the hemorrhoid back in. Unfortunately, my nails are long, which makes the maneuver trickier, in addition to making it very painful.

After the fourth failed attempt – please, someone kill me now! – I had no choice; I was already humiliated, frustrated and in total despair. I pondered upon the situation and decided that between being embarrassed (I had been plenty of times) and a colonoscopy, I'd rather stick with the first. So, I called Brian and asked to borrow his finger.

Needless to say, the whole situation was quite uncomfortable already and, when Brian burst into uncontrollable laughter, things got even worse. As soon as he managed to stop laughing, making me feel pitiful, his finger was of great help.

For a few days, I had some discomfort in that area. I could barely sit. If the chair was hard, oh God! But behold, the hemorrhoid eventually decided to stop being lazy and started working independently again, which was a huge relief.

There's just one more thing I need to get straight after this whole incident. Brian really needs to propose to me, otherwise I'll have to kill him. I definitely cannot let him live after witnessing this. Sorry, I just can't. I'm already searching the web for types of poison that leave no trace and cause no pain. After all, love is beautiful and I don't want Brian to have a slow, agonizing death. Despite his malicious comments about my personal tragedy and although he's been mumbling little comments to tease me, the way things are going, he'll need to attend a nursing school if he wants to stick with me.

26

Hi. My name is Amanda Loeb and I'm a hypochondriac. For most people, a dry mouth is a sign of thirst, but I can easily associate that to a symptom of leukemia. That's me, always trying to control my obsessive thoughts and compulsive acts. I've been doing therapy for two months now and I must confess it is helping a lot. I haven't checked my pulse yet today and I'll try not to. A few months ago, I'd do it 34 times a day. Yesterday, I only did it 15 times, which is a big step for me. It's been at least ten days since I last read anything at all about diseases. Actually, no, I lied. I went on a self-diagnosis website three days ago, but just to check if it's true that women who don't eat meat end up with protein deficiency, which may cause hair loss and dullness, as well as brittle nails. And, lo and behold, I've found out it's true! *At this time, I felt everyone stare at me, some in dismay, some with repulsion. So, I decided to go back to my introduction speech and to the initial focus.* I haven't been to a pharmacy for at least three weeks. When I need something, I practically tie myself to a chair and ask my boyfriend, Brian, to buy it for me. *I pointed at him, sitting in the last row.* He came with me today because it's my first day, and you know how it is. I feel like a child on the first day of school. I get anxious, which makes me think of diseases and medications. I'm really nervous and in need of support. *Everyone looked back and there he was, gorgeous, smiling and giving a friendly nod.* I still haven't been able to go a day without taking any medication. Yesterday I took two painkillers and an antibiotic, because I had an earache and, contrary to what doctors believe, I certainly had severe otitis. Yeah, it's true. I also do not trust doctors and their diagnoses. But, I believe I will soon. I understand this in an integral part of healing. I need to develop trust in health professionals; after all, they save lives every day, right? I know it'll take a while before I can celebrate my first month without taking any medication, then the third, and so on, until one day I can earn my golden pill, like some of you have, symbolizing a full year without anxiety attacks, an outbreak or a fictional disease. To tell you the truth, I'm anxiously waiting for this day to come. Which is very contradictory, because anxiety is my trigger. I become anxious, my body gets sick and I need to take medication to control myself. *I think this disease is a wild roller coaster – I thought, but didn't say that out loud; I didn't want to sound pessimistic on my first day.* It's been a while since I've had a panic attack. It's been weeks since I thought I was having a heart attack, aneurysm, or a liver crisis. *I paused to catch my breath and continued.* I also no longer think that every cell in my body is a potential cancer, much less that I'm suffering from some kind of degenerative disease. I don't have Alzheimer's, I don't have Parkinson's, arthritis, osteoporosis... *I spent a few minutes listing more than twenty diseases I thought I had in the past year.* Although I still believe one day I'll have all of these diseases, I try to control myself. I've done more than one hundred CT scans, had over 160 ultrasounds, and been to at least two hundred medical appointments. Seriously, I can prove it – *I said, proudly.* – This is it. I'm here because I know I need help. Hypochondriasis is my drug. Don't try it; I got addicted and freaked out. Everything happened too fast and all at the same time. I'm no better than a crack or heroin addict. I have a wonderful family who suffers a lot because of me. I've lost many friends and almost ruined my financial life. I have a good job, a great career, and I know this is all at risk. I also have a loving and dedicated boyfriend, who's taught me so much with his patience and understanding. You won't believe it, but a few days ago he was acting strange, which obviously made me very insecure and troubled (very easy to happen!). He disappeared two nights a week, and I knew he wasn't at work. So, I started to think he'd found someone else. You know, someone normal. When I was on the verge of a nervous breakdown, he showed up with a certificate. He'd spent all those weeks in training, to learn the Heimlich maneuver. He's so cute, isn't he? – *I said, all excited, while everyone graciously looked at Brian, who sported a proud smile.* – For all of this, I need to do everything in my power to stay well. Today is my 30th birthday, and I sincerely hope to live at least another 30 healthy and happy years. – *That's how I finished my first speech at Hypochondriacs Anonymous, with teary eyes and under an intense standing ovation from those who listened, among them, Brian and my mom.*

As soon as I finished, I had a huge surprise. Julia, Sarah, Robert, Jocelyn – who is quickly recovering – Marc, Lauren, Eric and Sophia walked through the door. Sophia had a birthday cake in her arms with two candles on it: 3 and 0.

They immediately started singing "happy birthday to you"! *But I hate birthdays.* Okay, I must admit I was very emotional and even cried. It was the best birthday of my life. Being with people who love me and help me, this is the best gift I could have asked for.

Brian waited for everyone to serve themselves and say hello to me, and then he approached. He looked especially handsome in his worn out jeans, pastel pink polo shirt and sneakers. He held his hands together, in the shape of a clamshell, in front of me. I smiled from ear to ear, trying to imagine what he had in there for me. He slowly opened his hands and, when they were fully open, I saw a small blue box from Tiffany & Co. with a silver bow on it. I took the box, as excited as a child on Christmas Day. As I started to untie the bow, he held my hands and whispered in my ear, only for me to hear: I love you! I really love you!

I had never smiled so much in my life. I was euphoric. I continued to open the box and saw a glow that only precious metals have. It was a gold necklace with the letters AB on it. How romantic. He's so romantic.

"How beautiful! Amanda and Brian." – I sighed.

"Nope."

"No? What is it then? Isn't it for Amanda and Brian?" I asked, surprised.

"AB. Your blood type." – he said, smiling, as I jumped onto his arms to kiss him.

About the author

Drica Pinotti, a Brazilian-born author, has been taking the literary world by storm with her witty perception of the modern female. With fifteen books published in Brazil and Portugal she is, now, debuting in America with her first romantic comedy, a hilarious New York fairytale titled "My Crazy (Sick) Love".

@dricapinotti
www.dricapinotti.com
Facebook.com/DricaPinotti